REDUCED

Robin Tidwell

Rocking Horse Publishing, St. Louis, Missouri

First printing, August 2012
Second printing, October 2012
Third printing, September 2014

ISBN 10: 1479196134
ISBN 13: 978-1479196135

Cover design by Shannon Yarbrough, St. Louis, Missouri

The characters and events in this book are fictitious.

www.RockingHorsePublishing.com

DEDICATION

To my fantastic husband, Dennis—who, from the very beginning with our first computer and through all the others that followed, still believed that I'd someday write a book.

Yes, honey, now you can say you were right!

ACKNOWLEDGMENTS

Besides my wonderful husband and family, I want to especially thank my awesome editor/proofreader, Peggy Linhorst, and my very supportive beta readers, LeAnn Areford, Bart Baker, Ann Hinds, Sharon Hopkins, Mike Williams, and Shannon Yarbrough.

Special thanks to LeAnn Areford, who kept yelling at me to "finish the book already, so I can read it!"

CHAPTER ONE

She took the phone call out in the hallway.

"No names. It's time. Are you okay?"

"Yes. I'll be taking the side roads."

"Good. Someone needs to be picked up. See you soon. Good luck."

Abby tapped her Bluetooth and disconnected. She stepped back into the locker room and cautiously peered around the corner. The office at the far end of the room had the curtains pulled shut tightly; she knew what that meant. She closed her eyes for a moment, saying a prayer, but only for a moment. It didn't pay at all to be unobservant.

She jumped when the curtain in the shower cubicle to her right moved slightly. A scarred, bleeding face looked out, directly into Abby's eyes, and a pale hand clutched at the curtain.

"Go," said the dying girl. "You can't help us." Abby turned and left.

She hurried down the hallway, ever vigilant. Her ears strained for the sounds of the living, her eyes moved rapidly as she watched for survivors. Or anyone. Finally outside, she broke into a run for her black truck parked in the back of the lot. She scanned the area, realizing how glad she was to have stopped in this particular parking space earlier in the day; there were almost no other vehicles nearby.

Checking both the bed of the truck and the cab before opening the door , Abby jumped into the seat, locked the doors, and strapped on the seatbelt. Making a rather wild turn and gunning the engine, she pulled out onto the road.

Be calm, she told herself; you have to think in order to survive. Once you get to where you're going, maybe you can relax a bit. Maybe. Everyone else will be there too; you'll be among friends—old friends, and good ones. The best. Well, most of them. Probably.

Abby raced down the street. There were a few cars on the side of the road, not many. Schools were still on summer vacation right now, but sports practices were starting up this first week of August. That's why Abby had been at the gym, starting her coaching job for the fourth straight year.

It was hot and humid, the sun bright overhead. Abby tried not to think of her boss and longtime friend, Deb, whom she'd left behind in that back office. She knew it was too late, even Deb had told her so. Get out, she'd said. Leave now. Go. And Abby had done so.

She pulled into the first gas station she saw ahead. Quickly she scanned the area. Two cars at the pumps, unoccupied. One, a red Camaro, by the door to the convenience store, engine idling. She parked by the pump farthest from the building, jumped out and automatically scanned her card in the machine. While the gas began flowing into the truck's tank, she realized that, in all likelihood, there was no one alive in that store. Certainly, she could see nothing from her vantage point.

Impatiently, Abby waited for the tank to finish filling, wishing that she had a couple of gas cans in the back. She knew she didn't have much time. Staying in one spot too long probably wasn't smart.

Abby clicked off the hose and, making sure that her .357 was tucked securely in the back of her jeans, walked towards the door of the convenience store. She opened it slowly, scanning the interior.

Surprisingly, there was a clerk behind the counter. A live one. One who was functioning, and appeared to be perfectly healthy albeit scared to death. Of course, thought Abby. Everyone is scared to death. Or should be.

As she walked over to a display of beef jerky and other snacks, Abby tried to give the clerk a reassuring smile. She began gathering packages of jerky, pretzels, chips, a few candy bars. In a quick moment, Abby saw another reason for the clerk's fear: three other people were standing by the beer case. Her green eyes narrowed.

They were survivors, yes. But they weren't normal. Probably hadn't been normal for some time, mused Abby, and it had nothing to do with what was happening now. The apparent ringleader was waving around a handgun and laughing loudly; he had slick, dark hair and pale skin. Eh, good-looking enough, thought Abby. Seems the two girls with him thought so, anyway. They were posing and giggling, couldn't have been more than 14 or 15. For a moment, Abby almost felt sorry for them. Then they turned, all three, and stared at her.

Her sympathy fled, and all her senses went on high alert.

These three weren't trying to buy booze, they weren't just hanging out. They were evil, all of them, with soulless eyes and carefully blank faces, looking for trouble. Abby wasn't thrilled to be the one to bring it to them, but she certainly wasn't going to back down.

"So," said the kid, obviously younger than Abby by a few years at least. "What brings you here this fine day?" His sidekicks/girlfriends/accessories just giggled. "I mean, what's a pretty thing like you doing here all by your lonesome?" He gestured with his sidearm, seemingly unaware of its presence.

Another careless gesture of the gun, and the blond girl hanging on his free arm moved swiftly to Abby's side, knocking the snacks out of her arms and onto the floor. Abby's eyes narrowed, but she said nothing.

The second girl, mousy brown hair in her eyes, looked at Abby and smirked. But Abby saw something else there now: the telltale signs, in her eyes, on her face. The girl brushed back her hair and Abby gasped.

In one swift movement, Abby shoved the blond girl to the floor and whipped out her gun. She shot the boy first; he was armed after all. Then she took careful aim at the second girl. Whispering, "I'm sorry," she pulled the trigger. She'd heard what would be in this girl's future and she wanted to stop it. The girl dropped like a stone. The blond was on her feet and running for the counter. "Stop!" shouted Abby. The girl spun in her tracks, and Abby fired again. It was over almost as quickly as it had begun. Abby took several deep breaths and willed her heart rate to slow.

The clerk stood up shakily from behind the counter. She'd disappeared as soon as the kids had started hassling Abby. "Are you okay?" asked Abby. The clerk nodded. "I have to go," Abby told her. "I suggest you do the same. Find someplace safe." The clerk nodded again, as Abby headed for the door.

"Wait," the clerk said, finally finding her voice. "Take whatever you need; no one else will be in today." She smiled crookedly. "I mean, it's all just going to sit here . . ." Her voice trailed off.

Abby didn't need a second invitation. She grabbed a plastic basket from a stack near the door, looking quickly out the bank of windows for any new arrivals, and began loading it up with peanut butter, beef jerky, and canned soups. She set the full basket by the door and started filling another.

Within minutes, she heard the sound of a revving engine and looked up to see the clerk's car leaving the lot, gravel flying. She ran outside and pulled her truck up to the door, loaded several baskets in the bed, then dragged out a couple cases of bottled water. She hesitated, then ran back inside.

Knowing she had to keep a clear head, Abby resisted opening a cold beer from the case she'd added to her stash, but she did pause long enough to light a smoke before pulling out onto the road. Her hands were shaking. Three people. Dead. How many more, she wondered, before it was all over? And how many more would leave blood on her own hands? She had to make it to Emmy's house. Alive, she added to herself, strapping on her seatbelt.

Traffic was light. Duh, she said. At that moment, it hit her: the sickness, the death, her friends, her family, the escape, the shoot-out at the gas station. Abby pulled over, dropped her head to the steering wheel, and cried.

Some minutes later, she stopped. Just like that. She had a job to do, probably several jobs yet, and she had no time to be sentimental. Or to remember. Get it together, she told herself. Now. So she did. She popped open a can of Pepsi, lit another cigarette, and got back on the road. Her cell phone rang.

"Abby, where are you?" came a whispered voice. "Hurry up!"

"Almost there, Emmy, hang on . . . about ten more minutes if all goes well." Abby pushed the accelerator, hearing an edge of fear in Emmy's voice and not liking that one bit. Emotions were running high. Both girls had forgotten the "no names" rule, but Abby was fairly sure that was a little overdramatic anyway. I mean, she thought, it's not as if "they" know who we are anyway.

The truck careened off the highway onto a lesser road, a two-lane blacktop. Abby righted the truck and pointed it in a straight line down the middle, really the only way to avoid the few scattered, abandoned vehicles on the shoulder. She pressed the accelerator, moving almost too quickly to take note of a few drivers slumped in their seats; most likely it was too late for them.

She pulled into a gravel driveway, ready to click her Bluetooth and call Emmy, but the front door of the old frame house flew open and her best friend came rushing out towards the truck. Abby lowered the window just enough to push the muzzle of the .357 through. "Stop," she said. Emmy skidded to a halt, and Abby studied her face, her dark blue eyes. "All right," she said. "Come on!" She lowered the window so Emmy could check as well, standard procedure in which they'd been drilled the last few weeks. Just this morning, it hadn't been standard at all.

Emmy ran around to the passenger door. Abby unlocked it and relocked it almost in one motion, and stuck her gun back between her seat and the console. The girls hugged, clinging together for a brief moment, then Abby spoke.

"Deb's gone. And Sam. The rest are waiting."

Emmy bit her lip, her eyes began to fill. "Okay." She took a deep breath. "We better go."

Abby turned the truck around, pulled back onto the two-lane, and turned right, avoiding the highway. From here on out, they were fugitives from whatever-the-heck was happening and the lower a profile they kept, the better for everyone. Once they all gathered, the situation would improve; how could it not? Friends for years, those meeting today at the prearranged site came from all walks of life, each bringing a different skill set, yet all united by one common goal: survival.

Robin Tidwell

CHAPTER TWO

The sun was in their eyes as they headed southwest out of the metropolitan area. The two-lane blacktop wound through the hills, thick trees on either side. Abby could remember this drive as a child, too excited to doze off as the car continued on for what seemed like a very long time.

Years later, when she drove herself down here, she was always just as eager to arrive. Under the circumstances, this time she was more apprehensive. No one really knew what was going on, except perhaps Cal, and she had been rather secretive from the beginning.

It was well into the afternoon when Abby and Emmy finally approached the old camp gates. The rusty metal hung crookedly and the stone posts were crumbling. It had been many years since the camp was in operation but, to them, it seemed like yesterday when they were last here.

Abby's phone rang. She tapped her Bluetooth. "We're here."

"Yes. Turn off the vehicle and step outside. Keep your hands visible, in the air."

Abby complied, but left the truck running. SOP again, unusual until a few hours ago. "Now the other one," said the voice in her ear. Abby motioned to her friend, and Emmy stepped outside too, careful to keep her hands high.

9

"Abby!" boomed a loud voice, as a woman stepped out of the trees. "We're so glad you could make it!" The woman stopped within feet of Abby, peering at her face, shotgun trained on Abby's midsection. Another figure had approached Emmy, similar weaponry quite visible.

Abby studied the woman's face, just as cautious.

Megan slung her shotgun over her shoulder and grabbed Abby in a tight hug. "I was so worried when I heard from Deb this morning."

Abby stared at her. "Is she . . ."

Meg shook her head. "No. She called right before she . . . right before." Abby took a deep breath and bit her lip.

"Come on," Meg said, "Let's head on inside. No one else is expected for a couple hours and there's a lot to do. Sandy here will keep an eye on things." She jumped onto the running board as Abby and Emmy climbed back into the truck. Sandy pulled open the gates as the truck rolled slowly through. Abby could see her in the rearview mirror, closing them back up and covering the shiny new hinges. More security. Few would think that there was anything behind the old gates, but they were still functional.

They drove past the old office and staff buildings, further into the camp itself, and crossed a rickety wooden bridge. The smell of cedar was heavy on the warm, still air. Off to the left, Abby could see the beginnings of a flickering campfire and a few tents already in place. Several figures moved around, setting up a kitchen area and a first aid station.

Abby parked at the end of a row of vehicles, mostly trucks similar to hers, all facing out. She noted at least one sentry keeping watch, high in a tree near the bottom of the hill by which the campsite was located.

The meadow itself was large and open, the center of the old camp. In better times, it was the place they all gathered to start the coming week, play games, and sometimes arrange to meet before a night out. The old fire circle was being put to good use once again, but the number of those coming together on this day had sadly dwindled.

Meg jumped down and hollered for some help unloading. Several people hurried over and emptied the truck bed. Abby and Emmy knew most of them; too many, however, were missing.

"Come on," Meg said. "I'll show you around and then we'll get your assignments."

The camp had a simple layout. Meg explained this was temporary until they had a full head count. Later, they'd spread out and incorporate more of the property itself into a defensive mode.

Two rows of tents were arranged parallel to each other. At the far end of one was the kitchen area, a large concrete pad with a raftered roof but no walls. Two stone barbeque pits were along one side, and a second wall held a plywood counter and several cabinets. Opposite it was the first aid station, similar in construct but much smaller.

The campfire that Abby had seen upon their arrival was now roaring and was the central gathering spot. One tent, larger than the rest and nearest the fire, was the command center.

They entered the tent, and were immediately enveloped in a hug from Calypso. "Abby and Emmy!" she exclaimed. "Two of my most favorite people!" She ran her hands through her short, red curls and waved her arms around. "As you can see, we've been busy getting set up, and now that you two are here, we can get down to business."

"Meg! Show these two to their tent and give them a chance to get cleaned up. We'll have dinner in about 30 minutes and then come back here to strategize."

The three left the tent and Cal went back to her lists and notes, promising to make time after the meeting to catch up with them and hear their news.

Meg took Abby and Emmy to their tent, just across from where they'd left Cal, then pointed to the low frame building on the far side of the meadow. "Showers are rigged up in the lodge. Sorry, three-minute limit," she grinned. "Oh, and the water isn't exactly hot . . . See you at dinner!" She stalked off, heading for the perimeter of the camp.

Abby and Emmy walked back to the truck to get their bags out of the back seat and headed for the showers. A few short, chilly minutes later, they emerged and, after a quick stop at their tent, joined the others in the kitchen area.

Dinner was served buffet style, some sort of stew and biscuits; Abby was so hungry at this point that she didn't much care what she ate but, after finding a spot at a long table, discovered that she had little appetite.

Few of her fellow diners were eating much. Most looked shell-shocked, and conversation was minimal. The only group who appeared even slightly animated was the cooks, mostly teenagers. A few children played quietly nearby in the grass. Several men were cutting and stacking wood, keeping the fires burning.

Abby pushed her food around on her plate for a few minutes, then resolutely ate. She knew she needed to, she knew all the things that she had to do, she just didn't really feel like it. Then again, she also knew that didn't matter. Her feelings. She couldn't afford to have any right now.

Finally, she dumped her empty plate into a tub of hot, soapy water and made her way to the central campfire. She paused to warm her chilly hands. Even with daytime August temperatures in the 90s, on the inside Abby felt like a block of ice.

She walked over to Cal's tent and slipped inside. Cal was there, of course, and Meg. Sandy was sitting in the back, her feet propped up on a stool. Emmy scooted over on a cot to make room for Abby. There was an impressive rack of weaponry standing by the open tent flap. One by one, the others drifted in: Lorie, Ted, Noah, Janey. That was all of them. No one else. So far, anyway.

Cal stood up and stretched and looked around at all of them. She smiled tiredly. "So good to see all of you. Really. After the last few days, or rather weeks, of preparation and waiting, especially after today . . . what some of you had to go through just to arrive safely . . . " Her voice broke and she stopped.

Taking a deep breath, Cal continued: "We all know why we're here. You've all been briefed, you know what must be done and how. Meg and I have finished your assignments, based on our assessment of your skills; if there are any questions about those, we can certainly discuss them. Meg?"

Meg stood up and handed out small squares of paper. "These are your duties for the time being. It goes without saying that you're also expected to remain vigilant for both outside and internal disturbances. There are a number of people here, outside this group of course, whom we don't know too much about. Most are friends or family, but some seemed to have hitched a ride, so to speak.

"We have a responsibility not only to those who came here for sanctuary, but to any others who may arrive." Her eyes met

Abby's for a brief moment before she continued, "There are a few of us who are not present. Some, we know will not be coming; for a few, we have lost contact."

Calypso said, "Meg and I have discussed this, and believe that it would be detrimental to talk further about those who are missing, at least out in the general areas."

One by one, everyone in the group nodded their agreement. Emmy tentatively raised her hand and spoke, "Can we ask who . . ." Meg and Cal exchanged a look.

Cal cleared her throat and produced another small square of paper. "Eve and Chloe will not be joining us. We have lost contact with Brad, Zoe, and Pops." She brushed her cheek quickly and blinked rapidly. Abby was stunned. She thought that surely . . .

"What?" Meg had said something; Abby missed it entirely. "Tonight," Meg repeated, "We mingle, we reassure, we perform our duties; we try to relax as best we can. Tomorrow the real work begins. Tomorrow, they'll be on the move and we must prepare for that, and more."

"Um, who are 'they'?" asked Emmy. Meg looked at Cal. Finally, Cal spoke.

"This stays right here . . ." Everyone nodded. Cal took a deep breath.

"Co-opCom."

Several in the group looked stunned. Some nodded, knowingly.

The Cooperative Commonwealth was the supposed new and improved US Government political party. Socialist by both nature and design, it had steadily encroached on the two majority parties until it wielded unprecedented power and control. The president himself was a member, as were the top representatives on the federal and state levels.

Guns or other weaponry were outlawed entirely, except for the military; travel was heavily restricted from zone to zone— in fact, none was allowed at all. Speech was monitored, everywhere, all the time, and one wrong word would get a person locked up for months at a time with no contact, let alone a trial or even official charges filed.

Rumors were rife: death camps, abortion-on-demand, government hoarding, secret deals with foreign powers, unspeakable torture of everyday citizens, spy drones used against those suspected of holding different viewpoints than those in power. Some of these proved to be true.

Over the last 10 years, Co-opCom had managed to infiltrate every level of government, to become involved in even small, trivial municipal politics.

"Six months ago when I first approached most of you, they partnered with Ultratron, the bio-chem company, to start work on a top-secret project. Only a handful of us had any kind of clearance whatsoever, and that was mostly just knowledge that this venture was in the works.

"We began to worry as their experiments ramped up and became more ethically questionable.

"We think we know what's going on, and we believe that we can fight it. But that's all I'm going to say tonight. We'll keep you posted on all developments."

The group remained silent. Some were no doubt thinking of those left behind, those who would not be able to be helped. Others were questioning their government, and their own wisdom in selecting or supporting it. And a few were simply trying to absorb the information and struggling for composure.

After a short time, Cal spoke again.

"Come, let's join the rest of the group outside. People want to talk, to share and connect. Let's try to clear our heads a bit and, and remember the others. Right now we are responsible, one way or another, for 47 people—people who are scared, and tired, and worried. Tomorrow there will likely be more.

"We'll meet again in the morning, 0700 hours."

Abby and Emmy were the first to step outside. Abby stretched, then automatically checked to see if her gun was secure. As the others followed them outside, the two moved closer to a hanging lantern and opened their papers.

Abby read hers and smiled. It was a rather grim look, but a smile nonetheless. Cal and Meg sure knew what they were doing: they put her in charge of scouting. She couldn't wait to start and, if she were to see some action, so much the better. Emmy held her paper up so Abby could see it too. Rather ironically, it read: Welcoming Committee. Abby smiled at her friend, a real smile this time. Perfect job for Emmy—someone had to be available to help settle any newcomers and get them assigned to work crews. It suited Emmy, the consummate hostess. In another life, of course.

Abby followed Emmy over to the campfire. Those who had already gathered looked at the new arrivals questioningly, but no one voiced a query. Good thing, thought Abby, since neither she nor any of the others in Cal and Meg's group had any real answers yet.

She grabbed a beer from a nearby bucket of ice that someone had thoughtfully provided and sank to the ground, legs crossed Indian-style. She lit up a smoke and leaned back on her hands, as casual as she could manage.

"Some party, huh? Is this the best you all could do on short notice?" Someone snickered, then a rolling laugh spread among the crowd. People began to relax, to let down guards that had been up since sunrise, or maybe before that. Conversation sparked, people introduced themselves, smaller groups formed and ebbed.

Abby talked to several people, keeping a watchful eye on the darkness beyond the firelight; she kept close tabs on Emmy as well, almost unwilling to let her friend out of her sight. She knew she needed to keep control of this, just like all her other feelings. But right now, she needed Emmy. Everything else was gone. Just gone.

CHAPTER THREE

Abby had finished her undergrad degree in just three years. She'd been at loose ends for a while after that, wandering around the Southwest for a few months, stopping when the mood struck and working at a few odd jobs.

Along the way, she picked up a few non-mainstream skills: tracking, sharpshooting, and an ability to blend into her surroundings and live off the land when necessary. All of which would actually become useful much sooner than she, or anyone, had expected.

Upon her return to Missouri, she settled down with a high school basketball coaching job and a conventional, suburban apartment, notable for nothing more than its ordinariness. She had no boyfriend, no live-in lover, not even a cat. Abby preferred to live with few attachments; her parents had died when she was not quite nine-years-old and she was raised by a short-tempered, elderly aunt of whom she had few fond memories.

She did, however, recall in excruciating detail the holidays and Christmases with no gift, no acknowledgment of the special day. She remembered her aunt yelling and screaming over trivial matters, such as Abby not making the bedcovers perfectly smooth or not folding the laundry to the older woman's precise standards. Her aunt was, Abby thought in later years, not so different than her own mother had been.

Of course, she had friends, good ones, the best. The kind with whom one could go for years with little contact, except on holidays or the occasional reunion, yet pick up the phone one day and begin a lengthy conversation about everything under the sun.

That's exactly what had happened three months ago, when Calypso called her.

"Abby. We need to talk. Can you meet me at the reunion park at 6:00?"

"Sure," said Abby. She had no plans after work, and Cal sounded worried.

She pulled into the parking lot early that evening, and saw Cal sitting on a picnic table about halfway down to the river. She made her way down the slope and sat beside Cal. "What's up? Everything okay?"

Cal continued to gaze out at the slow-moving water…and remained silent for a moment.

"Ab. You know where I work, right?"

"Of course," Abby responded, curious. "Some government office, right? Downtown?"

"Yeah," said Cal. "Some government office." She almost smiled. She turned and faced Abby.

"So. Here's the thing. We've been monitoring some unusual activity; nothing serious yet, at least the top guys there don't seem to think so. But I'm worried."

"Um, well…okay. Worried about what, exactly? I mean, that's pretty ambiguous, Cal."

Cal took a deep breath. "Something's wrong, Abby. I'm not sure, at this point, what it even involves. But it's big. Huge. I mean, like end of the world stuff, ya know? And I think we should be ready."

Abby stared at Cal. "Really? End of the world? Okay, Cal, let's say I know exactly what you're talking about. And let's say I believe you aren't entirely off your rocker. Let's take it one more step: who should be ready? And how? And for what?"

"Look," Cal countered, glancing around. "I'm not supposed to talk about this and, honestly, I don't have all the details yet. But there's talk. Talk of bunkers and contagion and maybe even little green men running around.

"I don't really know much. But I want us to be ready." "Who is "us"? The world? The country? Who?"

Cal bit her lip. "Just us, for now. The gang. All of us. Meg and I have been making plans."

"What kind of plans?"

"Plans to stay safe. To be prepared."

Abby thought for a minute. "Safe from what? And prepared how?"

"Look, Ab, are you in? If you give me the say-so, I'll tell you what I know. You can help. A lot. We want you with us."

Abby was silent. She wondered exactly what information Cal had obtained, and why the secrecy. She wondered, too, at the seriousness of all this and, yes, she wondered just a little at Cal's sanity. She'd always been pretty levelheaded, very organized and, after all, Abby wasn't entirely sure exactly what was in Cal's job description. Cal had always been pretty vague about that.

On the other hand, she'd known Cal for years and years. Cal had never been the hysterical type. Heck, once Abby'd seen her calmly stomp a copperhead snake to death after the thing slithered under her bike tire and made everyone jump.

"All right," Abby told her. "I'm in."

CHAPTER FOUR

The campfire burned down, the evening grew late. People had started to drift toward their tents. Abby got up and stretched and signaled to Emmy. The two walked back to their own tent, stopping to say good night to Cal and Meg.

Once inside, Abby sat down on her cot and pulled off her boots. She removed the knife sheath from her leg and placed it carefully under her pillow. The .357 went under the edge of the cot, on the floor, within easy reach. She slowly unwound her long, golden braid and brushed out her hair.

Both girls stretched out on their cots and said good night. Both expected sleep to be hard-won that night. Neither was proven wrong.

"Abby? Are you still awake?"

"Yes," sighed Abby.

"Can we talk about today?"

"Of course." Abby shifted onto her side, facing Emmy across the small tent, not three feet away. "Tell me what happened."

"When I got up this morning, I knew something was wrong. Mom usually gets up really early and she wasn't . . . she

21

wasn't in the kitchen. I didn't hear anything, so I went outside to check.

"The animals hadn't been fed, so I took care of them first. Then I walked around the house to the front yard, and there she was. Sitting on the ground. Staring at nothing."

Emmy stopped. She swallowed hard. When she continued, Abby could hear the tears in her voice and felt her own locked-up emotions begin to bang on the door.

"So I said, 'Mom?' And she—she—looked at me, but not at me, you know? And I asked her what in the world she was doing out there, like, you know, it was a normal day besides that.

"And she said, 'Go away, Emmy. Go.' So I did. I went inside and locked the door. And I pulled out my bag and checked it and called to check in with Meg and then I waited," Emmy finished in a rush.

"Oh, Abby, what have I done?" She began to cry.

"Em, don't cry, please don't cry." Abby jumped up and sat down on Emmy's cot, grasping her cold hands. "Em, please. You know there's nothing you could have done. You know it was too late. Your mom was right; you had to go, to leave her. She knew that."

"Yes, but Abby? After I followed the procedure and was waiting for you, I looked out the window. I know I was supposed to stay out of sight, but I looked. And she was gone."

Abby blinked. As far as she knew, that never happened. Wasn't supposed to happen. After a person got . . . whatever this was . . . they died. And stayed put. Didn't move again.

Cal needed to hear this, tonight. Not in the morning, but right away. First, though, Emmy needed her.

"Em," said Abby, firmly. "Look at me."

Emmy raised her tear-stained face to Abby. Her hands were trembling. Abby took Emmy into her arms and held her like a child, whispering into her ear.

"Em. Sweetie. I don't know what this means, honestly. But I do know that your mom is gone—she was gone when you talked to her, it was just too late. I am so very sorry. But, truthfully, we don't know a lot yet except this: there was absolutely nothing you could have done. Nothing."

After a few minutes, Emmy began to relax. Abby kissed her lightly on the forehead, told her she was stepping outside for a few minutes, and to go to sleep.

Then she pulled on her boots, strapped on her knife, shoved her gun into the back of her jeans, and went to pay a visit to Cal.

The tent flaps were open and Cal and Meg were bent over the table in the middle of the tent, looking at a rather untidy stack of papers. A lantern burned overhead. They both looked up and smiled worriedly when Abby rapped on the tent pole.

"Hey, Ab, what's up?" Meg greeted her heartily. "Thought you'd be asleep by now."

Believing that, most times, potentially bad news was more palatable when spoken quickly and plainly, Abby said, "Emmy just told me about what happened to her today. Her mom. She moved. She disappeared."

Cal and Meg looked at each other, then at Abby. "She moved? Or disappeared? What do you mean, Abby? This could be important," Cal told her. "Start at the beginning."

Abby realized how confusing that must have sounded, so she simply reiterated exactly what Emmy had said. When she finished, Cal sat down heavily. Meg put a hand on her shoulder.

"Cal, does this mean anything?" asked Abby. "Was this unusual, or unexpected? Or has it happened before?" She looked from Meg to Cal and back again. "What the hell? Where did Emmy's mom go?"

Cal sighed. "Abby, we don't know where she went, and we don't know if anyone else has, um, taken off or disappeared. We did know that this was a possibility, albeit a remote one. And," she added, "This is the first instance we've actually heard about.

"Sit down, Abby." Cal gently guided the younger woman to the bunk and sat her down. "With the older folks, and even perhaps those who were ill or on certain medications, this was discussed as a long-shot. The breakdown of blood vessels is so overwhelming that it takes everything, very, very quickly, and—disintegrates the body. Entirely."

Abby turned very pale. "That's not possible."

"Yes," said Cal, sadly, "it is now."

"Okay," Abby said, taking a deep breath and swallowing hard. "Great. 'Cause things weren't just jolly enough around here." Abby stood up to leave.

"Hey, kiddo," said Cal. "We'll make it. We can do this."

"Yeah," countered Abby. "We don't have much of an alternative, right?" She smiled crookedly and walked outside, back to her own tent where Emmy was finally sleeping.

She repeated her earlier drill: weapons stashed handily, she lay back down on her cot, arms crossed behind her head. Normally, Abby had no problems going to sleep, but this day was, she thought, about as far from normal as one could get. She remembered how it had started.

Up at 5:00 a.m., 30-minute workout, shower, breakfast while reading the news online and checking her email—all as usual. And then, there it was. From Cal, one word: today.

Her cell phone rang. Meg. Today. Crap.

Abby mentally ran through her checklist. She stowed her camping gear, already packed and stored neatly in the spare bedroom, in the back of her truck. It took three trips down the apartment building stairs, and she was no lightweight, no wuss. She could pack 100 pounds of gear for two solid days of hiking, if necessary. According to Cal, this might well be necessary.

She checked her weapons cache, one by one, and added these to the truck. The knife and .357 she'd become accustomed to carrying with her at all times during the last few months was part of her and needed no checking.

Abby turned off the breakers, shut down the water valves, and locked her doors. She really didn't think this would make much difference, in the long run, but it gave her something almost automatic to do in order to calm the part of her brain that was operating on warp speed.

She climbed into the truck and paused for just a few seconds. She fully expected never to see this place again, at least not in one piece. Whether she meant herself or the apartment, she wasn't quite sure.

Driving to work was actually fairly normal: the traffic, the stubborn red lights, the good-natured honking and sometimes blaring of one or two particularly impatient drivers. All par-for-the-course in the St. Louis area, especially during rush hour.

When Abby pulled into the high school parking lot 45 minutes later, she noticed there were about half as many cars there as usual. She found an ideal spot near the back of the lot, empty spaces all around it, and parked facing out. Standard operating procedure that she'd been studying, for this day at least.

It was just before 8:00 a.m.

With a watchful eye, Abby walked quickly toward the building that housed the gym. Once inside, she was on high alert. It was strangely quiet.

She moved down the hallway to the girls' locker room and opened the door cautiously. Hmmm. Business as usual, here at least. Then she looked closer. A few girls had finished their morning workouts and were heading for the showers; a few more were in the gym itself, getting some personal instruction from Deb, Abby's boss and longtime friend. Abby stepped through the doorway just as Deb finished speaking.

The girls left the gym with confused looks on their faces. Two were practically running, and one glanced over her shoulder, looking as though she were about to speak. She didn't, however, and the fire door banged shut behind them.

Abby looked at Deb questioningly. Deb nodded. They walked into the coaching office and Deb shut and locked the door, drawing the curtains closed over the bank of windows.

Deb was tall, taller than Abby, and a few years older. Her short, brown hair was a bit spiky, almost standing straight up. She was athletic in build, as a coach should be, and had a direct, no-nonsense manner with her "girls." She still often considered Abby one of them.

"You got the call?" Abby nodded. "Yes."

"And you're ready?" A drop of blood appeared on Deb's cheek. She quickly brushed it away, but not before Abby noticed her movement. "All right, then. You know where to go, what to do?" She coughed and cleared her throat.

Abby grew tense, standing on the balls of her feet, her muscles taut. She waited.

"I'm not going, Abby." Deb looked a bit pale. What looked like a scratch suddenly appeared on her cheek. Then another. "Abby! Pay attention!"

Abby started to move, to speak. She had a lump in her throat and could do neither. She just looked at Deb.

"Abby," said Deb, sadly. "Oh, Abby . . . tell everyone I said . . . just tell them I love them all."

"But, Deb, come on, I mean—I mean, come on!" Deb grew increasingly paler; there were more scratches on her face. Her eyes . . . dear God, her eyes—

"Get out, Abby. Leave now. Go." And Abby fled.

She paused once, to look back at the office. That's when her cell rang again. It was Meg.

She took the phone call out in the hallway.

CHAPTER FIVE

They all gathered in the "command center," early in the morning. Most appeared tired already, as no one had gotten much sleep. Too many questions, too few answers. Thankfully, the cooks had gotten up early and put the coffee on; Abby had finally given up on sleep and gone for her usual morning run. Now she was holding a steaming mug, sipping, waiting for Cal to begin.

"All right," said Cal. "I'm going to start at the beginning. I'll take questions as they come, but let's try to stay on topic.

"You were all approached three months ago with vague talk about a kind of Armageddon…or rather, the possibility of one. I purposely didn't give anyone any details, mostly because I didn't have much information myself.

"Meg and I talked. We decided, knowing each of you personally and for quite some time, that you were the people we could see making a difference.

"Basically," she added, "You were the ones we wanted with us when all this went down."

"But I have one question." Cal looked around the room. "Does anyone want out of this?"

Silence.

Of course they weren't leaving. No one spoke, no one moved. They were in for the long haul, whatever that might bring, whatever might happen next. Cal knew what she was doing, and besides, there was nothing else out there; they'd all seen that for themselves.

Cal took a deep breath. "Okay, here we go.

"First, you all have your assignments. Those duties begin immediately. I'd like all of you to check in with me twice a day." She looked at Abby. "Some of you may not find that possible, but we can cross that bridge later.

"Second, we expect more refugees to show up, today and maybe over the coming week. Possibly after that as well, but it's doubtful. Emmy, that's your department; meet and greet, so to speak." Cal smiled.

"And finally, I'm going to tell you what's happening."

Muscles tensed. Smiles, tentative at best, faded. Someone cleared his throat, nervously. The silence was total and complete. "The disease itself is Venal Atrophic Dissolution. Its creator was Dr. Edward Roberts. They call it VADER." Cal managed a small, ironic smile.

"The initial symptoms are, as most of you have seen firsthand, a general feeling of unease followed immediately by facial pallor. The whites of the eyes become blood-filled and usually the face begins to show signs of…cracking. That last usually happens progressively faster over several minutes.

"Death is imminent, and painful, but at this point absolutely nothing can be done. All arteries and veins have, um, dissolved, but the brain is the last organ affected.

"The important thing is this: if you see any of these signs, on anyone, anywhere, you must immediately detain the individual and report in as soon as possible. It's doubtful that there will be a case here; it seems to have begun and ended quickly, from what we can tell by monitoring the outside. In other words, no one here has been affected or that person would already be dead."

Noah stood up and cleared his throat. "If I may, Cal?" She nodded assent. "As Cal said, we've been monitoring this via the Internet, not only since we've been here but for the last few weeks. There have been small pockets of these cases, worldwide, since the middle of July. There has been almost no media coverage, and that was quickly silenced. Co-opCom, we presume, put on the pressure.

"Those earlier outbreaks were, we believe, tests. This one, the big one, was a mistake. A very, very tragic mistake with unfathomable consequences.

"However, I've been working toward this end for some time. I've gathered a lot of data and quite a bit of information, but it will take time. I hope to discover not only exactly the cause, but if there's a cure or a vaccination. It could be that we here are all simply immune and, if so, I need to know why." Noah sat down and Cal asked if there were any questions.

Several hands waved, and Cal took each in turn. Most were desultory, few dealt with specifics of this…this plague. VADER. What an apt name, thought Abby. And created by an Ultratron employee. She idly wondered what had happened to Dr. Roberts but, having heard a great many things about his controversial company over the last few years, didn't really care.

Ultratron had been very secretive about its numerous projects and contracts in the last decade, but the media portrayed it as an altruistic organization, funded in part, at least, by the government.

Janey spoke next. "Cal, when you all say 'outside world,' what exactly do you mean? Is there anyone left besides us?"

Cal bit her lip and looked first at Meg, then at Noah. "Not many," she said crisply. "There are a few groups, like us, small and in scattered locations. However, we can only keep in touch as long as communications stay up. We're not sure how long that will be."

They absorbed this in silence.

Thirty minutes later, after a few more desultory questions, the meeting was adjourned. They all wandered outside, into the sun. No one spoke.

Ted headed over to the kitchen area to check on breakfast; it was a rather automatic response, he had a job to do and so it must be done. Besides, he thought, food was pretty important for everyone! A chef in his former life—sheesh, was that only yesterday—Ted was an excellent cook, be it over a 12-burner gas range or a campfire; didn't matter much either way.

He quickly checked on his "assistants," the teens and almost- teens, and rang the bell for breakfast.

Abby ate quickly, barely aware of what she was eating but, in a testament to Ted's skill, she decided it was delicious. She headed back to Cal and Meg's tent, at the latter's request, for some detailed instructions on what exactly was needed from her.

Meg was on her phone and Cal was fiddling with a stack of papers; Meg gestured for Abby to sit, so she did. Surprisingly, she realized, she hadn't checked her phone for messages or mail since she'd arrived. Assuming there would be none because, after all, it was kind of the end of the world, she pulled the phone out of its holster.

There was an email from Deb, sent early yesterday morning. Abby hastily put the phone away. She couldn't read that now. Maybe later. Maybe when she was alone.

Meg ended her call and came and sat beside Abby.

"Kiddo, here's what we need you to do. We're gonna have to expand our camp; like Cal said earlier, more folks could be heading this way. The first part is easy—check out the main areas of the camp, see which sites are usable and which ones might need some repair. We'll get a crew on that right away, if Brad . . . when Brad gets here." She paused briefly.

"It goes without saying that you're also to keep an eye out for any, er, trespassers. Use your own judgment, Abby, but make sure you report back here as soon as possible after any 'incidents'. In fact, for these first couple days, until the whole place has been checked out, I expect to see you here before lights out, 'kay?"

Abby nodded.

"All righty then," said Meg. "See you at dinner and, Ab, be careful . . ."

Abby left the tent and went back to her own. She grabbed her water bottle and a light daypack, filling it with ammo, a blanket, an extra pair of socks, and a small first aid kit. She reached under her cot and pulled out a long, hard plastic case. She unlocked it, opened it, and paused for a moment, mulling her choices.

The Mossberg. Perfect. She added shells to the daypack, quite a few, and double-checked the shotgun. Relocking the case, she slid it under the cot and headed for the commissary.

Lorie was behind the makeshift counter just inside the door to the old lodge. "Shower or supplies," she drawled, seconds before she took note of Abby's accessories. "Right. Got you covered, so to speak."

She knelt down behind the counter, knees popping, and came back up with a couple of granola bars and a package of jerky. She'd been expecting Abby, as Meg had briefed her last night.

Lorie carefully made note of the supplies going out and said, "There ya go. Be careful out there." Abby shrugged; it was just a job. She truly didn't expect any problems, yet, but was a little on edge all the same. Still, she smiled at Lorie and stowed the food in her pack.

"All familiar territory today, Lorie," she said. "See ya!"

Abby walked over to the kitchen area to fill her bottle from the pump. Thank goodness this place had always had well water although, if Brad didn't get here soon, they might not be able to reach whatever was left once the storage tanks were empty. She spotted Emmy.

"Hey, Em, I'm off for the day—I'll be back for dinner. Stay close, okay?"

Emmy smiled. "Sure, Ab. Busy day so far, plan to keep it that way! Take care . . ." The girls hugged, and Emmy turned back to her small group of new arrivals. Abby set off down the gravel road to her first stop.

CHAPTER SIX

The brush was thick and trees towered over Abby's head. Using her knife, she slowly made her way back into the old campsite, cutting just enough to allow herself passage. It took her nearly twenty minutes to move as far as the abandoned fire pit, around which was just a bit of cleared space.

Alert to any sounds, Abby stopped and surveyed the immediate area. Nothing, not even the sound of birds, no movement except high in trees where a light breeze blew. She took a swig from her water bottle and sheathed her knife.

Scanning the steep hills, Abby saw no signs that any humans had been here recently, probably not for several years. All the same, she made her way to the covered shelter, stacked with old picnic tables, cautiously and carefully.

One table was off to the side, upright and fairly sturdy looking. She laid down the Mossberg, safety off, and sat beside it. Mentally, she began to take notes on the location, the layout, and the condition of this particular site. Abby had trained herself in memorization, both visual and verbal; she would have no difficulty relaying any relevant information back to Cal at the end of the day, no matter how many locations were involved.

Within minutes, Abby stood up and, grabbing the shotgun, made her way to the small, nearly dry, creek bed a few yards away. On the other side was a cabin of sorts; she'd already noted the silent and abandoned look to the place, but she had to be sure.

Without making a sound, Abby stopped at the screen door, a little to the left of the frame. Hooking one finger in the handle, she yanked the door open and cocked her weapon. That sound, often, was enough to at least startle a person and give Abby some shock value as an unknown entity.

The cabin was empty.

There were two bunkbeds, one on each side of the doorway, near the back; two windows, one on either side of the building; and a large hole in the roof. The floor was covered with sticks and leaves and dust. There was nothing, or no one, else.

Abby stepped outside, made a quick check, and clicked on the safety. Shouldering the gun, she made her way down the creek bed for nearly a hundred yards before turning back. That was enough. Time to move on.

Remembering the layout of the camp from years earlier, Abby recalled that she could climb the hill to the east and come back down an old trail behind the main office and staff quarters. She almost missed the cutoff, however, because of the vast overgrowth. Again, quite obviously, no one had been on this particular trail for some time.

She knew the buildings themselves had been scoped out a few weeks ago, when Cal and Meg and Sandy had first checked on the feasibility of coming here. She wasn't worried about them; she just wasn't sure how thoroughly some of the nearly unknown backcountry up there had been scouted. She clearly remembered a small cave, up in the limestone, about two hundred yards higher than the old office building.

Yes. There it was, almost obscured by brush. All of it looked natural, not contrived by human hands. Or other hands. Abby was brought back to reality for a short, sharp moment. She'd almost forgotten the "why" of this mission.

Deciding it was time to rest after her brief lapse, and after stopping to listen and watch, she peered into the opening of the cave. Nothing but cobwebs…nothing at all had disturbed the chalky white dust on the floor.

Abby sat down, cross-legged, with the Mossberg at her side, safety off and ready to grab at a second's notice. She slung her pack to the ground and placed the .357 beside it.

Munching on jerky and granola, she decided that now might be the time to read Deb's email. She reached for her phone, but yanked her hand back almost immediately. Nope, she thought. Not now. I have to focus on the job at hand.

Basing her knowledge on the events of the last 24 hours, Abby realized that things could change in a heartbeat, and what seemed a peaceful interlude at the moment could very well turn deadly. She needed her wits about her.

Brushing some crumbs to the ground, Abby stood up and stretched, loaded up her gear, and headed down the hill. Ever vigilant, she continued to watch and listen and move as silently as possible. When she reached the road and crossed the bridge, she glanced over at the encampment.

There seemed to be a few more tents erected since this morning, she noted; perhaps four? No, five. Obviously that meant more people, but it was difficult to tell at this distance as everyone was gathered on the far side for lunch. Abby continued down the road; checking her watch, she thought she could probably tick at least two more sites off her mental list before heading in for the evening.

The sun was directly overhead and the temperature was climbing. It was August in the Midwest, after all. There was barely a breeze and the humidity was high. Abby paused to drench her bandanna with water, then tie it around her head for a bit of relief. Just a few yards farther and she broke off the road to follow a creek.

This time she could hear the birds and see the sun trying to penetrate the tree canopy overhead; the slight breeze was welcome. Senses alert, Abby walked cautiously through the almost-dry creek, easily avoiding the few puddles. Perhaps twenty minutes later, she arrived at her destination.

This campsite was in the middle of an overgrown meadow, rimmed with platform tents. Upon closer inspection she discovered that, while the frames appeared to be in decent condition, many of the dozen or so tents were sporting rotting and sagging canvas. Not really surprised, Abby carefully circled each one, shotgun at the ready, before checking the interiors.

At the far end of the meadow was a covered shelter, similar to the one she'd seen at the first site but larger and better equipped. Some of the built-in cabinets were hanging open, pots and pans lying on the floor; Abby assumed animals had gotten inside and made the mess as she still had seen absolutely no sign of humans.

The two fire pits were in good repair, as one would expect stone to be; the wooden tables seemed to be intact but filthy. She walked across the nearby footbridge to the gravel road; the old totem pole was still standing, but faded. She turned and went back to the campsite.

Up on the hill, just east of the shelter, was the latrine. A newer version than what Abby had been accustomed to years earlier, its maximum capacity was fewer than a dozen people. She had heard, however, that these newer ones included a storm shelter of a sort. That was her focus.

Not thrilled about actually going inside, considering that this was, after all, a latrine, Abby hesitated then flung open the cellar- type door. Naturally, it was dark, but she could see the stone stairs descending.

Straining to both see and hear, she unclipped a flashlight from her pack and shined it down those stairs.

CHAPTER SEVEN

Abby slipped into the kitchen shelter at the far end, nearest the trees. Dinner was over, the sun was taking its final bow, and the entire camp was gathered. Ted had the floor.

"And so," he concluded, "For the time being, we're okay on provisions. Meals will be served at 8:00 a.m., noon, and 5:00 p.m. We have a full crew at the moment, but some of you may find your assignments changing as things progress."

Ted took a seat, wiping his brow. He wasn't much on speaking in front of large groups, and this one had doubled in size just since this morning.

Janey stood up next. Abby didn't know her well, but certainly had heard of her expertise with firearms and other assorted weapons. A former Marine, Janey's short hair and no-nonsense attitude, along with her diminutive stature, made for quite a contrast.

"Defensive training will begin in the morning at 0900 hours," stated Janey. "Before you leave here this evening, please pick up your assignment sheet; this will tell you to which group you belong and, therefore, what time you are expected to arrive. Do not be tardy.

"We'll start with basic self-defense and hand-to-hand combat. We'll move on to non-mechanized weapons, then handguns. Regardless of any training or experience in which you may have previously participated, everyone will start at the beginning.

"Any questions? Good." Janey strode back to her seat near the front of the shelter.

Meg introduced Sandy. "Sandy is in charge of security here. That means when she tells you to do something, you do it. There's a reason for it, and our safety here depends on her. Those assigned to Sandy's watch will have a brief meeting as soon as you all are dismissed." Meg stomped off. She wasn't much on small talk but preferred to get to the point.

Lorie stood up and smiled. She was so friendly and open that she put everyone at ease, even strangers. Her success at sales in her former life made her an ideal fit to run the commissary and keep track of supplies; very detail-oriented, she was also honest to a fault.

Lorie explained to everyone how the commissary system worked. Each person was accountable for their purchases, although there was no money involved. Since everyone worked at different jobs around the compound, everyone contributed. However, she added, there would certainly be limits simply because no one was sure how and when supplies would be replenished or for how long certain things would be available.

"Your personal items are, of course, yours to use as you see fit. But I will caution everyone on being conservative and making things last as long as possible. We will try to keep all necessities available, but there may times when this is impossible. Please try to be understanding and patient."

The group remained silent as Lorie made her way back to her seat and Cal stood up near the front. They all seemed rather shell-shocked and Abby completely understood that. Kudos for Cal and Meg for calling this meeting so soon, not only so everyone could begin immediately to work together, but before people had entirely recovered from this disaster and therefore were less likely to question or derail all the earlier planning.

Meg tapped her on the shoulder. "Glad you got back, Abby." She gave her a quick hug. "Come over to our tent after the crowd here thins out, 'kay?"

"If there are no more questions," Cal said, "Please see Meg for your work assignments before you leave. Have a good night, everyone." She turned and left, but her progress out of the shelter was slow as many wanted to speak with her.

Abby pushed her way through the crowd until she found Emmy. "Hey, you," she said, squeezing her shoulder. "How'd everything go today?"

"Abby! When did you get back? I was so busy all day, first we had a new family come in right after breakfast, then I spent a few hours showing them around and helping them unpack. This afternoon three more people came in and, well, I pretty much did the same thing!" Emmy was clearly caught up in her role, a perfect fit as Abby already knew.

The girls walked back towards their tent. "I'll introduce you at the campfire tonight, okay, Abby?"

"I have to go see Cal and Meg," Abby replied, "But sure, I'll see you either here or there...let me just drop off my pack, and I'll be back as quick as I can." Emmy went inside to light the kerosene lantern and hang it on the outside pole, and Abby continued on to the command center.

Cal was, as usual these days, bent over a table filled with papers and her laptop. Fortunately, the generators in the old lodge behind the campsite were still functioning and they'd rigged up a charging system of sorts for certain electronics. The cell towers were still up and operational and, while the Internet seemed to still be plugging away, there were very few updates and many error messages.

In other words, no news. The latest stories were almost 48 hours old and no one had any answers then, only questions. And so it continued.

"Hey," said Abby. Cal looked up and motioned her inside. "How'd it go today?" Cal asked. She spread out a map of the area on the table, displacing several stacks of paper. "Show me."

Abby picked out a pen and circled the first site she'd scouted, labeled it, and gave her report. Then she hesitated.

"I went back up behind the old office and staff house. There used to be an old cave up there, a couple hundred yards behind the buildings. It's pretty overgrown, impossible to see unless you know it's there. Kind of a small opening, but it expands if you go back farther."

"I didn't go much past the entrance, but it's definitely empty." She took a deep breath. "I think it's best that it remain unmarked. Just in case."

Cal nodded. "I'll brief Meg and Sandy, of course, but it goes no farther."

Abby continued with the second location, labeling it as she had the first one and giving her detailed description. Meg arrived just as they were discussing the newer latrines and their storm shelters.

"Not where I'd want to be, exactly," said Abby. "I mean— it's a latrine, ya know? And it's small, maybe hold 20 people for a short time and not very comfortably. But it's secure."

"Smelly, too, I'd imagine," said Meg with a wry face. Abby confirmed that guess with a grin and a nod.

The third site that Abby had inspected was up on the hill almost directly across from their current location, past another meadow and behind the remains of an old dining hall. Abby had poked around in rubble briefly before climbing the hill and she told Cal that there was nothing useful to scavenge. Meg nodded. She'd been there earlier in the week when she'd brought down a load of supplies.

"Now, the site itself is workable, at least for some of the group—by the way," Abby asked, "What's our count up to now?"

"Fifty-six," replied Cal. "And," she added, "No word from Brad . . . yet."

"So," Abby multiplied quickly in her head, "With an average of, say, three per tent, this site can accommodate just over half of us. Site Number 2 could hold the rest, but it needs some work—more so than this one.

"That is," she looked questioningly at the other two, "If we need to move farther back into the woods?"

Meg and Cal exchanged looks. "We've been mulling that over all day," said Cal. "We're pretty well-established here in the meadow and folks are beginning to settle in, but it feels awfully exposed."

"To what?" Abby asked.

Cal sighed and picked up her laptop. She opened it, turned it around, and handed it to Abby.

Facebook, Abby thought. Of course. She almost smiled. Then she saw exactly what Cal was showing her. She scrolled down, reading quickly.

"Itssss the ZOMbIE TAKOVER!!!!!!!"

"No more then you disserve, you Chritsan haters!"

"imma get my big guns out for this!"

"GOD told me to warn you and I did!"

"WTF???????"

Then she saw it.

"I know who you are, Calypso, and more importantly—I know WHERE you are, right this minute! Better look out . . ."

Abby blinked. She read it again.

"Cal, who is this?" she asked. Meg looked worried. Cal wrung her hands and started pacing.

"I don't know," Cal said simply. "He's blocked. Or she's blocked. It's a fake name, a fake profile. I mean, it says Dan, but we know it's not. I think. Dan's profile is still there, but so is this one, the fake one."

Abby was beyond irritated. Really? People had time for crap like this now? Sheesh.

"All right," she said. "Tomorrow morning, first thing, I'll take a crew over to site Number 3 and they can get started. I'll go on up the hill behind it and check it out more thoroughly."

"Exactly what we were thinking, Ab," said Cal. "And what about the second site you checked out yesterday? How much work needs to be done?"

Abby mulled it over for a moment. "That one needs canvas more than anything; I suppose we'll have to scavenge it from another site, and that means going further down the road to Number 4 . . ."

There was a commotion outside; Meg stuck her head out of the tent flap.

"Well, I'll be . . ." she said in wonder, "Here comes the cavalry!"

Brad and Zoe and Pops had finally arrived.

It was late when the group finally disbanded. Brad had kept them spellbound with his tale of their travels, then there had been tomorrow's plans to finalize and everyone needed to be brought up-to-date on the latest news.

Abby went back to her tent and got ready for some much-needed sleep. Emmy was still out, helping Pops get settled in his tent. Abby lay down on her cot, still thinking through all the details for tomorrow's project. She finally fell asleep, still worrying about that message on Cal's computer.

Morning broke; it was hot and humid already, nearly the moment the sun rose. Abby stretched and yawned and sat up; she reached over to wake Emmy.

"Hey, sleepyhead, up and at 'em!"

Emmy moaned and pulled the covers over her head. "Feels like I just went to sleep," she mumbled.

"C'mon," Abby told her. "Move! We've got a ton of work to do today."

"Yeah, yeah." Emmy slowly sat up and rubbed her eyes. "M'kay. I'm up."

The girls grabbed their things and headed for the showers first, then breakfast. A truck was being loaded over in the parking area; Brad's truck was still packed from last night. A group was milling around, getting organized to start off to Site 3 to begin the necessary repairs.

Once they'd finished, Emmy caught up with Lorie to help list and divide supplies and Abby walked over to the parking area. The trucks were loaded and the crew was ready, so Abby jumped onto the running board of Brad's truck.

"Hey," she said. "Recovered yet from all your traveling experiences?"

"Not a chance," he grinned. "But ready for more!"

"Let's hope not," Abby retorted. "I, for one, couldn't stand the suspense." Part of Brad's story last night had involved driving along a muddy riverbank, high above the Missouri River, slipping and sliding and coming perilously close to the edge. Abby didn't mind heights, as long as she wasn't in a vehicle. The thought gave her shivers.

When they arrived at the site, Abby briefed Brad while the crew unloaded both trucks. Making sure both her knife and handgun were secure, she checked her Mossberg and started climbing the hill behind the tents.

It was cooler in the trees than it had been in the meadow, but not by much. There were a few birds flitting around, some small animals scurrying through the underbrush. Abby idly wondered how much longer it would be before they'd have to declare open season on certain edible species. Yuck. She could do it, had done it, but simply wasn't fond of wild game. Wuss, she told herself. Get over it.

She'd nearly reached the top of the hill, one of the tallest in the entire camp. Truthfully, she wasn't completely sure where the legal boundaries were located but she guessed that it didn't matter much anymore. Most of the trees were cedars, but there was one majestic oak that stood out. Swinging a rope over the lowest branch, just out of her reach, Abby began to climb.

Obtaining her goal after several minutes, Abby hooked one leg around the branch upon which she was sitting. She pulled a pair of binoculars out of her pack and began to survey as far as she could see, starting with the space closest to her.

No unusual sounds, no movement that could be attributed to humans. Or anything else besides smaller animals. Good, she thought. So far, so good.

Using the rope as a guideline, Abby came down rather more quickly than she'd gone up. She could have joined Brad and his crew for sandwiches, but instead rummaged through her pack for a couple granola bars. Finishing her lunch with half-a-bottle's worth of water, Abby stood up and dusted off her jeans.

Within less than 45 minutes, she was back at the base of the hill, checking in with Brad.

The crew was finishing up lunch and, Brad told her, all the repairs on the unit were done. He was going to check out the old shower house nearby and see if that could be fixed up as well, and was moving part of his crew down the road to Site 2. Abby's cell phone beeped.

"Ab, how's it going?" came Meg's voice.

"Fine," Abby told her. "I'm off in search of canvas and Brad's moving right along here. Looks like we can start the move tomorrow, unless something else comes up."

"Great! Gotta go, be careful!" Meg hung up and Abby clicked off as well.

"See ya," she said to Brad.

Some two hours later, Abby was still hacking through the scrub growth, trying to get to the last campsite. Obviously, this unit had been abandoned long before the others; she wasn't very optimistic about finding anything here that they could use.

When she finally emerged into a clearing of sorts, about halfway up the rocky hillside, she was positive that it had been a wasted effort.

The tent frames were bare, some crumbling into termite dust. Old leaves littered the floors, and she smelled a skunk odor, faint but definitely present. She made her way over to the kitchen shelter. The cabinets, surprisingly, appeared to be intact; there was nothing strewn about. Empty, she guessed. Then she saw the padlocks.

Removing a small axe from her belt, Abby struck at the first lock until it broke and fell to the ground. She opened the cabinet doors, which squeaked from disuse, and there they were. The cabinet was stuffed with canvas, presumably the missing tent covers but, given their size, only one or two could possibly be stored there. She hastily moved to other four and broke the locks.

Eight. Altogether there were eight large rolls of canvas. Jackpot! She put the axe away and called Brad to send someone to the base of the hill; on second thought, she asked for an extra person to help drag these down to the road. They were quite heavy and bulky and smelled like mold. No matter, thought Abby, they'd air out just fine as long as that skunk stayed away.

By 4:00, Abby was back with Brad's crew at Site 3, stretching canvas over the repaired tent frames. Just before 6:00, everyone piled into the trucks for the short trip back to the meadow.

Abby had a few minutes to check in with Emmy and get cleaned up, then she joined the rest of the group for dinner. Cal stood up as soon as everyone was served and cleared her throat to get their attention.

"Tomorrow," she said, "We're moving."

CHAPTER EIGHT

The buzz of conversation grew louder as people's faces registered surprise and shock. Most of them had been there just a couple of days, some had arrived after that, but all were at least beginning to feel comfortable and safe given the circumstances. Many questions had yet to be answered, and there was a constant undercurrent of fear. This was too much.

"Hey," said Meg, loudly. "Listen up, folks!"

The group quieted somewhat as Cal continued, "Late yesterday I received a message. I'm not sure from whom it came, but that person was pretty clear: he or she knows we're here and warned us of that fact.

"There's no easy way to say this. It's a threat, and we're too exposed out here in this meadow. We're moving tomorrow, to higher ground. Meet up after dinner with your work crew, and we'll get this done in an organized fashion. We'll go over more details tomorrow night and hopefully be able to answer some of your questions." Cal stepped out of the light, out of the shelter, and the general conversation became louder.

Abby quickly finished her dinner, waved to Emmy, and made her way to the command center. Meg arrived just as Abby sat down and started giving her report to Cal.

"Here's the layout," she began, making a simple drawing of Site 3. "The tents are all on the hillside, not very spread out but some are higher than others. Brad's crew cleared out the paths in between them all, so movement is easy. The shelter is at the base of the hill, by the road, and since it's just as large as this one, we should have no problem gathering everyone at once.

"I suggest we keep most storage in the shelter at Site 2, maybe even reinforce that as needed. It's back a lot further in the woods, even though it has road access."

"All right," Cal said. "Let's take a look at all this and go over the particulars as soon as the others arrive."

Abby stepped back further, into the shadows. She opened her phone and scrolled to Deb's text message from three days ago. She could barely hear Meg and Cal's conversation as she focused on the screen.

"Abby. It's too late for me. I know this. I'm not sure what's happening, but I don't feel too bad yet—just strange. I wanted you to leave, not knowing what else was coming. And now—"

That was it. The message had ended abruptly; Abby felt as though she'd been punched in the stomach, hard. She took a deep breath, surprised to realize that she hadn't actually taken a breath at all for several minutes. Later, she could think about this, about Deb. Right now she had to get control of herself and try to figure out what Deb had meant by "strange" and how she had known it was too late.

Voices intruded on Abby's thoughts. Everyone else had arrived and so she joined them, carefully putting her phone back in its clip.

"Hey," said Meg, "Listen up, guys! Here are your bunking assignments, effective tomorrow. We'll be splitting up the command, since we're gonna be at two different sites starting tomorrow. Meals will be as one group, at Site 3; so Ted, you'll be there along with your cooking crew. Cal and I, and Abby and Emmy, will be quartered there too.

"Lorie, Brad and his gang fixed up the old shower house yesterday, which includes the laundry room. Since we don't have enough power for that, we'll be installing the commissary in there. That puts you at Site 3 as well.

"Okay, Emmy has the lists of who will be at each site. As soon as the crews finish up this evening, around 2030, she and Cal and Pops will be making the rounds, letting everyone know where they're moving to.

"Any questions?"

There were none. This group had worked together often over the years and, although the circumstances were completely beyond their collective experience and imagination, the duties and schedules were quite similar.

"Right," said Cal. "See you in the morning, then. Ted, breakfast at 0600 tomorrow, yes?" Ted nodded. "Good night, everyone."

Back in her own tent, Abby checked the list for tomorrow's move. There were eight of the black trucks, altogether; that meant that Abby would have six passengers. A tight fit, but doable given the truck's double-cab design. All the personal gear would easily take up the bed, but she already knew there'd be more than one trip. First, they'd load up with communal provisions: food, water, medical supplies, building materials.

The second trip would consist of the generators, gasoline, and weapons cache. Finally, a third trip for the personal items. It would be a long day, Abby knew, which was why they were starting so early. Still, she couldn't relax just yet; she had to pack, too.

Fortunately, Abby traveled light. A few pairs of jeans, half a dozen t-shirts, a couple jackets, an extra pair of boots; besides some winter gear, which was stowed temporarily in a special after-market case under the bed of her truck, this was nearly her entire wardrobe.

Once she had her clothing stowed in her frame pack, she turned to her gun case. Starting with the Mossberg, she carefully cleaned and oiled each one, checked her ammo stash, and gently replaced each in its soft case.

Abby had just stretched out on her cot and was setting the alarm on her watch when Emmy finally arrived.

"I'm beat," said Emmy, as she plopped down on the edge of Abby's cot. "And I still have to pack!"

"Yep, you do," Abby grinned. "Go ahead, I'll supervise." She made herself comfortable and slyly shoved Emmy onto the floor with her foot.

"Hey!"

"C'mon, Em, you can talk to me while you pack; tell me all about your rounds tonight. What's everyone think about all this?"

"Well," Emmy said as she began to stuff clothes into her pack, "They're scared, but not as much as you might think. After being here for a few days, and knowing—or, rather, not knowing—much of what's going on out there, they seem to have confidence in us. I mean, they're mostly all here because they knew us, or someone they were close to knew us.

"There is that one couple, um, Tom or Tim or something, and his wife, Alana. I think they just sort of followed someone into the campground. But it's okay," she added when she saw the look on Abby's face. "Noah said he'd heard of them from Janey, a few months ago."

Abby relaxed and lay back down on her cot; in her tension, she'd not only sat bolt upright but had one foot on the ground.

If Noah was vouching for them, it was okay then; she'd mention it to Cal tomorrow.

At last Emmy finished her packing and she, too, lay down on her cot. Abby yawned and stretched. Another long day was coming, and there were still so many unanswered questions.

By 0900 hours, the first convoy of trucks was loaded and headed to Sites 2 and 3. At the crossroad, three of the eight vehicles turned off and continued down the road further to unload the medical and building supplies. The remainder stopped at Site 3.

Abby was already there; she'd gone ahead of the group to check that everything was still secure at both campsites. Emmy had driven her truck for this load. Everyone got to work immediately, unloading and storing food and cooking gear. One truck backed up to the old laundry room to pack away extra supplies in Lorie's new commissary.

Within an hour or so, all the trucks were empty and heading back to the old camp. Ted and his crew remained at Site 3 to put together a quick lunch for everyone and make sure the water jugs were full and coffee was brewing.

Abby wiped sweat off her neck and paused for a moment in the hot sun. She and Janey were loading the last of the rifles, and Abby had been particularly impressed with the cache of HK416s that Janey had, somehow, managed to acquire.

A moment later, Janey came trotting around the corner and Abby almost couldn't believe her eyes.

"Okay, spill—how the heck did you get one of those?"

"Ha," said Janey. "Don't ask, don't tell! Give me a hand here, will ya, and stop gawking." Between the two of them, they lifted the M2 Browning into the truck bed.

"Sheesh," Abby said. "Do you really think we're going to need one of these?"

"Don't know," Janey told her, "But I'd rather have it and not need it. And at this point, who knows?" She shrugged. "C'mon, let's go."

The two girls climbed into the truck after Janey had carefully covered the M2. "Um, Ab. No one knows about this but you, okay?"

"Of course." Abby drove over to the stack of ammo boxes and they began to load them, pausing only to wet their bandanas and tie them around their heads.

At last they reached Site 3, and stopped for lunch. It was much hotter now, pushing 100 degrees Abby guessed, plus the humidity. It was good to sit and rest in the shade for a short time.

One more trip and they were finished with the move by 1600 hours.

Abby plopped down under a tree, wiping sweat from her face. At least it was a little cooler up here by the tents. Almost everyone had rolled up the sides to try to get at least a little breeze moving under the hot canvas, but it was a mostly futile effort.

She could hear some light-hearted bickering as people unpacked and staked out their own personal territories. No voices were actually raised, however, as no one had enough energy left to actually complain too much.

Emmy came up the path and sat down beside her. "Man, that was tough. All Ted's girls wanted to bunk with him and I had to practically drag a couple of them out of his and Lorie's tent. Sheesh, you'd think they'd have better things to think about!"

Abby grinned. "And how did Lorie feel about all this?"

"Oh, she's still down in the commissary, sorting and checking. Hey," exclaimed Emmy, "I think I'll go tell her! She'll love it!"

"Where do you get your energy? I don't even feel like going down for dinner. Blech, it's too hot for anything else today." Abby shifted and made herself a bit more comfortable.

"Oh, no you don't," said Emmy, pulling her friend to her feet. "You have to eat, same as everyone. You can crash later."

"Fine," Abby retorted. "Remember this when I get you up in the morning!"

The two moved down the path to the meadow; they saw Lorie coming before they reached the shelter. "Hey," said Emmy, "Hope you don't mind, Lorie, but I had to put a couple of Ted's cooks in the tent with the two of you. They were pretty insistent and all and I knew, even though you—hey, ouch!"

Emmy glared at Lorie and rubbed her shoulder. "That wasn't nice!"

Lorie was blushing. "Knock it off, Em," she said, putting her arm around Emmy. "And keep it down, will you?" she pleaded.

Abby just stared off into space and grinned. So that's how it was, huh? Boy, could she have fun with this!

The three got their plates from around the fire pit and found seats together. "I wonder what tonight's meeting will bring," said Abby. "Surely we've got to find some real-life contact with the rest of the world, and probably pretty soon."

"No idea," said Emmy. "I do know that I'll be tied up most of the evening checking on everyone; probably go over to Site 2 as well."

Just as they finished eating, Cal stepped up to the front and raised her voice for everyone to listen up.

"I know that you have questions. I'm going to answer as many as I can, but you should know that we just don't have a lot of answers yet." Hands flew into the air. Cal nodded at a big, burly man.

"Hi," he said, standing up. "I'm Mack." He twisted his baseball cap in his hands. "I guess my main question is this: what the heck is happening?" He sat down amid several shouts of "Yeah, what's going on?" and "Tell us!"

"Well," said Cal, her eyebrows raised. "Let's start off with the top question of all time, shall we?" There were a few polite laughs, but not many. Everyone was deathly quiet, waiting to hear the answer.

"Here's what we know," Cal continued. "First, I'm going to use the word "infected." We're not sure if it's actually an infection per se, but that's as close as we can come right now. Second, some people are infected, others are not; at this point, we don't know why. Third, it appears to be fatal.

"Yes, I know that many of you have seen friends and family become ill and die in a short time. You know that's what happened, but a few of you have also reported that the body you saw had later disappeared. I have no answer for that.

"Next question. James?"

"How do we know if someone has it?"

"Symptoms that we know of include scratches or scarring suddenly appearing on the victim's face, minimal bleeding, followed by weakness and a trance-like state. Death is within minutes." Everyone looked around nervously, trying to see faces more clearly in the lowering light.

Candy stood up next. "How do we know everyone here is okay? I mean, some of us don't know everyone and well . . . what if someone here is infected?"

Cal smiled reassuringly. "We don't think that's a danger, Candy. We think that if anyone here was infected, we'd know by now."

"Why did we move out of the meadow?" someone shouted.

"This area is easier to defend ourselves, with the hill and the trees," said Cal. "It was a simple matter of safety and security." Though she was a bit surprised by the question, she didn't show it; she had thought that, last night, the mention of a potential threat would lead any thinking person to see the point of moving.

"What about food?" said another anonymous voice, this time a woman.

"We have enough for now," answered Cal, "And there are plans to obtain additional supplies. Some of you will be a part of that over the next few days.

"As long as we can move about the general vicinity, outside the camp itself, we'll be fine for quite some time."

There were few additional questions, as most were tired and worn out from not only moving the camp that day but also from several days' worth of fear and anxiety. The group finally disbanded, and the dozen leaders met at the commissary for further instructions.

CHAPTER NINE

"Lorie, Brad, Janey, and Abby are going into town tomorrow," said Cal, starting the meeting off quickly. "Two trucks, just in case. Your primary purpose is to scout out anything that's happening, any people around, but no contact. Plus, scope out any supplies you think we might be able to, er, acquire.

"Zoe? You can take over for Lorie tomorrow. And Emmy, I need some help with these reports and schedules."

Sandy spoke next, which was rare. "As per Cal's request, we're stepping up patrols for at least the next week or so. I've added two crews, one at night and one during the day; that means at all times we have three people keeping an eye on things in our immediate area, and four on the camp perimeter.

"It's going to take some work to keep all the slots filled, and I might have to ask some of you to sacrifice a little sleep.

"That's all," she smiled shyly and stepped back. "Noah, do you have anything for us?" asked Cal.

"Sorry to say, I don't. Not much, anyway. I did want to check with you about setting up a small lab in one of those shacks at Site 2. Brad said he could fix it up for me pretty quickly.

"And, um, I'm going to need blood samples from all of you . . ." His voice trailed off a bit when he saw a few of them turn pale.

"We'll talk about the details tomorrow, Noah," Cal said hastily as she grabbed Meg's arm to steady her. "Brad, what time will you all be heading out?"

"Right after breakfast," said Brad. "Can't wait!" He smirked at Abby and she stuck out her tongue at him.

By 8:30 the next morning, both trucks were pulling out of the camp gates; Sandy was there to carefully close them and then disappear back into the woods. Brad and Abby rode in silence for several miles along the winding road.

They saw nothing out of the ordinary until they reached the main road. There, cars were in the ditch, at least one was rammed into a tree, and several had crashed into each other. But there were no people. No bodies.

Both trucks pulled into the gas station at the corner of the main road and the highway. Brad and Abby jumped out, guns at the ready, while Lorie and Janey tossed out plastic gasoline cans and began to fill them. They filled the truck tanks as well.

Moving as one unit, the four walked carefully towards the building, eyes roving ahead and to the sides, constantly watching. Once inside the doors, the still-functioning air conditioning was cooling as well as surprising. Of course, most machines were automated and the gas pumps themselves ran on electricity, but still, in a world where everything else had changed so drastically . . .

There were bodies here. Nearly a dozen, in various poses, but all with the same telltale signs of the mysterious symptoms so far documented. Two cashiers, the rest customers. Perhaps a manager, or a delivery guy. After several days, it was getting hard to tell.

Determining that the area was secure, Abby began to empty the coolers in the back of the room. As she stacked cases of water, soda, and beer, Lorie searched for and found a wheeled platform used for stocking heavy items. The two loaded it up as much as they could.

Janey and Brad found and secured the back exit, along with the adjacent parking area. While they kept watch, Abby and Lorie pulled the trucks around to the back. The four worked in shifts, loading and guarding, until the beds were full, then Abby and Lorie went back inside.

Finding the storeroom, the pair discovered many cases of convenience-type foods, unopened, as well as canned goods; the type of fare usually available in gas stations everywhere. They started the process all over again, loading, unloading, guarding, this time stopping when both backseats were filled to the top.

"Not much of a 'town' trip, Brad," teased Abby. "And here I thought we were going to see some big city lights, you know, maybe dinner, dancing."

"Huh," said Brad. "Next time, if you're a good girl."

Abby lightly punched him. "Schmuck."

The four arrived back at the camp within an hour. It had taken some time, as they used the heavy trucks to gently move several abandoned cars off the road so the next trip would be a bit easier. They left the trucks at Site 3 for unloading and returned to town in two empty ones for the second phase.

This time they bypassed the gas station and kept going, crossing under the highway. They saw no signs of life but presumed that anyone would be just as cautious as they. The small convoy turned south at the intersection.

The four-lane, pseudo highway was less congested than the smaller road, but they could still see many cars along the shoulder. Here, however, while driving slowly out of necessity, they also spotted several bodies. Having been exposed to the hot temperatures for several days, the smell of those corpses was overwhelming.

Abby rolled up the windows and turned on the air conditioning. "Phew," she said, gagging a little. Brad merely nodded; his face had a greenish tinge.

They drove past the old drive-in on their right, a junkyard on the left. The road opened up a bit, with fewer parked cars, so Abby rolled her window down and lit a cigarette. After a couple more miles, businesses began to appear on either side of the road.

Janey and Lorie were behind them by about 50 yards or so when they reached the town itself. They closed up the gap, and both trucks proceeded slowly, all four of them keeping a close eye for movement and listening for any sounds.

Brad had a particular destination in mind. At last he directed Abby to pull into the parking lot of a strip mall. He signaled Janey to follow him as he stepped out of the truck, handgun at the ready. The two of them scoped out the electronics store as Abby and Lorie backed the trucks closer to the building.

Janey tested the door, which was unlocked, then covered Brad as he ducked inside; she quickly followed. Moving cautiously, the two secured the interior. Janey kept watch as Brad moved to the back, to the storeroom.

From which he returned, running, as a wild honking noise arose outside in the parking lot. Janey was right in front of him and both burst through the door.

Abby and Lorie were standing on the running boards of the trucks, shotguns cocked and aimed at a strange figure.

It was impossible to determine the woman's age; indeed, the only way they could tell that the person was female was due to her outfit: a somewhat faded print dress, work boots, a cardigan sweater in spite of the heat and, of all things, an old-fashioned gas mask.

She was, however, pointing the business end of a rusty old rifle at Abby and Lorie.

"Hey there," said Brad quietly. "Why don't you put that gun down and we'll talk." He cringed, knowing that he sounded exactly like some actor in a cheesy cop movie.

The woman turned her head from side to side, taking in the four people directly in front of her, all with guns trained in her direction. "Oh, hell," she said, and set her rifle down.

As the others relaxed their guard a bit, she took off her gas mask. "I s'pose if you all can breathe the air here it's safe after all. Name's Millie," she added. "Don't imagine you all can tell me what in tarnation's going on?"

Brad holstered his gun and approached the woman; the girls stood by, ready for trouble if it came. He stopped several feet from her, and studied her face. Nothing. Well, nothing except a few wrinkles and some faint age spots. She appeared to be well past retirement age, although feisty and rather spry. He frisked her as a matter of protocol, then stepped back, gathering his thoughts.

"Well, sonny, dontcha have any questions for me?" asked Millie.

"Uh, yeah," Brad cleared his throat. He could feel the girls smirking at him from behind his back. He cleared his throat again and looked at Millie. "Are you alone?"

"Yep," said Millie. "Except for Bob. Hey, Bob!" She put two fingers to her mouth and whistled long and loud. Everyone jumped, guns brought back to firing position.

A very large, very black German shepherd came bounding around the corner. "This is Bob," said Millie.

Janey was annoyed at herself for being so tense, and annoyed with Millie for scaring the daylights out of everyone. Abby and Lorie felt rather the same way. Brad, however, was smiling and rubbing Bob's ears.

Lorie stayed outside, keeping watch while Brad questioned Millie at length. Janey and Abby returned to the electronics store to search the storeroom.

Satisfied at last that Millie was indeed exactly what she appeared to be, Brad joined the two inside. As per his instructions, the three of them began carting boxes of two-way radios and CBs out to the trucks. They also raided the store's supplies of batteries, particularly rechargeable ones. Abby found two cases of heavy-duty cable, and Janey found three packed with outdoor LED lights.

Last on their list were the binoculars and high-powered telescopes, but when they finally had everything packed, Millie asked, "Didja see my solar panels back there?"

"What?" Lorie turned to look at Millie. "They don't carry those; you have to special-order them."

"I did," said Millie. "Well, Ed did, rest his soul."

"Who's Ed? And where is he? I thought you said you were alone!"

"I did and I am. Ed's my late husband. He passed two weeks ago yesterday. I was sure they'd be here by now, and a good thing too."

"But . . . never mind," said Lorie. "Hey, Brad! Check that storeroom again. Millie says there might be solar panels back there."

"Hang on." Brad trotted back into the store, returning quickly. "Janey, Abby, come give me a hand with these!"

Sure enough, Millie's panels were there. They loaded the boxes along with everything else and were ready to move on. Bob jumped into the front seat next to Abby; Brad shrugged and got into the back with Millie.

"Where to, boss?" asked Abby.

Brad mulled over the question for a minute. On the one hand, they still had some ground to cover; on the other, they now had Millie with them…and Bob.

"Let's head back to camp. We'll decide after that."

The two trucks pulled out onto the four-lane and turned north. There was no need to move vehicles on this wider stretch of road, so they made good time. Before long, they were inside the camp gates and Sandy had called Meg to tell her about the extra passenger. Cal and Meg met them at the old office building. They were prepared for almost anything, handguns at the ready.

"Bob," said Millie. "Stay here. I'll be back in a jiffy." She got out of the truck a little stiffly and waited to be introduced, hands at her sides. She wasn't dumb.

"So," boomed Meg, "What's going on?" She and Cal assessed the group and, not seeing any signs of duress or force, relaxed a bit. Especially when they got a good look at Millie, in her dowdy housedress and sensible shoes.

"This is Millie," Brad told them. "We found her… um, she found us over at the electronics store."

"What's your story, Millie?" asked Cal.

Millie reiterated what she'd told everyone else earlier. Brad nodded at Meg. All the details matched, and Millie didn't sound like she'd rehearsed; she was about as threatening as a loaf of bread. Which, Brad thought, reminded him that they'd missed lunch.

"Millie, you're welcome to stay here with us, but I want to cover a few ground rules first," Cal told her. "Meg and I are in nominally in charge, but there are a group of us who act as the central command; you've already met these four. Sandy is our head of security; she's the one who called in for clearance.

"You'll be assigned a tent, and a work crew. You do nothing on your own, but report to us whenever you see or hear or find something unusual.

"Why don't you ride back to the campsite with me, and Meg can follow us; that way I can answer any questions you might have."

Millie looked tired, but relieved. "Sure, I'll be happy to stay. No one's left back in town, far as I could tell. And I can follow directions and take orders, if I have to—I'm a hard worker, been one all my life. But what about Bob?"

"Who's Bob?" asked Meg. Abby opened the truck door and Bob came bounding out to stop directly in front of Meg. He sat down and wagged his tail.

"Meet Bob," said Millie.

CHAPTER TEN

Abby and Brad ate sandwiches, brought by Cal, as they all drove back to town for the third time that day. Millie had given them a description of her house, along with directions. She said they couldn't miss it, since the front yard was full of the pink flamingos that Ed had, inexplicably, been fond of since his retirement.

"Full" was perhaps an understatement. Even Janey gawked at the sight. Lorie just laughed. "I had a grandmother who loved those things," she said. "Her neighbors weren't very happy, though."

Brad punched in the alarm code that Millie had given them. In spite of the older woman having told them that she'd seen no one at all for several days, at least no one who was alive, they still moved cautiously.

Abby and Janey moved through the small house, room by room, checking for intruders. Assured that all was well, the four congregated in the sunny kitchen.

"Under here," said Brad, "Is Millie's storm shelter. Let's get this table and rug moved, and see what we can find."

Within half a minute, the four of them were descending the wooden stairs, flashlights on, stopping at the bottom in a concrete bunker. Janey switched on the overhead light. They all blinked.

Three walls of the room were lined with metal shelves, bolted and anchored. The shelves were filled with canned goods, batteries, flashlights, bottled water, coffee, and packages of freeze-dried meals. Two entire units were devoted to boxes of ammo, all types. The fourth wall was covered in gun racks. Fully stocked.

One corner held a comfortable-looking bed, unmade; in the center were a small wooden table and two chairs.

"Wow," said Lorie. "Ed must have been expecting a war." "Yeah, well . . . that's kind of what he got," said Janey. "Come on, let's start moving all this stuff. Looks like we hit the jackpot!" Almost everything was still packed in its original cardboard case, which made the task much easier. Still, it took an hour just to heave it all up to the kitchen where the group stopped for a few minutes to rest.

"Looks like we'll miss dinner, too," grumbled Brad, looking at his watch. "Up and at 'em, folks, let's go!"

Abby stood up. "What's that?" They all froze. "Did you hear anything?" They strained to listen.

"Probably a cat," said Lorie. "I've been wondering what happened to all the animals, you know, pets."

"Starved or running wild, most likely," said Brad. "I'm not going to go around rescuing cats, anyway. Yuck."

"There it is again. It sounded like . . ." Abby moved to the back door; they all drew their weapons. Easing the door open just a crack, Abby paused. She heard it again. There was movement behind a bush near the steps; a flash of pink. Abby quietly walked down the stairs, toward the sound.

Silence.

"Hello?" said Abby. "Is somebody there?"

She heard a sniffle, and then a tiny voice said, "Grammy?" She clicked on the safety of her .357 as she realized that Lorie was just steps behind her. Slowly she reached forward and moved just one branch.

A small, dirty, tear-streaked face looked back at her. Tangled blond hair and big blue eyes stared at Abby; the eyes, fortunately, appeared normal and there were no wounds on her cheeks. The small girl, perhaps four years old, hiccupped.

"Where's my grammy?" she asked.

Having replaced Millie's rug and kitchen table, the four of them sat down to discuss the newest member of their group. Member she was, since she seemed to be permanently attached to Abby and refused to let go of Abby's neck. None of them quite knew what to say or do.

"She's not infected," ventured Lorie. "And we certainly can't leave her here, alone."

"Duh," said Janey. "Guess we just figure it out as we go.

Maybe one of Ted's girls can babysit or something."

Abby loosened the little girl's arms just a bit so she could breathe better. "She asked for her grammy. Do you think that's Millie?"

Janey got up and stretched. "Dunno. S'pose we'll find out when we get back and, speaking of back, we need to be heading that direction."

At this point Brad, who had been lost in thought, jumped up too. "Janey, you and Lorie go get the trucks and bring them around back. We'll get loaded and head out. Ab, guess you're babysitting for the time being." He grinned.

"Great," Abby said.

Thirty minutes later, they were ready to roll. Brad drove this time, as it was impossible for Abby to do so with a small child still holding on tightly to her neck. As they pulled out of the small driveway, Brad called Meg to let her know they were on their way.

"Oh, and Meg?" he said. "We have an extra passenger . . . about three years old."

"Wonderful," said Meg. "Don't tell me it's another dog. Bob already knocked over a pot of Ted's stew and since I was the one who hollered at him, he's stuck to my side like glue now."

"That's okay," Brad told her. "Abby's babysitting this one. See ya soon." He laughed when he broke off the connection.

Abby absentmindedly stroked the little girl's back. "I wish she'd talk, Brad. This doesn't seem right."

"Well, I don't know," Brad said. "She must've been through quite a lot the last few days. I wonder where her folks are . . ." His voice trailed off.

"Yeah, let's not go there." Abby hugged the little girl, who had begun to sob quietly. "She was at Millie's house, and asked for her grammy, don't forget. I assume that Millie knows who she is; maybe she can get her to talk?"

Brad shrugged. "We'll know soon enough."

They arrived back at camp without incident. Abby was relieved, as she thought they'd had enough of those today anyway. And, they were in time for dinner, which made Brad happy.

As soon as they stopped, and Abby disentangled herself and her passenger from the seat belt, Millie rushed over to her. "Oh my goodness gracious, you poor little thing!" she said, and took the small girl from Abby. Abby massaged her neck for a moment as everyone crowded around, asking questions.

"This," said Millie, "Is Miss Juliet. No, she's not my granddaughter; Ed and I never had any kids, but she comes over to play all the time. Well," she corrected herself, "She used to . . ."

"Now, you all just go on and eat. I helped out Mr. Ted there with dinner and it's something awfully good. I'm gonna take little Jules here and get her cleaned up and all." Millie marched off to the shower house with her young charge before anyone could ask any more questions, Bob trailing behind.

Abby started over to the fire pit, noticing that Ted looked a bit harassed. She heard him muttering as he served her plate, something about "that woman," but she let him be and focused on her dinner. She sat down next to Pops, who was eating diligently.

"So," she said, "How's it going over at Number 2, Pops?"
"Just fine," he answered around mouthfuls of cornbread.

"Damn, this is good. That woman sure can cook." Somehow, Abby didn't think that his comment and Ted's about "that woman" were at all similar. She grinned.

"I don't know, Pops, looks like Ted's a little bent out of shape over there."

"Eh, whatever," Pops retorted. "Kid could still stand to learn a thing or two." Ted, the kid in question, had had his 30th birthday several years ago. "Anyways, I like her. She speaks her mind and does what's needed. Don't have to keep after her like I do some people." He glanced across the way at Candy.

"That one, for example. Not a day goes by already that I don't find her slacking off, wandering around. We gotta keep an eye on her, Abby."

Hmm. Interesting. Abby hadn't paid much attention to Candy; she barely knew her, in fact. The younger girl struck

Abby as being a little entitled, a little lazy perhaps, but not particularly a bad person. However, after Pops' comment, she decided she better keep a lookout just in case.

Emmy walked over and sat down. "Hey, Ab, heard you had some excitement today."

"Yeah, you could say that." Abby filled Emmy in on the day's activities.

"Well," said Emmy, "We had a little fun here today too. First, Millie's arrival created something of a disturbance; Pops' jaw dropped when he saw her and well, I think he likes her, don't you?" She poked him playfully in the ribs, grinning.

"Aw, Emmy Lou, I don't either. And stop poking me!" Pops turned his attention back to his food, his face reddening. "But she sure can cook!"

Abby got up and took her plate to the dish bucket at the other end of the shelter. She looked up and saw Millie and the little girl coming her way and, when the Juliet saw Abby, she broke into a run.

"Juliet," Millie called. "Mind your manners!"

Juliet skidded to a halt and dropped her eyes. After a moment, she looked up at Abby and took a deep breath. "Pleased to meet ya, Miss Abby." Then she threw herself into Abby's arms. Again.

Abby had to admit that having a small child hanging on her was a bit more pleasant when said child had had a bath and was wearing clean clothes. She smiled when she saw the girl's outfit of an extra-large camp t-shirt that Lorie had found somewhere in the commissary.

Millie finally caught up and coaxed Juliet to come with her and eat some supper. It didn't take much convincing; the little girl was evidently very hungry. However, she was still barely speaking.

Juliet cleaned her plate and used her napkin, setting it carefully to the side when she was finished. When she saw Noah approaching the table, however, she ducked her head.

"Come on, honey, let's go to our tent now," said Millie. "Dr. Noah here wants to take a look at you."

Juliet shook her head vehemently, curls hiding her face. "Want Abby," she said.

"But honey, Grammy's here. Come on." Millie stood up and tried to pry the girl from the bench, but it was no use; Juliet stubbornly refused to budge.

"No," she said. "Abby."

Millie looked over at Abby and shrugged. Abby sighed and walked around the table to Juliet. "Let's go, little one." She picked up Juliet and turned to follow Noah. This should be fun.

Millie walked along beside them and the four went down the road to Site 2. A crew had moved another cot into Millie's tent and delivered a bundle of bedding for Juliet. Abby sat down on the cot, still holding the little girl.

"Juliet," Millie said, "Dr. Noah is just going to take a look at you and make sure you're feeling okay. You know, just like Dr. Dennis used to do."

Noah opened his standard black bag and took out a roller thermometer. Abby was always slightly surprised when she actually saw Noah being a doctor—back in the day, she never would have imagined it. She pried Juliet's arms from around her neck and, in one smooth motion, turned the little girl around to face Noah. Bob the dog laid in the corner, watching with interest.

"Okay, little one, let's take your temperature, real quick-like." Noah looked in Juliet's eyes, her ears, and her nose. He examined her hands and her arms and legs; he listened to her heartbeat and her lungs.

"Well, there you go, Juliet. Best I can tell, you're fit as a fiddle."

Juliet smiled, shyly.

"And," said Noah, "Here's the obligatory lollipop!" "Thank you," said Juliet.

Abby helped Juliet unwrap her treat while Millie and Noah stepped outside to talk. Abby sat with Juliet, just holding her, as the light waned and katydids began to sing.

Finally, she realized that Juliet had become quite heavy. She looked down, and the little girl was fast asleep. Abby stood up and laid Juliet on Millie's bed while she spread out the sheet and light blanket and put on a pillowcase. She moved Juliet into her own bed and tucked her in, then lit the kerosene lantern and turned it down low. She tiptoed outside to tell Millie and Noah good night.

They'd finished their conversation and Millie went inside for the night; Noah insisted on walking Abby back to Site 3.

"It seems Millie has known Juliet's family for a number of years," he told Abby. "I'm assuming her parents are gone; Millie said she never saw them, and for the last few days she's been scoping out most of the town.

"At any rate, if her parents are still alive they weren't doing a very good job of taking care of her. And she's four years old, by the way; just had a birthday a few weeks ago."

"So what happens to her now?" asked Abby.

"Well, Millie has agreed to take care of her, as much as she can. Juliet knows her well, so that's good. And Ted has said a couple of his helpers would be willing to babysit sometimes."

"Oh," said Abby. She was almost, just a little bit, disappointed for some reason.

"But, Abby . . ." Noah stopped. "Juliet really seems to have taken to you. I think it would be a good thing for her if you're around as much as you can manage.

"In fact, when Millie was giving her a bath, Juliet talked about you quite a bit."

"Really?" said Abby. "I've barely heard her say two sentences."

"Well, she knows Millie and the rest of us are strangers. And Millie said she's rather shy most of the time. Nothing she won't probably outgrow, eventually. But, I'd like you to take on as much of her care as you can; work out some kind of, um, custody arrangement with Millie. She's willing, she knows her limitations; besides, she said you kind of resemble Juliet's mom, you're even about the same age." Noah finished his speech.

"So, what do you say, Abby?"

Abby thought for a few minutes, as they continued to walk down the road. She'd never thought about having kids. Ever. Of course, this wasn't like having a child, really. After all, she'd be "sharing" with Millie. And she was apt to be gone out in the woods, scouting or on guard duty, or making trips around the area.

Likely most of the work would fall on Millie. Or Ted's babysitters. But still . . . it was an interesting proposition.

Abby stopped. Good Lord, what was she thinking?

"Noah, I don't think this is a very good idea. I don't know the first thing about kids, especially four-year-old girls. And I'm out in the woods half the time, or scrounging around town or wherever.

"I don't think this'll work."

"Sure it will, Ab. You'll see. It'll be fun! And Millie is here, she can take over whenever you're gone. Besides, think of the things you can teach Juliet...c'mon, Ab, say yes!"

Abby was silent for a few minutes.

"All right, fine. I'll do it. But I'm telling you, Noah, you might want to consider someone else. Maybe Zoe. Or Candy. Or someone!"

Noah gave Abby a quick hug. "Knew I could count on you!" He grinned. "And congratulations, it's a girl!"

Abby rolled her eyes and started walking again.

CHAPTER ELEVEN

Abby jumped out of bed and pulled her gun out from under her pillow. She heard the scream a second time as she was pulling on her boots; she flew down the path, in the dark, and reached the bottom of the hill almost before that second scream ended.

"Stay put," she told Emmy. "I'll let you know if I need you." She knew from whom it was coming; it was Juliet, down at Site 2. She ran down the gravel road, more by instinct than sight as no moon was visible.

As she dashed across the bridge, she could see a group of people gathered outside Millie's tent. She brushed aside the flap and went inside.

The lantern was burning brightly and Millie was rocking Juliet, trying to quiet her; Noah knelt beside the cot. Fortunately, Juliet had stopped screaming but she continued to sob loudly and tried to flail her arms and legs. Millie held her tightly, but it wasn't working.

"Millie," said Noah. "Try to wake her; she's having a night terror, not surprising under the circumstances, but she doesn't realize what's happening or where she is now."

Millie bent her head close to Juliet's ear. "Honey, come on, wake up." She shook the girl gently. "Juliet, wake up!"

The little girl gave one last shudder, then relaxed. Her eyes opened and she stared up at Millie. She stopped crying. Noah moved closer and stroked her hair.

"There you go, little one. Everything's fine now. You just had a bad dream, didn't you?"

"Y-yes," said Juliet. "Want Abby."

Abby had stuck her gun in the back of her jeans as she'd entered the tent, noting not a single threat that could be dealt with via weaponry. However, she'd had zero experience with a child's nightmare, or anything else to do with children for that matter, and so she was a bit nonplused when faced with Juliet's request.

Noah turned to her. "Well, Abby?"

"Of course," she said. That was simple enough. She took Juliet from Millie and sat down on the cot.

Millie stood up and stretched and yawned. "Dang it, I'm too old for this commotion," she said. "I need my beauty rest." She crawled back into bed. "Young lady, you wake me if you need to, but I reckon you'll be just fine." She rolled over and was asleep again almost immediately.

Abby blinked. Now what was she supposed to do? Noah came back from telling the crowd to go on back to bed, that everything was fine, and she looked up at him.

"And?" she asked.

"Well, Abby, I guess you have a little girl for the night. Or what's left of it. See if you can get her back to sleep, and maybe sleep some yourself.

"You've really got to stop this running around in the middle of the night . . ." He grinned and disappeared into the darkness outside before she could call him any one of the several names on the tip of her tongue.

"Well," she said.

She looked at Juliet. Juliet looked back at her. Abby smiled. Juliet smiled back.

"All right, Toots, let's get you all tucked in. Again." Abby laid Juliet down and pulled up the covers. Juliet rubbed her eyes and yawned.

"Abby, will you stay here with me?"

Abby sighed. "Sure, kiddo, scoot on over so I can lie down." It had been a long night already. Wait a minute. Abby realized that she probably shouldn't put a loaded gun under a little girl's pillow, safety locked or not. Then she thought that, probably, it would be a bad idea to have a loaded gun in the tent. However, she was unwilling to imagine having to need that gun within seconds, and still be trying to find the ammo and load it.

"Juliet," she said, pulling out the gun and showing it to the little girl. "Um, I know you're only four but you know what this is, right?"

"Yes," said Juliet. "A gun."

"Good. And you must never, ever touch a gun, right?"

"Right."

"Especially this gun."

"Okay."

"Now," said Abby, "I'm going to set this gun under the cot. You are not to touch it. This is very important, okay?"

"Okay." Juliet rubbed her eyes again. "Abby?"

"Yes?"

"Will you tell me a story?"

Abby sighed. Did she know any stories? Well, yes, but for little kids? She thought about it for a minute. The Three Little Bears? Dogs? Wait, that wasn't right. The Three Little Pigs. Of course!

She snuggled next to Juliet and began. "Once upon a

time . . . " But Juliet was already asleep.

Early the next morning, Abby woke with a start. It took her several seconds to realize that she wasn't in her own tent, then another moment to gather her memories of the previous night.

She carefully disengaged her arm from beneath Juliet and eased to a standing position. She stretched and yawned, then made her way quietly outside and across the bridge. Within a few minutes, she was climbing the hill to pick up her shower bucket.

After a quick shower and fresh clothes, Abby went in search of coffee. The fire crew was hard at work and Ted was directing his cooks; he paused to hand her a steaming mug. She sat down at a table and waited for Cal and the others. After all the excitement yesterday, the usual nightly meeting had been postponed until this morning.

Emmy sat beside Abby. "How's the little girl this morning, Ab?"

Abby yawned. "Sleeping, I guess. She had a nightmare or something last night."

"I heard. Well, we all did, actually." Emmy looked down at her coffee. "I'm glad you could be there for her, Ab. Poor little thing, she must be so scared."

"Well, yeah. I mean, we're all scared, Em. I mean, well, you know." Abby was a little rattled, having just now appreciated that they all might just be in a really big jam, something it might be impossible to work their way out of any time soon.

Finally Cal arrived and the meeting began. Abby was grateful to have something else, something practical, to occupy her thoughts.

"All right, here's where we sit: Noah is still working with me, trying to access files and checking on the overall situation.

It appears that, as you know, it's not confined to just our area, or even the entire US. It's global." Cal paused for a moment, then cleared her throat.

"What this means is that we're on our own. We're also trying to connect with additional groups that may be out there; this is Meg's department, but she's not having much more success.

"Sorry to say, in a nutshell, we're still pretty clueless."

Everyone was silent. There was really nothing to say. They all, each one realized, had been hoping for better news without being aware of that hope. And, too, what had seemed almost surreal the last few days was rapidly becoming a new existence, for the duration.

"So," Cal continued, "Here's what we're going to do. Almost everyone will remain with their assigned duties, unless there are any objections?

"No? Good. We'll be sending out salvage crews over the next week, starting tomorrow. Brad's going to compile a list of needed materials, and Lorie will provide a list of needed supplies for the commissary, along with Ted's requests for the cooking crew.

"The fire guys will be off in the woods as much as we can spare them, getting wood for the winter. Yes, I'm aware that it's just late August, but you all know as well as I do that the weather in Missouri is weird at its best." She smiled. "At any rate, we need to start thinking and preparing. That electric grid isn't going to last much longer. Neither are the cell towers."

Well, thought Abby. This should be interesting. Most of them had grown up without cell phones; CBs and walkies worked just fine, after all. But they'd sure all gotten used to cells pretty quickly; and the Internet. Wow. On the other hand, there wasn't much online at the moment; no one seemed to be around to post any new information, or they didn't have any in the first place.

Cal wasn't finished, but Abby needed more coffee. She refilled her mug and strolled over to the edge of the shelter, lighting a cigarette.

"Emmy," said Cal, "I'm pulling you off hostess duty—we aren't likely to get any new folks in here, unless we pick up one or two like we did yesterday. You'll work with Lorie over at the commissary most of the time, but I also want you to sit in with Meg and me in case we have any, um, disagreements with anyone. You know, help mediate." Cal was well aware that she tended to be all business, and Meg could be rather blunt; Emmy would provide a little more conciliation.

"Okay, that's it for today. We'll all kind of take it easy around camp here today, a little R&R, and meet at the commissary tomorrow after dinner.

"Oh, and I need to see Abby and Zoe for a minute."

Everyone got up to leave, pleased at the thought of having no schedule, at least for a short time. No one even thought to ask any questions or for clarification of anything Cal had said. The part about not knowing much at all had temporarily shocked them a bit.

Abby put out her cigarette and fieldstripped it. She and Zoe sat down with Cal.

"All right," said Cal. "Zoe, since you have your degree in forestry and have been using it for quite a few years now, I want you to take over the fire crew.

"Ted's been nominally in charge, since he uses them for the cooking fires, but starting today we're going with cold lunches so the crew can be out in the woods most of the day.

"We need to go pretty far out, but still stay on the property; we certainly want to keep our cover here, nearby. I also need you to make a plan as to what areas and when, so Abby can know where you all are while she's out and about. That way, in case we need to communicate and radios are down in your location, Abby can find you."

"Got it," said Zoe. "I'll have the info to you by lunchtime today."

"Sorry to make you work when everyone else is off today," said Cal with a smile. "I'll make it up to you and Brad later."

The petite redhead blushed. Everyone knew she and Brad were an item, even though they mostly tried to hide it. Zoe left and Cal turned to Abby.

"Congratulations," she grinned. "I hear it's a girl."

Abby groaned and put her head down. Why did everyone keep saying that? Cal laughed.

"Okay, okay. Sorry." She looked anything but repentant as she grinned at Abby. "Seriously, though, how do you plan to handle this?"

"Me?" said Abby. "This wasn't my idea—and besides, Noah said that Millie was going to take care of Juliet, that I'd be like a backup person or something. And Ted's girls said they'd babysit too. What am I supposed to do?"

"Well, Abby, clearly she's attached herself to you. And while she knows Millie, and has since she was a baby, it's you she wants.

"I've seen her run to you, speak to you, and hang on to you for dear life—not to mention last night, as soon as she became coherent she asked for you. Not Millie."

"Geez, Cal, don't you ever sleep?" grumbled Abby. "No," said Cal, "Not really."

"Again, what exactly do you want me to do?" Abby asked, yet she feared the answer.

"Glad you asked," said Cal with a snicker. "She can stay with Millie at night; I'd rather you be free in case, er, anything urgent comes up. But the rest of the time, when you're in camp at least, I'd like you to take charge of Juliet.

"Millie is no spring chicken, if you didn't notice, and she just can't keep up with a four-year-old all day."

"What about when I'm in the field?" asked Abby. "She'll have to stay here, either with Millie or someone else."

"Absolutely," said Cal. "We'll make arrangements for that. I'm sure you'll get lots of help. Speaking of . . ." Cal got up to leave as Juliet came running to Abby.

Millie was close behind the little girl, Bob at her side, and she sat down beside Abby. "Whew! She practically ran all the way here! Hang on a minute, honey, let Grammy catch her breath and we'll get us some breakfast." Juliet obediently sat down on the bench.

"Abby can help me," said Juliet.

Millie looked at the younger woman. "Maybe, but you have to ask her first."

"Abby, will you help me get breakfast?"

"Sure, kiddo." Abby stood up and Juliet took her hand and smiled up at her. Huh, thought Abby. How hard could this be?

She helped the little girl fill her plate with bacon and scrambled eggs, but was stumped when it came to the coffee. She was pretty sure that caffeine wasn't the best thing for a four- year-old to drink. Ted came to her rescue, and offered Juliet a mug of milk.

"Thank you," said Juliet. Abby smiled at Ted in relief. The two sat down and Juliet ate her breakfast.

"So," said Millie cheerfully, "What do you two have planned for today? Just so you know, I usually lie down for a bit right after lunch...and so does Juliet. Sometimes."

"Um, what do we have planned?" Abby looked nonplussed. "Uh, for instance?"

Millie took pity on her and patted her shoulder. "It's okay, dear, it can be quite a shock taking care of a small child all day. You just bring her back to my tent after lunch for a bit. Maybe take a walk, or play a game?"

"A game?" Abby repeated. She sure didn't remember playing games at that age; heck, she couldn't remember even being that age!

"Yes, a game. Like hide and seek, or tag, or catch; Juliet loves baseball. Oh," Millie added, "Guess we don't have any baseballs around here. Well, maybe just a nice walk then."

Abby loved a challenge but this . . . this would take some doing. She looked at her watch. 9:00 a.m. That left, oh, a few hours at least. Surely she could handle a small girl for that amount of time.

"Right," said Abby. "Come along, Jules, we'll find something to do." She lifted Juliet off the bench, told her to tell Millie goodbye, and showed her how to put her dishes in the waiting tub by the fire pit. She whistled for Bob and they climbed the hill to Abby's tent.

"This place," said Abby decidedly, "Is a mess. Jules, you can help me clean up; whatever I hand to you, set it on Emmy's bed. Yes, that one," she added, as Juliet pointed.

Within a few minutes, Abby was able to make up her bed, left in disarray from her hasty departure in the middle of last night. She swept the floor and showed Juliet how to hold the dustpan. When they were finished, Abby started to slide out her gun case.

"Oh. Right. You're four, aren't you Jules?" The girl nodded. "Hmmm. Well, it's a bit of an early start, but under the circumstances . . ." Abby opened the case, and when Juliet looked inside her eyes grew wide.

"First," Abby told her, "Never, ever touch these, or this case, or any other gun, ever, unless a big person tells you to, got it?" Juliet nodded solemnly.

Abby took out what she needed and closed and locked the case. Pushing it back under the cot, she sat down on the floor. Juliet followed suit.

First, Abby pulled out her .357, checked the safety, unloaded the gun, and began to clean it. Juliet watched her every move.

"What's that called, Abby?" Juliet asked. So Abby explained the parts of the handgun and exactly what she was doing. Before reloading, she handed the gun to Juliet.

The little girl was surprised at how heavy it was and almost dropped it into her lap. But she didn't. She hung on to it and turned it over, carefully examining it.

"That's enough for today, Jules. One more thing: never, ever point a gun at a person unless you intend to shoot him. And you better have a darn good reason." Well, Abby thought, maybe that's a little too much for a four-year-old. But she shrugged it off; the world had changed, and a little knowledge, even of things so unthinkable just a few days ago, certainly couldn't hurt.

Abby reloaded the .357, checked the safety, and stuck it back in her jeans. She pulled her knife out of the ankle sheath and began sharpening it, while Juliet watched. When she was done, she replaced the knife and stood up.

"Come on, Jules, let's go for a walk."

CHAPTER TWELVE

By noon, Abby and Juliet had arrived back at the shelter for lunch. They'd tromped through the creek just beyond Site 3 until they reached the meadow where the first camp had been set up initially. They walked down the gravel road, all the way back to Site 1. Along the way, Abby pointed out different trees to Juliet, explaining that since trees were usually the biggest thing in the woods, it would be good to recognize particular kinds and shapes.

They were in no real hurry; it was a beautiful day, not too hot for late August and slightly overcast. They stopped frequently to listen to the birds singing, or just to rest for a moment and sip some water.

However, when it was time to head back, Juliet was clearly too tired to walk much farther. She climbed up on a nearby rock and then onto Abby's back.

Millie saw them arrive and came out to meet them. "Oh, mercy, is she okay?"

"Of course," Abby told her, "She's just tired. We had a nice long hike, didn't we, Jules?"

89

Juliet blinked. "Oh, yes, Grammy! We had the most fun! Abby took me for a walk, just like you said. After we cleaned her guns, of course." She jumped down. "What's for lunch?"

"What?" said Millie. "Guns?"

"Well, yes," said Abby. "She does have to learn, you know. Especially now. And," she added hastily, "She didn't actually do anything, just watched me clean them. And she had a lesson in gun safety."

"Yes, Grammy, Abby said to never, ever touch guns unless I was with a grown-up and they told me to. And she told me all about trees and birds and things too!"

Juliet skipped off to wash her hands and was back at Abby's side in a nanosecond. Millie just stopped and stared at them.

"Well, mercy me!" she exclaimed, shaking her head. She took Juliet off to get sandwiches and milk, Juliet chattering the whole time.

Abby felt like she could take a nap as well, something she never did. She wondered just what else she was supposed to do on this "day off." She grabbed a sandwich and wandered over to a tree and sat down.

An hour later, Abby awoke with a start. Emmy had just sat down beside her and she, too, jumped a bit.

"What the heck," said Emmy. "Did I scare you? I thought you were asleep!"

"Wow," Abby replied. "Had no idea one small kid could wear me out like that." She rubbed her eyes and stretched. "That's more work than tromping around in the woods by myself all day long."

Abby picked up her forgotten sandwich and wolfed it down. She took a swig from her water bottle. "So, what's next on the agenda for our day of leisure?"

"I don't know," said Emmy. "I've been helping Lorie all morning and I'm tired of sitting still. Hey, want to go to the lake? No one's been there yet, far as I know."

"Well," said Abby. "I don't know, Em. I mean, I haven't had a chance to check it out yet and I don't think anyone else has, either. It might not be, you know, safe."

"Come on, Ab. We can both scout it out; you know I'm up to it!" Emmy stood up and pulled Abby to her feet too. "I'll run find Meg and let her know we're going, and meet you at the tent." Emmy took off, full of energy.

Abby shrugged. It would be something to do, guaranteeing that she wouldn't fall asleep again, like some, well, four-year-old! She climbed the path to their tent to gear up for the hike.

Thirty minutes later, Abby and Emmy set off for the lake. Bob decided to join them, apparently; the big German shepherd wasn't much for taking naps. They walked past the old campsite but, instead of going left towards the old office buildings, they turned right to cut through past an old barn. A short time later, they found the overgrown entrance to the path that led up yet another hill, then around to the lake. Bob took turns running ahead of them, then dashing back, barking joyfully every few minutes.

It took nearly an hour to hack their way through the undergrowth and finally reach the lake. They had paid close attention to both the trail itself and the surrounding woods, and the girls had neither seen nor heard any signs of humanity. However, before they stepped out from the trailhead into the clearing, Abby stopped Emmy with a tap on the shoulder; using hand signs, she told Emmy to wait just a moment.

Abby pulled out her binoculars and scanned the lake itself, and just beyond, all around the perimeter. She set them aside and, using only her eyes and ears, repeated the process. Bob sat down obediently, watching and waiting.

Satisfied that no one was close by, she motioned for Emmy to follow her. They stepped out into the cleared area, gazing at the sparkling lake.

Lake Atwood was nearly nine acres in size, and about one-third of the shoreline was a sandy beach; the rest was ringed by trees and rock outcroppings. There was a falling-down shelter to their left and a dilapidated boathouse opposite.

The girls walked down to the edge of the gently lapping water and splashed some of it on their hot faces. They started walking around the shoreline, watching and listening. Before long, they came to the gravel road leading up a hill to the old barns. Trees had naturally fallen to block the way and the road itself was full of weeds. It was obvious that no one had been up there in years.

They turned around and walked back to where they had come out of the tree line, and further, until they reached the large rocks. Seeing and hearing nothing but the few wispy clouds and the songs of native birds, the girls went back to the old shelter and beach area.

Abby pulled some beef jerky out of her pack and handed some to Emmy. Bob lay down and gave her a pitiful look, so Abby handed him a piece as well. They drank from their water bottles and relaxed under the scant amount of shade.

"Nice and quiet here," said Emmy. "But you know, I haven't been swimming in ages . . ." With that, she was up and stripping off her boots, jeans, and t-shirt. She ran for the water and plunged in, but came up immediately, sputtering.

"D-dang, that's cold!" She shook her head, her brown curls flattened, and wiped water out of her eyes. "Brrrr!"

Abby laughed. "What did you expect? Spring-fed, remember?"

"Yeah, I remember, but still! It must be 95 degrees today and you'd think the sun would have warmed it up a little. Come on in, Ab!"

"Nope, no thank you! But Bob appears to be enjoying himself." The big dog was paddling close to shore; within a few minutes he landed on the beach area and shook himself mostly dry. Abby walked to the edge of the water and, removing her boots and rolling up her jeans, placing her knife on the sand beside her, put her feet in the water. It was nice and cooling.

Just a few short minutes later, Emmy came out and sat next to Abby, drying in the sun.

"Wish we could just stay here," said Emmy. "It's so nice and quiet."

"Hey," said Abby. "Look!" They saw a fish jump into the air and then disappear; then another. "At least the lake is still stocked."

"Too bad I don't have a pole," said Emmy, stretched out on the sand, unmoving.

"Yeah," said Abby. "'Cause I can see you hustling up to go fishing right now." Emmy mumbled something, under her breath, and rolled over.

Abby nudged her with a foot. "Don't go falling asleep now, we have to be heading back. I'm going to go take a look at the boathouse, I'll be right back."

Abby walked around the outside of the old building. It wasn't in great shape, but still standing. She stood on tiptoe and tried to see inside the one grimy window, but it was too dark. She circled back to the door.

It was padlocked, but Abby was sure she could simply wrench the handle off the door itself; the wood was practically falling apart already. Grasping it tightly with both hands, she twisted once, then again. She staggered backwards, almost falling, when it came loose.

The wide door swung open as Abby pulled her gun out and clicked off the safety; better prepared than something else, something worse, she thought. Nothing, or no one, rushed out and Abby gave herself a minute for her eyes to adjust to the darkness inside.

Surprisingly, the tall racks to both her right and left were full of canoes; paddles were stacked along the back wall, and from the rafters hung a few dusty old lifejackets. In the center was a jon boat. Cobwebs were thick, and the floorboards creaked as Abby stepped inside for a closer look.

Fifteen minutes later, she woke up Emmy and the two girls, and Bob, were on their way back to camp.

Juliet saw Abby and Emmy coming up the road before anyone else and, with her grammy's permission, ran to meet them. She jumped onto Abby, nearly knocking her over, and began asking questions almost immediately.

"Where'd you go, Abby? What did you see? Did you miss me? I missed you!"

Abby rolled her eyes at Emmy. "Slow down, Jules. Give me a minute, okay?" They reached the shelter at Site 3 and Abby unloaded the little girl and then sat down. It was nearly dinnertime and people had begun to gather. Jules promptly climbed into Abby's lap.

"We went to the lake today, Jules. It's a big, beautiful lake over that way." She gestured vaguely in the direction from which they'd come; it occurred to her that it might not be a good idea for Juliet to decide to try to go there herself. "And we saw boats, and fish," Abby finished.

"Fishes!" exclaimed Juliet. "My daddy took me fishing once." Her small voice trailed off and she stuck her thumb in her mouth, snuggling against Abby. "I miss my daddy."

Abby felt an unexpected lump in her throat as she hugged the little girl tightly.

Folks were starting to eat and Millie came bustling over. "Come on, Juliet, let's go eat. You need to give Abby some time to rest and you can see her after dinner." Juliet went along with her grammy and Abby went to get her food, wondering what the evening held in store.

The command group met again in the commissary, that being the space which offered the most privacy, should they require it. The mood was much lighter than all the previous meetings; the day off for nearly everyone had made a huge difference in their outlook.

"Okay, folks, listen up!" said Meg, breaking into the general chitchat. "Here's our plan for next week.

"September 1st is in two days. That gives us just two months, more or less, until the weather starts to really cool off and things might get a bit uncomfortable.

"I know you're all wondering just how long we're going to be holed up here, especially if we're getting ready for winter. Cal?"

Cal stood up. She looked tired.

"Noah and I have been going over all the intel we've gathered so far. He'll talk to you in a minute about some of that. What we've decided, with input from Meg and Sandy, is that we're all much safer here than anywhere else; at least for the foreseeable future.

"This is why we're going to plan on staying put. Through the winter, at least. So, in order to do this, we're keeping Zoe's crew on firewood duty; the cooks will tend their own fires. Brad and his group are going to be winterizing as much shelter as they can manage, but priority goes to storage facilities, either building or repurposing.

"Some of you may have to pull double duty and pitch in wherever you're needed most on a particular day, but all-in-all we'll keep assignments as regular as possible. I want everyone to check in each morning after breakfast for any changes."

Cal paused for a moment and looked at her notes. "We'll be sending a crew into town to scavenge every morning, at minimum, until we have the supplies we need. And Sandy will be doubling her security team.

"That's all I've got for now, except for individual assignments. Noah, you're up."

Noah's tall, lanky frame almost reached the rather low ceiling as he stood and moved to the center of the room. "Well, he said, "I think we may have a handle on this whole scenario."

Silence. Complete and utter silence greeted his statement. Apprehension shone on the faces of everyone in the group. For several months they'd all lived with the possibility of a mysterious occurrence, for nearly a week they'd hidden away after escaping the consequences. For a few hours today they'd almost been able to stop wondering, to halt their fearful thoughts.

Noah cleared his throat. He looked around the room slowly. "Biological," he said.

"I'm sorry," Noah apologized. "That's all I've got." He shrugged. "I know it's not a disease, per se, and I know it's neither bacterial nor viral.

"I don't think anyone here can catch it, and I don't think we'll be seeing any new cases. In other words, everyone still living appears to be immune."

Silence. Again.

Minds were racing, taking in all the implications of Noah's report. Some looked baffled, others appears slightly dazed. Meg's booming voice brought them all back to reality, this new reality.

"So, what you're saying is that you think you know what it's not, but there's more work to do to find out what it is, right?"

"Yes." Noah looked relieved. "Exactly. I think we're pretty safe, for now, but I need to run more tests and go back over the information. I know there's a key, I just have to find it.

"And," he glanced around, apprehensively, "I'm still going to need blood samples from all of you. Later, I'll probably have to expand it to the entire group; but I'd like to keep things under wraps, just us, for the time being."

Meg seemed a bit pale, but she put on a brave face. "Okey dokey, then. Who's next? Cal?"

Cal stood up. "That's really all for tonight folks; we'll keep you updated as we go along and please, remember not to let this out of the group. We don't want to start a panic.

"I am, however, going to call a meeting after breakfast tomorrow. Some folks are getting restless, and I want to give everyone the option of staying here for the winter, or not. That'll give us an idea of numbers and a way to come up with a better plan if we can manage it.

"Abby, Emmy, I need to see you two for a minute. Oh, and Janey, you too."

Everyone filed out after Noah took his samples, most heading for the campfire, some to their tents. It was barely 8:00, but in the valley there it was starting to get dark. Abby stepped outside for a moment, lighting a cigarette and wishing she had a beer. She went back inside just as Janey was leaving.

"See you in the trenches," said Janey, winking.

Abby raised a questioning eyebrow, but continued through the door. She figured she'd know soon enough what Janey was talking about. She sat down beside Emmy, to whom Cal was speaking.

"All right then, we'll start tomorrow, Em. You and Pops and Lorie can head out after breakfast. I wish I could spare someone else, but it can't be helped just now.

"Abby," Cal continued, "You're going to have it pretty rough the next couple days but, like I told Emmy, that's just the way it is. I'll know more, of course, after we talk to everyone in the morning.

"I need to know what's going on around our perimeter; yes, I know that the immediate area is safe, but I think we need to expand our borders, so to speak. Things are going to get a lot rougher, I'm afraid."

Abby looked up, still wishing for that drink. "How far out?" she asked.

"All the way up, top of the hills," replied Cal. "Especially after we see who's staying and who's leaving. You should probably plan on an overnight, but I'd rather you not do two in a row."

"Sure," said Abby. "No problem." She thought for a minute. "I'll head out in the morning and start with Pioneer. No reason not to make it back down in the afternoon, far as I know."

"Here," said Cal, handing Abby a two-way radio. "Just a matter of time before we lose cell coverage; surprised it hasn't happened yet. Oh, and some extra batteries." She rummaged around in a box behind her and pulled out a few.

"Lorie's over at the commissary waiting for you, to issue whatever you'll need. I'll see you in the morning before you leave." They all stood up to walk outside. It had gotten quite dark by then, but the campfire over by the shelter offered more than enough light to see the way. Emmy and Cal continued on, but Abby turned the corner to the commissary door.

She knocked and entered, all at the same time, only to see Lorie and Ted jump apart. Both looked guilty, and Ted was blushing. "Shall I come back later?" asked Abby with a grin.

"No, no." Lorie busied herself with some paperwork. "We were just, you know . . ."

"Ha," said Abby. "Oh yeah, I know. Ted was just er, getting supplies for tomorrow taken care of, right?"

"Right," said Ted, straightening up. "Thanks, Lorie, I'll see you later." Ted walked out quickly, closing the door carefully.

Abby burst out laughing. "You two! Do you really think no one knows what's going on?"

"Well, no." Now it was Lorie's turn to blush. Then she turned to business. "Okay, here's what I've got for you. What else do you need?"

Abby scanned the list. Jerky, granola, Gatorade, dehydrated meals . . . all the essentials. Two extra canteens. Coffee, of course. "Looks good, Lorie, I should be all set."

"Great, let's head out then; just let me lock up." The two left the commissary and walked towards the fire pit. "I'll see you in the morning, Ab, I think I'm just gonna go crash." She yawned, a little obviously Abby thought.

"Yeah, right! Sleep well, I'll see you in the morning." Abby smacked the other girl playfully on the shoulder. "Tell Ted I said good night!" Lorie climbed the hill and Abby kept walking, finding a spot next to Emmy near the fire.

Emmy handed her a beer. "Just what I needed," said Abby. "Long day."

"Ain't over till it's over," said Emmy, pointing toward the small girl running for Abby. Bob was hot on her heels.

"Abby!" said Juliet. "I missed you!" She plopped into Abby's lap and began chattering about her evening. Bob kept pushing Abby's free hand with his nose, wanting attention. Sheesh, thought Abby; she sure was popular tonight.

Finally, though, Juliet began to tire. She slumped against Abby and sleepily asked, "Abby, will you come tuck me in?

Abby stood up with some difficulty, having Juliet's almost 40 pounds in her arms, and whistled for Bob who had trotted off to sniff something interesting. She looked around for Millie and spotted her talking to Ted. She grinned. She supposed Lorie was still waiting . . .

Millie caught up to them as Abby and Juliet headed down the road to Site 2, Bob following in their wake.

Abby tucked in Juliet and told her good night, then she and Millie sat outside on the steps. "I hear you're taking off tomorrow, Abby. Will you be gone long?"

"No, just for the day; I should be back by dinner, maybe sooner." They sat in silence for a few minutes, gazing at the stars and listening to the whippoorwills.

Then: "Juliet really loves you, Abby. I'm so glad she's taken to you and that you help me out with her. She can be a handful." Millie chuckled.

"Well, um, thanks," said Abby. "She's a sweet kid." Decidedly uncomfortable with the way this conversation was turning, Abby stood up and said good night to Millie. Bob scrambled to his feet. "Stay," said Abby. Bob lay back down, next to Millie. They both watched Abby walk away into the darkness.

CHAPTER THIRTEEN

Cal waited until most had sat down with their breakfast before she began the group meeting. "We've had some new developments since the last time we all got together. First, there are 61 of us now, plus Bob." She smiled, and Bob sat up, wagging his tail. He was parked, as usual, next to Abby; Juliet was on her lap.

"The command group met last night and we've made a decision to stay here for the winter. It's going to involve a lot of work, and probably some hardship. However, in light of some of our information, we believe it's the best plan.

"I want to give you all the opportunity to choose, of course, as to whether you wish to stay or to leave. If you stay, you'll be assigned duties much like you have the past week; if you decide to leave, we'll outfit you with as many supplies as we can spare and wish you the best." Cal paused for a moment.

"I'd like your decisions by dinnertime tonight."

There was a low buzz of conversation that quickly grew louder. Several hands were raised, a few questions shouted out.

"Hey, Cal! What if we leave and want to come back later?" "What do you mean by "duties?" Do we have to work more or something?"

Cal stood on a bench so she could see everyone and began to call on folks with questions; Abby could hear some of the murmuring, particularly since she was sitting near a couple who seemed to be somewhat at odds with the announcement. They seemed to have their heads together quite often, whispering.

"James, we haven't really discussed anything about leaving and coming back; we'd hope that you'd have a detailed plan before leaving, but of course we wouldn't turn anyone away if they decided to return." Cal kept her face carefully blank and answered the next question, "Yes, there would necessarily be more work involved if you choose to stay. Winter isn't going to be easy here."

Most people seemed at ease and the questions had slowed when Abby got up to leave. She had her pack ready, and she slung the Mossberg over her shoulder after depositing Juliet on the bench next to Millie.

"'Bye, Abby," said Juliet. She reached up and hugged Abby and looked very sad.

"It's okay, little one. I'll be back for dinner. Behave yourself." She chucked Juliet under the chin and turned to find Emmy, but her friend was busy helping Cal field a few more questions. Abby waved and started off down the gravel road.

She found the beginning of the old trail up Pioneer Hill fairly easily, but still had to use her knife to hack away quite a lot of undergrowth. She left as little evidence of her passing as possible, knowing she wasn't breaking a trail but merely scouting the territory.

Abby climbed for a good two hours, stopping once for a water break. Fortunately it was cool in the trees; birds were singing and occasional small wildlife would crash through the brush. She was confident that there were no humans nearby, but was alert for any changes.

Finally reaching the top, Abby paused for a breather. She glanced around first, making sure she was alone, then sat down to stretch her calves and her shoulders. She took a long drink of water and snagged a handful of granola from her pack. Finally, she took out her two-way radio and called Meg to check in and give the all-clear.

That accomplished, she sheathed her knife and began to explore. There used to be a couple of old shacks up here, somewhere, but Abby hadn't been up here for at least a decade.

She stumbled on an old fire pit first, some distance from where she'd stopped to rest. Literally stumbled. Chiding herself for not paying attention, Abby knelt down to get a closer look. Nope, this hadn't been used in forever, probably.

A short distance away, she located the remains of the old shelters. The roof of one was completely down, in several pieces, the weathered, gray wood barely visible under a canopy of greenery. Only two of its walls were standing, and neither appeared very sturdy; they, too, were covered in vines and brambles.

The second shelter had fared a bit better. The roof had a gaping hole, but was attached, and all four walls were supporting it. The screen door was missing entirely, so Abby was easily able to shine her flashlight inside and take a closer look.

The scent of cedar trees was heavy, but not enough to mask the distinct odor of skunk. Blech, thought Abby, I'm asking Cal for a raise when I get back down. She stepped back hastily and continued to look around.

Some time later, well past the lunch hour, Abby sat down and gathered her thoughts, memorizing her report while she ate. The site could be used, certainly, but would take a lot of hard labor to clear the area; not to mention shelter repairs. Still, not bad she decided, considering the neglect and lack of use over the years.

She stood up, prepared to descend, and chose to take the other trail back down the hill. It was as disused as the one she had come up, but would put her at the back of Site 2. Might come in handy to have a route both directions.

The trail, as it turned out, was both rockier and more overgrown than the first one. Abby spent a good deal of time hacking her way down and, often, climbing over rocks instead of going around them via the trail itself.

Completely forgetting the basic safety rule of stepping on an object, rather than over it, Abby lost her balance and fell heavily onto her wrist. Immediately, an excruciating pain shot up her arm, much worse than a sprained wrist alone would warrant. With a small cry of shock, she grabbed the knife that she had dropped and slashed the head of a copperhead snake. She flung the body into the woods and stopped short, panting.

Great, she thought. What a moronic move that had been.

First, she checked the wound; not deep, but it didn't matter as far as the poison was concerned. Fortunately it was on her hand, so she could keep moving if she was careful. She splashed some water on the bite and wrapped it tightly with her bandana. She decided not to immobilize her arm itself, as she'd need it for balance to continue her descent.

Abby got her breathing under control, checked the immediate area for any friends or relatives of the diseased, and stood up. Her pulse was beginning to accelerate, but not much. Her hand was already swelling.

She fumbled with her left hand to activate her radio and called Meg. Feeling like a complete greenhorn, Abby succinctly told Meg what had happened and gave her location.

"All right, Ab," Meg told her, "We're on our way; you better stay put, okay?"

"Nope, can't," said Abby. "It'll take you guys at least a couple hours to get up this trail, probably more. It's in pretty rough shape. If I keep going down, we're bound to meet up quicker."

"Fine," said Meg. "Cal won't like this but, well, do what you gotta do, Abby. We'll be as quick as we can. I'll grab Noah and see who else is available.

"And be careful!"

Abby clicked off the radio and continued down the trail, keeping a better watch now and moving rather slowly. She took regular sips of water and kept monitoring her pulse but, within half an hour, was beginning to feel a little light-headed and somewhat nauseous.

She stopped to rest after another half hour, dousing her hand, still wrapped, with cool water. That seemed to help. Her radio crackled to life.

"Abby, how're you doing? How bad is it?" Cal sounded worried, of course.

"I'm doing okay," Abby responded. "Pulse is high, but no major problems. I'm wrapped and taking it slow. How're you guys coming along?" She was starting to feel rather uncomfortable and was really wishing she was back at the camp about now.

"Based on the topo map and your previous location, we should be meeting up in an hour or less. It's not so bad down on this end."

"Okay," said Abby. "See you soon." I hope, she added to herself after signing off.

Another 30 minutes and Abby was about down for the count. She stopped again, worn out from the pain and maneuvering down the trail. This time she took a few Advil and doused her hand with water, but didn't sit down; she wondered if she did that whether or not she'd be able to get back up and keep walking.

Finally she just stopped, slumped next to a tree, and picked up the radio again. "Cal? Are you there?" Then it got dark for Abby, very quickly. She heard a crashing noise not too far in the distance and weakly reached for the Mossberg.

Abby floated in and out of consciousness for what seemed like hours, but by the time Cal and Meg and Noah had gotten her down the trail to Site 2 she was coherent again.

She looked around at her rescuers. "Man, do I feel stupid or what? Can I walk now?"

"Nope," said Meg. "Why start now? I mean, we carried your sorry butt all the way down that hill; I won't be able to move for days after this. Besides, you scared the bejesus out of us up there, ranting and raving about some pretty weird things. The least I could do is haul you the rest of the way...your highness."

Abby smiled and relaxed a little, still wincing in pain. The trio carried her to Millie's tent, which was the closest one, and Millie was waiting for her.

"Oh, you poor dear, let me get you all set up here," Millie said, fussing around the tent, tucking Abby into her own bed. Noah unwrapped Abby's hand for a closer look than the cursory exam he'd done on the trail.

"What time did this happen, Abby?"

"Around 3:30. Too late for antivenin, right?"

"Yes," Noah said. "But you kept it wrapped and wet, so that'll help the swelling. Did you take anything?"

"Yeah, about four Advil, around 4:00 or 4:30. Damn, this hurts. First time one of the little suckers ever nailed me."

"I'll give you something stronger, but here, Millie has some dinner for you. You'd better eat first, then take these." Noah handed her two pills. "They'll probably knock you right out."

"Someone call for an ice bucket?" asked Emmy from the doorway.

"So, Em, how was your day?" asked Abby, still with a sense of humor although it was dwindling fast. Emmy put Abby's hand in the bucket and began talking about the outcome of the morning's meeting, who was staying, who was leaving.

Abby couldn't focus and, before Emmy even got close to finishing her monologue, was sound asleep.

Early the next morning, Abby groaned and sat up. She blinked and looked at her hand, trying to piece together the fuzzy memories. Ah, yes. Hand. Snake. She lay back down quickly.

A second try found her examining her hand; still swollen, and bruised. She tried to flex it. Wonderful. That was her best shooting hand. She hoped she wouldn't be out of commission very long. She tried sitting up again. There, that was better.

Millie stuck her head through the tent flap. "And how's our patient this morning?"

"Starving," replied Abby. "And sore."

"Well no wonder, after what you went through yesterday. And falling asleep before you could even eat your dinner!" Millie set a plate down on Abby's lap. "There you go, dear. Dr. Noah said he'd be by in a few minutes, so eat up!"

A small, curl-framed face poked itself inside the tent, eyes wide. Juliet flew to Abby's cot but stopped short. "Abby, are you okay?" She looked scared.

"Yeah, Jules, I'm fine. It's okay, come here." Abby patted the cot. "You can sit down right here."

Juliet slowly climbed up next to Abby, then threw her arms around her. Abby used her good arm to hug the little girl, then gently moved her aside a bit so she could finish her bacon and eggs. She was dying for coffee and a smoke, but that would have to wait until Noah showed up.

Next through the flap was Emmy. "Hey, lazybones, up and at 'em!"

"What is this," Abby grumbled good-naturedly, "Some kind of 'welcome back' party?"

"Nope," said Emmy, "We had that last night, only you slept through it."

"True," said Millie cheerfully. "That nice Dr. Noah was here most of the night, checking your vitals and all, and Juliet got to have a sleepover with Miss Lorie. Emmy and me, we took turns icing your hand and giving you sips of water."

"Yep." Emmy gently hugged her friend. "I just came by to tell you I'm off to town with the rest of the gang. I'll check in when we get back, might not be until dinner. Behave yourself!" And Emmy was off.

Within minutes, Noah appeared. After he checked Abby's hand, he took her blood pressure and asked a few questions. "Well, looks like you got pretty lucky. The swelling isn't too bad, nor is the bruising, and you don't have a fever. However, you've got to take it easy for a few days at least; move around if you feel like it, do what you feel up to but stop if anything changes.

"And," he added, "No more scouting trips for at least a week. You need to stay close by. I mean it, Abby."

Abby rolled her eyes. "Fine. Whatever. Now can I get up and go find some coffee?" She was already halfway off the cot.

Noah sighed. "Sure, but don't forget what I said. I'm watching you." He winked. "Hey Millie, find this girl her boots, she's heading out!"

Abby walked down the road at a brisk pace, heading for Ted's coffee. She really wanted a shower, too, but that would have to wait a few minutes. She was glad that Millie had insisted Juliet stay behind, she needed some time to recuperate.

Sipping coffee and lighting a smoke, Abby parked herself on a bench. Several people stopped to ask how she was feeling, but they seemed to sense her reticence and quickly moved on. She could see some people carrying belongings to the nearby trucks, lined up and waiting to help those leaving.

Cal sat down beside her. "So, we have a bit of an exodus. Not too bad, really."

"How many are going?" asked Abby.

"About half," Cal replied. "Millie and Juliet are staying, of course, and 17 of the others. Surprisingly, James decided not to go; Candy's hanging out with him now, by the way." The two watched the last bags being loaded. Abby wasn't particularly sorry. She didn't know any of them well, most were friends of friends, people she'd never met except recently and she hadn't had time to get very friendly.

"We need to keep an eye on that one," said Abby, referencing James. "Who is he, anyway?"

"I agree," said Cal. "And he's someone who used to work with Meg. She's concerned too. How's the hand?"

"It's okay," said Abby. "I think I'm going to head to the showers and get cleaned up."

"Good idea." Cal stood up and walked away to see off the group that was leaving.

Abby climbed the hill to her tent and sat down, just for a minute, on the edge of her cot. She thought she just might lie down for a bit, then get her shower bucket and go back down. Next thing she knew, she was awakened by a loud thump.

She jumped up and reached for her gun, which of course wasn't under her pillow as usual. In a flash, her hand went to her knife instead.

Noah turned red and looked guilty and scared, all at the same time. "Oops, sorry. Didn't realize you were up here."

Abby started to breathe again. "Sheesh, Noah, you about got yourself shot; well, if I knew where I put my gun."

"Oh, yeah, about that—Meg took it off you when we picked you up yesterday on the hill. She said she'd get it back to you when she sees you. Guess she's been busy with the folks leaving."

"So what's all this?" Abby gestured to the pack Noah had dropped.

"Oh, um, we're having to double-up I guess. Cal had everyone down at Number 2 move up here. It's easier, really." Noah paused. "If you don't mind, that is?"

"Of course not, silly. It'll be like old times." "Yeah," said Noah. "A long, long time ago."

Abby tried to help Noah get settled in an extra bunk, but he made her sit back down and told her she needed to rest. She insisted on at least taking a shower and, since it was near noon, having lunch. She gathered her things and hiked down the hill, wondering if having a doctor living with her and watching her every move was going to be worth it or not.

CHAPTER FOURTEEN

Juliet spotted Abby the minute she'd sat down with her sandwich and came trotting over, Bob hot on her heels. She sat down beside her and started asking Abby questions about the hike, the trail, what she found, what she saw, and the snake. Juliet tried not to look at the bandage on Abby's hand, however. She was a little afraid.

Millie came puffing up to the table. "There you are, you little scamp! You need to slow down when Grammy's with you." Millie sat down heavily. "Abby, do you think you could watch Juliet this afternoon? I don't think she's gonna take a nap today. Unless you need to rest?" Millie looked a little hopeful.

"Sure," answered Abby. "I crashed right after breakfast, so I should be fine." She turned to Juliet. "What would you like to do today, little one?"

"Well," said Juliet. "Could we look at your guns again?"

"Mercy!" Millie exclaimed.

Abby smiled, just a little, then quickly became more serious. "Sure, Jules, but we have to cover all the safety rules again. Do you remember them?"

"Yes!" said Juliet. "Never point a gun unless you in-intend to shoot it. And have a darn good reason!"

"Oh dear." Millie fanned herself and looked a bit faint. "Very good, Jules," said Abby. "Now finish your sandwich."

Juliet rapidly ate her lunch and within minutes the two were climbing the trail to Abby's tent. Abby let Juliet help drag out the gun case from under her cot and showed her how to open it, reiterating that she must never do so without an adult's permission. She showed Juliet the rags and oil and other cleaning implements, as well as the spare ammo.

Just then, Meg appeared at the doorway, carrying the Mossberg and Abby's .357. Abby had to admit, she breathed a sigh of relief. Not that she didn't trust Meg, completely, but she'd felt like part of her had been missing.

"What are you two doing?" asked Meg. "Gun lesson?" Meg seemed to think it was the most natural thing in the world to teach a four-year-old. Maybe especially in this world.

"Yep," answered Abby. Juliet just stared at Meg. She was still shy, and she hadn't seen much of Meg since she'd come to the campsite.

Meg sat down with them to listen as Abby unloaded the .357, took it apart, and began to clean it. Juliet watched her every move and nearly forgot about Meg.

"Abby, can I hold it again?" asked Juliet, when Abby was finished.

"Sure." Abby handed the gun to the little girl, and Juliet checked the safety before she began to examine the weapon. Surprised, Abby smiled and looked at Meg.

"Very good, Juliet," said Meg, laying her hand on Juliet's blond head for a moment. Juliet didn't flinch, but she didn't respond either. "Well, I'm off, got more on my plate than delivering guns today. See you all later!" And Meg was out the door.

"Bye, Meg," whispered Juliet, hardly daring to look up.

Abby took the gun from Juliet and loaded it; she stuck it back in her jeans and reached for the shotgun, repeating the cleaning process while Juliet watched. Abby allowed the little girl to examine it too, although it was much too heavy for her to hold. Again, Juliet checked the safety immediately.

After cleaning and sharpening her knife, and sheathing it in the ankle strap, Abby stood up and held out her hand. They were almost outside when Noah appeared.

"Not so fast there, Abby. Time to check you out again." Abby sighed, but sat back down on her cot. "Make it quick,

Noah, we have things to do."

"Oh? Like what? Take it easy, right?"

"Yes, yes," Abby answered, impatiently. "Just a short walk, down to the meadow."

Noah finished up before replying. "Make sure it's short, Abby, and try to rest up when you get back. Everything looks okay for now; how are you feeling?"

"Anxious to be out, doing something," Abby retorted. Then she relented a bit. "Fine, all right. I'm okay, a little tired, a little sore. Otherwise, like I said, fine."

"Okay then," said Noah. He pulled a lollipop out of his pocket and handed it to Juliet.

"Thank you, Dr. Noah," said Juliet shyly.

"Hey," said Abby. "Where's mine? Where'd you get that anyway?" She looked at him suspiciously.

"Oh, I have my ways. Besides, only non-cranky patients get lollipops these days. Have to ration them, you know!" Noah ducked out as Abby threw a pillow at him. His pillow.

"Come on, Jules. Don't forget your lollipop!"

When they reached the bottom of the trail, Abby saw Meg nearby supervising the unloading of items from Site 2. She angled over that direction and spoke quietly to Meg, just out of Juliet's hearing.

"Sure thing," boomed Meg. "You two go have a good time!" And Abby took Juliet's hand and they continued on their way to the old meadow.

Once there, Abby looked around until she found an old soda can that had somehow dodged the clean-up efforts. She set it in the long grass near the tree line, then she and Juliet walked away as Abby measured out a 25-yard distance. She figured she'd better start out slowly.

Juliet sat down next to Abby, finishing her lollipop and wiping her hands on the grass. Abby looked at her bandaged hand and tried to flex her fingers. Nope, not working. Anyway, with the bandage on, there was no way she could properly hold the gun or pull the trigger. She looked at Juliet.

"Jules, do you see that can?"

"Yes," said Juliet promptly. Abby handed her the gun. "Now, listen to me carefully. Point the gun at that can."

Juliet tried hard, but the gun wobbled precariously. "Here," Abby showed her, "Use two hands, like this."

Juliet put her other hand on the gun and managed to hold it steady.

"Good," said Abby. "Now, hand me the gun." Abby set it down on the grass beside her and took Juliet onto her lap. She picked up the gun again and instructed Juliet to hold it with both hands, while she wrapped her own hands around Juliet's.

"I'm going to have you release the safety, when I tell you, then you're going to fire. Okay?"

Juliet's eyes were as big as saucers. "Really, Abby? I get to shoot your gun?"

"Yes, little one, and I'm going to help you. We're going to aim for that soda can over there, okay? Ready?"

BANG!

Juliet hung on to the gun and didn't flinch when the loud noise exploded from the barrel. "Again," said Abby.

BANG!

They couldn't hear the shot hit, but saw the can fly into the air. Abby clicked the safety back on and lowered the gun, setting it beside her. "Are you okay, Jules?" She turned the little girl around on her lap so she was facing her.

A single tear rolled down Juliet's cheek. She threw her arms around Abby's neck and nodded her head.

"Jules, talk to me! Are you okay?"

"Y-yes," Juliet sniffled. She looked up at Abby. "It was really loud."

Abby smiled. "Yes, it was, but you'll get used to it."

"Does that mean I get to shoot it again?"

Abby and Juliet walked back to Site 3 an hour later, having fired and reloaded several times. Juliet hit the can almost every time, with Abby's guidance. Abby assured her that soon she'd grow big enough to handle the .357 all by herself, but she continued to drill the little girl in gun safety until they got back to Abby's tent.

They cleaned the .357 and reloaded once again; this time Juliet got to help. Abby was exhausted, just from the short hike down to the meadow and back, and was rather disgusted with herself for wanting another nap.

She did, however, lie down on her cot, and Juliet offered to tell her a story. Before Abby could wonder what, exactly, was going to happen to the princess and the frog, both of them were sound asleep.

They woke up when Emmy crashed into the tent, just back from her trip to town, wondering why they seemed to be missing dinner. Abby stood up and stretched, and so did Juliet, imitating her hero.

Emmy laughed at them. "You two are so cute! Come on, let's eat, I'm starving. And I'll tell you all about my day!"

They got their plates from the dinner line and sat down. Millie hustled over. "So what have you two been up to all day?" she asked. "I heard some interesting noises coming from back over yonder."

"Abby let me shoot her gun!" Juliet exclaimed. "It was fun! Then we took a nap. Please pass the salt."

Millie rolled her eyes. "Juliet, honey, you shouldn't tell tales."

"I'm not, Grammy. I really got to!"

"Well, um, yes she did," said Abby, a bit sheepishly. Maybe she should have asked Millie first, or least let her know ahead of time.

"Oh, my heavens!" said Millie. "And here I figured that .357 of yours was too heavy for her. Well, I'll be!"

"You'll be what, Grammy?" asked Juliet.

"I'll just be, that's all. Humph." Millie stalked off.

"Oops," said Abby. "Jules, I think we're in trouble."

"It's okay. Grammy never stays mad for long. Could you please pass the salt, now?"

Emmy handed the shaker to Juliet. "So, I was going to tell you about today, when we went into town? Everything went fine, we drove in, well, Pops drove and I rode shotgun. We took two trucks, in case . . . well, just in case." She glanced at Juliet and decided she better censor herself, well, just in case.

Emmy was just working up to her story when Millie returned. "Uh-oh. Here comes Millie again."

"Abby," said Millie. "I had an idea you were up to something, but under the circumstances, I'm not really mad. I was just surprised, is all. And Juliet is awfully young.

"But here." She handed Abby a small package wrapped in brown paper. "Let her use this; it'll be a lot easier for her to get consistent practice without wearing out her arm.

"Juliet, honey. This was Gramps' Glock .22. He'd want you to have it, if he knew all that was going on now. Abby'll teach you how to take care of it and use it, and you be sure to listen good, okay?" Millie wiped away a tear and gave Juliet a hug before she walked quickly away.

"Wow," said Emmy. They were all quiet for a minute.

"Jules," Abby said, "We'll go take a look at this after we eat, okay?"

"Okay," answered Jules, digging into her dinner. Emmy continued her story and the girls sat and talked for a bit. When Jules began to get a little restless, Abby took her back to the tent and they opened the package.

Jules squealed. "It's just my size! Abby, do you think it'll be as loud as yours?"

"Probably not," Abby smiled. Jules looked a little disappointed. While Abby familiarized herself with the weapon, Jules took out the cleaning supplies. Together, they took the Glock apart and cleaned it, although it was in surprisingly good condition.

"Tomorrow we'll go see if Lorie has any ammo for this." Abby looked up as Noah walked in. "Hey there, roomie. I was just about to walk Jules back to Millie's tent."

"Not so fast; time for a check-up." Abby sighed. Always so business-like, that was Noah. Or rather doctor-like. Sheesh.

Everything checked out, although again Noah cautioned her to rest more. He asked about her fluid intake and handed her a couple more pain pills. "Take these before you go bed. After the day you had, you'll likely need them and if not, at least you'll get a good night's sleep."

"Yes, Doctor," Abby said mockingly. "Come on, Jules, let's get you to bed." The two stepped outside and Noah sat down wearily on his cot.

He knew he was there for a reason; hell, he wanted to be there. What was the alternative, after all? But he was tired; tired of spending a good part of every day trying to figure out what was happening, and tired of fielding silly questions from some of the group as to what symptoms they were having at that particular moment. And he was tired of worrying and wondering about the patients he'd left behind, most of whom were likely dead. Or missing. Or both.

Noah stretched out on his cot, not even removing his boots, and drifted off. He slept straight through till morning, never hearing Emmy or Abby returning, but his dreams were populated with shadowy figures.

CHAPTER FIFTEEN

A week passed; Abby's hand returned to nearly normal in appearance, but was still quite stiff. She had continued to take Juliet out for target practice every day and Lorie had indeed found ammo for the Glock. Juliet wasn't able to hold the weight yet and still shoot with any kind of accuracy, but she was mastering the prone position as well as seated.

Pops and his crew had ventured into town every day and brought back a plethora of supplies; Emmy had even discovered some kids' storybooks to bring back for Juliet. Brad was busy preparing buildings, shelters, and tents for the coming season and Janey had practically deforested a large swath up on Sunnytop.

One morning as he was leaving the tent, Noah told Abby to come down to his "office," a particular table under the shelter, for her final all-clear. He watched carefully as she flexed her hand, pronounced her fit, and instructed her to keep exercising the hand as much as she felt able.

Abby grinned and scooted off the bench. "Finally! Come on, Jules, time for your next lesson!"

"After breakfast?" asked Juliet. "Of course, after breakfast."

The two finished up quickly, dropped their plates in the dishpan, and headed off down the road. "Abby, are we going to shoot today?" asked Juliet.

"Nope," said Abby breezily. "Today we're going to learn how to walk."

"You're silly," said Juliet. "I'm not a baby; I already know how to walk!"

"Yes, but do you know how to walk like an Indian?"

Juliet thought about this for several minutes. "No, but Bob doesn't know, either!" Bob was, as usual, accompanying them today.

Abby realized there was no way she had the patience to teach a dog how to do this, so she wasn't going to argue the point. She stopped at the old meadow and had Juliet sit down with her. They faced each other, several feet apart; Bob lay down nearby and rolled in the grass.

"This," said Abby, holding her hand up, palm out, "Means 'stop'. This," she said, holding her hand out with palm up, "Means 'come here'."

"Well, duh," said Juliet.

"Duh?" asked Abby. "Where did you get that from?"

"From Emmy. She says it all the time, like when something is ob-obeeus."

"I see. And the word is 'obvious'. With a 'v'. And yes, she does say that a lot." Abby tried to hide her smile. "But I bet you know what this one means." Abby held her finger to her lips.

"That means 'be quiet'," said Juliet. "Like an Indian, right?" Abby nodded. "And this?" She cupped her hand to her ear.

"Duh," said Juliet.

"Okay," said Abby, grinning openly now, "You and Bob stay here and watch for my signals." Abby walked a fair distance across the meadow. She wanted to see just how good Juliet's eyes were, even though she'd been making pretty consistent hits on 25-yard targets.

She began to signal. Stop, go, stop, go. When she held her hand to her ear, Juliet paused and looked around; when she held her finger to her lips, Juliet imitated her. Finally the little girl and her canine companion reached Abby. She was impressed with Juliet, of course, but also realized that Bob had done his part admirably as well.

"All right, Jules, you did very well. Remember, it's important to pay attention to everything around you, all the time. Especially when you're in the woods scouting with a partner; you need to know what's going on.

"Now, I'm going to sit down here. You run on back to where you started, and try to sneak up on me." Abby sat down and turned her back. Juliet and Bob took off at a run.

"Go!" called Abby.

At first, she could hear the pair as they rushed through the long grass; then all was silent. She resisted the urge to glance behind her. Then, a telltale swish…and another. Silence again. Abby waited patiently.

She could hear nothing, not even Bob's trademark panting. She strained her ears. There it was again. A faint noise, unheard by most. Then Juliet giggled. Abby smiled. She calculated that Jules was about 20 feet behind her.

Then, suddenly, small arms were around Abby's neck and Juliet was shouting, "Gotcha, Abby!" Abby nearly fell over, between surprise that Jules had, indeed, sneaked up on her and the little girl's weight pulling her to the side. She laughed and grabbed Juliet and began to tickle her. They rolled around in the long grass, with Bob barking and trying to join in the game.

They finally sat up and Abby began plucking grass out of Juliet's curls; Juliet returned the favor, always imitating Abby.

"Now what?" asked Juliet.

"Now we go into the woods," answered Abby.

The trio walked down the road to Site 1. Abby had taken Juliet as far as the tree line some time ago, but they hadn't ventured into the campsite itself. When they approached, Abby had Juliet walk behind her. Bob brought up the rear.

"Jules, walk as quietly as you can, and stay close to me, okay? Do exactly what I do. If you have a question or need something, tug on my shirt."

"Okay," answered Juliet. Her eyes were big.

They walked silently along the dirt road; there were old leaves still lying on the edges, and deadwood could be seen leaning against other, more viable trees. A quail flew out of the brush in front of them and Juliet jumped a little, just barely stopping herself from grabbing Abby's shirt.

Bob watched the bird longingly, but stayed on course.

They arrived in the semi-cleared area by the fire circle and the forest seemed to close around them. It was quiet and cool, but a few birds still sang in the trees and a few small, unknown animals rustled through the leaves.

Abby stopped and she and Juliet sat on a log. Bob wandered off, looking for that quail. "Now what," asked Juliet apprehensively.

"Now we eat lunch!" Abby told her. Juliet brightened up immediately as Abby shared some jerky and granola from her pack.

"This is good," said Juliet, taking a gulp of water from her bottle. "I like the woods, Abby!"

Abby smiled and tousled Juliet's curls. "I'm glad, little one. As soon as we finish, we're going to right back there." She pointed to a faint trail leading off from the back of the campsite.

"Remember, Jules, quiet like an Indian and be sure to listen and look." Abby stood up and Juliet followed. Bob came trotting into his place at the end of their line.

They walked for several minutes down the trail, Abby using her knife to hack at a couple interfering branches. They came across a log blocking the path and Abby stopped, signaled Juliet, then pointed at the log. Then she spoke.

"Jules, whenever you see a log or a rock or anything else in the path, be sure to step on it, not over it. Sometimes snakes like to lie on the other side and you don't want to step on one."

"Is that what happened to you, Abby?" Juliet whispered. "Yes. I wasn't being careful." Abby flexed her hand, definitely wishing she had been more cautious that day.

They both stepped onto and over the log without incident, but Bob seemed to disregard the instructions. He bounded along for a short way, almost disappearing from view, but turned back and walked behind Juliet again.

After half an hour or so, Abby stopped and she and Juliet looked around. The trail ahead rose steeply to continue up the side of Tank Hill, but Abby decided they'd better head back.

She needed to go up there herself, but figured it might be better to wait another few days. And to be sure to leave Juliet back at Site 3 with Millie. Probably not a good hike for a four-year-old and besides, she might have to overnight it and do some repairs up there.

"Come on, little one. Time to turn around. This time, you lead," she told Juliet.

The little girl was beside herself with excitement. She carefully started walking, trying to remember everything Abby had told her earlier in the day. "Abby," she said seriously, "If you need something, tug on my shirt, okay?"

Abby smiled. "Of course."

They reached Site 1 without any problems; Abby was pleased to see that Juliet remembered the log and that she moved very, very quietly for a small child. Slowly too, as it turned out. It took them nearly twice as long to get back to the old fire pit.

They stopped for a few minutes to rest, and to take a few swallows of water, then headed back down the gravel road and out into the sunshine.

Back in Abby's tent, Juliet took off her shoes and placed them precisely next to Abby's boots. Then she climbed onto the cot next to Abby and handed her a book. "Will you read me a story, Abby?"

Nearly asleep by the end of the book, Juliet rolled over and closed her eyes. Abby stifled a yawn and strolled down to the shelter, in search of coffee.

Brad was there, also needing both a break and some caffeine. "Hey stranger!" he said. "How's the snakebite?"

"A little stiff," answered Abby. "But I'm ready for some action."

"I heard you had plenty today—how's the kid holding up?"

"She's fine," said Abby. "And, by the way, she has pretty good aim with that little Glock of hers. You might want to be careful . . ."

"Well," Brad drawled, "I was doing some shooting myself at that age; I might be able to give her a run for her money."

"Right, you Texans are all alike. Killed your first bear at age five, huh?"

"Naw," retorted Brad. "My first buck, though."

"Heathen."

"Injun."

Abby stuck out her tongue. "So, you got anything for me? Besides the tanks, that is?"

"How'd you know I wanted to start that next?"

"Lucky guess," said Abby. "The grid will be going out any minute and the pumps will be down. If the tanks aren't holding, none of your magic will keep water flowing. I'd hate to have to cart it in from the lake."

"How soon can you go up there?"

"Day after tomorrow suit you okay?" Abby quickly calculated the supplies and tools she'd need to wrangle from Lorie and how soon she could pack. Plus, it wouldn't hurt to give her shooting hand one more day to rest, just in case.

"Sure, that'll work. Gotta run, see ya around." Brad went back to his crew, busy winterizing the showers and commissary.

Abby went in search of Millie, and found her doing some mending in the tent she was sharing with Pops. Abby grinned. Such a domestic scene. Pops was on his cot, snoring away.

"Hey, Millie, how's it going?" Abby sat down on the step. "Why, hello Abby! What in the world are you smiling about?" Millie tied off her thread and snipped the loose end. "Don't you be thinking there's any hanky-panky going on— mercy, I can't ever get a good night's sleep with that racket going on over in the corner.

"Is Juliet sleeping? What did you all do today?"

Abby told her about their adventures, including how impressed she was with the little girl's aptitude. Then she told

Millie about her upcoming trip, stressing that she'd likely be gone overnight but would be reachable by radio.

"Don't you worry about us. I've been taking care of kids for a long time. Juliet'll miss you, but she'll be fine."

Abby stayed for a short time, catching Mille up on Juliet's sayings and doings, then walked back to her own tent. Juliet was just waking up.

Juliet helped Abby pack for her trip, asking question upon question as they worked. Abby showed her how to make a bedroll and told her what foods should be taken along; she covered the basics of radio transmissions when Juliet began to experiment with the two-way device. Abby found that the little girl was a good listener and after a while she realized she was talking more to herself. Juliet, however, seemed to take it all in, and was eager to learn.

The morning, as Abby set out, was cool and damp. She knew it would heat up as the day went on, probably about the time she reached the top of Tank Hill and there was less tree cover. In spite of the early hour, Ted had coffee on the fire and he wished Abby a safe journey.

From the back of Site 1, Abby began to climb the hill. It was steep and rocky, barely a visible path, so she unsheathed her knife and began to hack at the undergrowth. Some, she noticed with a mixture of pleasure and chagrin, were blackberry brambles. Two hours later she was nearing the summit and stopped to rest.

Suddenly, it all washed over her in unrelenting waves, memories, thoughts, grief. Abby sat down abruptly and dropped her head into her hands. She would not cry. Would not. No time, no inclination. Really. Besides, it made her nose stuffy and she certainly did not have time for that. Okay, girl, she told herself. Breathe.

Several minutes passed while Abby simply breathed and tried to relax her muscles. She closed her eyes and tried to picture a serene, joyful place; the same place she often revisited in her mind.

The problem was that the place was this place, in a different time, a different world. And so she simply remembered.

CHAPTER SIXTEEN

Seven-year-old Abby got out of the old Pontiac and looked for her friend, Emmy. There were girls milling all over the place, some crying, some clinging to their parents. Others ran up and down the path to the cabins, ignoring the counselors' cries of "Walk, please!"

Abby scuffed the toe of her sneaker in the gravel parking area and looked down. She hoped Emmy would show up soon. She was used to being away from home, either on a vacation with her parents or staying with her dad for a weekend, but she wasn't too sure about this camp place.

"Abigail," said her mother, sharply. "Come here and get your suitcase!" Abby walked to the trunk of the car and hefted the suitcase, wondering what she was supposed to do with it. Just then, a counselor walked over and introduced herself.

"Hi," she said. "My name's Cal. What's yours?"

"Um, Abby . . ."

Cal looked at her clipboard. "Okay, Abby, you're in Cabin 1, with your friend Emmy. I believe she's already here. Let's go take a look, okay?"

Abby perked up a bit. She looked back at her mother, who made shooing motions with her hands and told the little girl that she'd be right there. Abby took Cal's offered hand and they climbed the path.

Emmy was chattering away with a group of girls and Abby hung back, shyly. But Emmy saw her, and came right over. "Abby, I saved this bed for you! Here, give me your suitcase." Emmy stowed it under the cot. "Now, you're all set!"

Abby's mother arrived, with her daughter's sleeping bag and pillow, and Emmy took over making up the cot. "Yay! Come on, Abby, let's go outside!" She grabbed Abby's hand and pulled her out the door. Abby looked back, fleetingly, but her mother waved her along and said she'd write to her soon.

Abby and Emmy had a wonderful time that summer; they learned to swim, although Abby didn't care much for the water, and they went hiking and had cookouts. They made crafts and went canoeing. Abby was sad to leave after just a week.

The next summer, the girls went back to camp. Abby was even more excited, riding in the "way back" of her parents' new station wagon, watching the trees and hills go by as if they were moving and she was not. Her face brightened as they approached the shiny new camp gates, swung open in welcome, and a counselor checked off her name on the list.

That was the year they met Pops.

Abby and Emmy considered themselves experts on camp now, and they took turns telling all the "new girls" about their adventures. Abby still wasn't as outgoing as Emmy, but she was rapidly coming out of her shell. It was her idea to go on a nighttime hike.

The girls sneaked some crackers and carrot sticks out of the dining hall at dinner one night; they hoarded some cookies from one of the other girl's care packages, and soon had a small band of four willing to join in on the fun. Emmy set her travel alarm for 3:00 a.m. and stuck it under her pillow, so none of the counselors could hear it.

When the bell on the clock rang at the appointed hour, Abby was already sitting up in bed. She watched as Emmy fumbled underneath her pillow and shut off the alarm, then rolled back over, still sleeping. Abby pounced on her, shushing her quickly. "Come on, Em, get up! Let's go!"

Emmy grumbled a little, but finally got up and put on her sneakers. All the girls had slept in their clothes so they'd make less noise getting ready. The six of them tiptoed outside, careful not to slam the screen door on the cabin. They started giggling as they climbed up the steep path, stumbling in the dark. They didn't dare turn on flashlights just yet.

They hiked for what seemed like a long time. Abby thought that surely Pioneer Hill must be a mountain, reaching up to the sky. She'd been curious about it, though, and wondered what was at the top. The sun was just barely peeking through the early morning clouds when they reached the summit.

"Look!" said Abby, pointing in excitement. There were two shelters in a small clearing, three-sided, made from the native cedar trees. Abby trotted over to investigate, but the rest of the third-graders were tired indeed and sat down on the ground to rest. They huddled together in the morning chill and most of them appeared quite miserable and more than a little frightened.

Abby soon rejoined them and sat beside Emmy. "Now what?" she asked. The girls all looked at her, but no one spoke for a minute.

"I wanna go home," one of them cried.

"I'm scared!"

"We're lost!" wailed another.

Even Emmy looked a little less excited about the adventure than she had earlier. "We can go back, if you want."

"But, where's the path?" asked Michelle, a new girl.

The girls looked all around. Try as they might, no one could find the exact spot. Finally, Abby pointed. "There." They all stood up and started for the trail, but Abby stopped. "Let's keep going, over that way!" She started walking east.

"No way," said Michelle. "I'm tired and I don't like this and we're going to get in trouble!" She looked at the others and they nodded in agreement.

Emmy ran back to Abby. "I'll go with you, Abby. Let them go back if they want. Let's have some fun!"

Michelle and her group started down the hill; they eagerly crashed through the brush, trying to hurry without appearing to be as scared as they felt.

Abby and Emmy set off past the shelters. The sun was fully up now and it shone down through the leafy trees, brightening Abby's golden braids. Emmy followed, looking around, trying to identify the many bird calls. Abby didn't like birds. She was concentrating, however, on the trail in front of her and trying to walk silently, like an Indian. The day before, their group had had a session with a counselor named Meg who told them all about the Indians who used to live there.

After an hour or so, Abby realized that the trail was dropping; they were going down the other side of the hill. She stopped, and so did Emmy. "I'm hungry," Abby said. "Let's stop for a few minutes." The girls dug some cookies out of their pockets and tried to decide what to do next.

"Abby, do you think we're really going to be in trouble?" asked Emmy. "I mean, I'm having fun and all, but . . ."

"Yeah," Abby replied. "But, hey, as long as we're already in trouble, we may as well keep going, right?"

"Well, yeah," answered Emmy, "But we've been gone a long time."

"Yep. Probably, oh, half a day or so," said Abby, wildly overestimating their travels. It was actually about 8:30, the time the rest of their group would normally be finishing breakfast and starting their activities for the day. Neither of them had a watch and they hadn't yet learned to depend on the sun or the stars for figuring either time or location.

"Hey, let's go this way for a while," Abby exclaimed, pointing east again. The trail they'd been following had begun to wind in a northerly direction, as well as descending, and Abby was up for more adventure. She focused for a moment and pictured the layout of the camp. She was pretty sure that, if they stayed on the current path, they'd end up in another part of camp. She wanted to see something new, something different.

And she was correct. If they had continued on that same path, they would have found themselves within minutes of another group of girls, safe and sound. And Cal would not have sent searchers out to look for them. And they would have been in a lot less trouble.

Abby shook her head, rubbed her eyes, and gathered her thoughts. Time to push on if she wanted to reach the top by lunchtime and set up camp. Funny how, all those years ago, she and Emmy had approached this same spot by very nearly the same trail.

And, of course, meeting Pops for the first time. Abby remembered, smiling, how she and Emmy had finally stopped from sheer exhaustion. They'd somehow traveled into midafternoon that day, reaching the top of Tank Hill, where they both promptly fell asleep.

Which is why they never heard the shouts of the search parties.

When the pair had awakened, they were starving; the cookies were long gone, they'd even resorted to eating the carrots at some point. They'd wondered aloud if they'd ever be found, or doomed to wander forever…and then they heard the noise.

Whatever it was, it was coming closer and it sounded big. Like maybe a grizzly! Abby chuckled at the memory. There were no grizzlies in Missouri; no monsters either, which they'd also imagined in their heightened state of fear.

"Well, well," said a deep voice. "Looky what I found!" An older man climbed down off his sorrel gelding, which stamped its foot impatiently. "I'm assuming you two must be Abby and Emmy. My, my, but there are a lot of folks out looking for you." He picked up his two-way radio. "Break 1-4. Pops here. I got your munchkins. We're up here on Tank. Be down shortly."

He clicked off after receiving confirmation and looked at the two girls. "Come on, then. Let's get you back downstairs." He loaded Abby and Emmy onto his pack horse, Sara he called her, and both girls burst into tears.

Abby shook her head again, as if to clear the memories. She really had to get moving, and she did; this time, no more stopping and no more thinking. She had a job to do, in the here and now.

But she did chuckle when she recalled just how very much trouble they'd gotten into that day.

Abby finally approached the old water tanks, warily, as the sun shone directly overhead. She circled them, watchful and on edge, finally convinced that the area was relatively safe. The ladders were tested, carefully, and as long as she was up there she pulled out the binoculars to scan the immediate vicinity. She paid special attention to both the east and the south, as her location was on the very edge of the property.

As instructed, Abby radioed into check with Meg. "It's Abby. Here and clear."

"Great, Ab! How's it look?"

"Fine so far. I should be down by noon tomorrow, but I'll check back tonight after dinner."

"Sounds good. Meg out."

Abby clicked off as well and made camp. She set her bedroll under a nearby cedar; she liked the smell and the low branches would keep off the heaviest of the morning dew. She cleared a small area for a fire. She wouldn't need much, just the right size for a coffeepot. It would cool off overnight, but not enough to need a very big fire and it was still pretty dry. She wouldn't risk keeping it burning all night.

Abby found a few rocks to frame her fire pit and gathered some nearby deadwood, sorting it into three stacks by thickness and length. After digging out her lunch package, which Ted had handed to her this morning, she set her backpack next the bedroll and ate lunch. Resisting the urge for a beer, knowing she'd get sleepy, she popped open a Pepsi for the caffeine and ended her meal with a smoke.

Smiling again at the memory of her and Emmy's last adventure up here, Abby got to work. There were two huge galvanized water tanks, set close together. She inspected each one carefully, then pulled out a blowtorch and began the laborious task of resealing the seams.

It was hot work, necessitating several water breaks but, by late afternoon, Abby was finished and the tanks were freshly sealed. She was thankful that the tops were intact, since crawling around on blazing steel was sure to result in burns to various body parts; besides, she simply wasn't into perching that high off the ground without a decent handhold.

Darkness came later up here than it did in the valley, so Abby started her fire before exploring the weeds at the base of the tanks. Within a few minutes she found the pipes leading out and down to the pump house below, in the main part of the camp near Site 1. She'd follow those downhill in the morning, checking for leaks and breaks.

Abby stretched out by her little fire and opened a beer. It wasn't very cold, but good just the same. She lit a smoke and was thinking about dinner when her radio crackled to life. "Abby, you there?" It was Meg, and she sounded upset. Abby grabbed the radio and pushed the talk button.

"Yeah, Meg. Go ahead."

"Juliet's missing. Millie thought she was with Candy, then Candy and James showed up at dinner without Juliet. No one knows where she is."

Oh good heavens, thought Abby, trying to focus. "But she's only four, for crying out loud! How do you lose a four-year-old?"

"Well, apparently it's pretty easy," retorted Meg. "How the heck should I know? I don't know anything about little kids. Sure, I can handle older ones, but this—wait, hang on a sec."

Abby had jumped to her feet and was pacing; she finished off her beer and seriously considered a second one, but she likely would be called to do something here shortly and she needed to have her wits about her. So much for a relaxing evening in the woods, alone.

"Abby?" Meg came back on the radio. "Millie put her down for a nap, then fell asleep herself; she sort of remembers Juliet waking her and telling her she was going with Candy, but now she's not sure. Candy hasn't seen her at all."

Abby didn't answer. She was listening to a sound in the woods. Once again, she flashed back to hearing a sound in the woods when she and Emmy were little girls and Pops had shown up on his horse. This time there was no horse, and no Pops.

But there was Juliet. And Bob.

CHAPTER SEVENTEEN

"Meg. She's here. I'll call you back."

Abby put down the radio and Juliet ran to her. Her face was dirty and scratched, as were her arms. Her jeans were damp up to her knees and she rubbed tears from her eyes as she broke into a smile.

"I knew I'd find you, Abby! I walked all the way, up that hill and then this hill. I told Grammy I was going with you and everything! But I didn't bring my gun. You said not to touch it unless a grownup told me to and so I didn't touch it, Abby, I didn't!"

"Oh, Juliet!" Abby let out a breath that she didn't realize she was holding as she hugged the little girl tightly. "You scared me—and everyone else! They're all out looking for you down there." She set Juliet down beside her and told her to stay put. She picked up the radio and called Meg back. She lit another cigarette to calm her nerves.

"Yes, Meg. Yes, she's here. I don't know how she got here. No, I can't believe she got this far either. She says she told Millie. What? Well, okay. Fine, yes. That'll work. Okay, Abby out."

Abby turned back to Juliet. "All right, little one. Let's get you cleaned up, then you can tell me everything. But," she added sternly. "Don't ever do anything like this again! You could get lost, or . . . you could get lost for good in these woods. You might not find me the next time, so don't do it again!" Juliet nodded soberly.

Abby dribbled some water out of her canteen onto a fairly clean bandana and wiped Juliet's face and hands. Instructing the girl to strip down to her underwear, she rummaged through her pack for a t-shirt and socks. Juliet was obedient and silent, shivering in the rapidly cooling night air.

With a flashlight, Abby checked Juliet for any injuries; all were superficial scratches which she dabbed with an antibiotic ointment from the first aid kit. More extensive doctoring could be done tomorrow, when they returned to camp. Abby quickly wrapped the girl in the overly large shirt and helped her put on the socks.

"Are you hungry?" she asked. Juliet nodded eagerly. Abby handed her a water bottle and made her a comfy nest on the sleeping bag, then built up the fire a bit. While they waited, Abby lit a smoke and leaned back on her hands, watching the little girl.

"So," she said. "Tell me what happened."

Just as Meg had said earlier, Juliet had laid down for a nap but, missing Abby and not tired enough to actually sleep, she'd gotten up and told Millie she was going to find Abby. Half asleep herself, Millie had misunderstood the little girl and hadn't given it another thought—until Candy showed up at dinner without Juliet.

Juliet had remembered that Abby was going to check the water supply, but she couldn't quite remember where that was—she only knew it was up on a big hill. So she'd walked down the road, farther from Sites 2 and 3, and found a nominal trail up the back side of Pioneer. When she started going back down, she panicked a bit and stopped; she tried to remember what Abby had told her about the woods and the hills.

Around 3:00, best Abby could calculate, Juliet had started down the hill but found another path leading upwards. This one had taken her across to Tank Hill, where Abby had set up camp.

Other than the scratches, Juliet was in surprisingly good shape. True, she'd been walking for some time and had gotten lost, but she'd also gotten found again. And under her own steam. She'd kept going until she reached her destination, and Abby had to admire that fortitude.

She got up and stretched, surprised that Juliet was still awake, and dumped a can of stew into a pot, setting it on the fire. She opened another can and set it down for Bob. She wondered how to address this apparent issue; Juliet certainly couldn't be allowed to roam everywhere, alone.

While they ate, Abby called Meg back and told her that Juliet was perfectly fine, and they'd be back down in camp by noon. After she cleaned their dishes and banked the fire, Abby said, "Come on, little one; bedtime." She rolled them both up in the sleeping bag and closed her eyes, snuggling with Juliet.

"Abby, are you mad at me?" came a tiny voice.

"No, sweetie, I'm not mad. I was just scared and worried about you. Go to sleep now, we'll talk in the morning."

It was still chilly as the sun rose, barely visible through the curtains of mist swirling around the trees. Abby and Juliet crawled out of the sleeping bag, and Abby stirred up the fire while Juliet gathered some wood nearby.

After breakfast, and coffee for Abby, the two girls packed up the camp. Juliet's jeans were still damp, as were her sneakers, but Abby shrugged; she'd be uncomfortable, but okay. Natural consequences, right? Seems like she'd heard some parents talking about stuff like that once. Maybe. At any rate, it couldn't be helped. They started down the hill, following the line of water pipes.

Juliet's job was to scout ahead a short distance, looking for water or dampness. It was difficult to tell between the fog and the dew, but Juliet managed to stop Abby every ten feet or so, pointing to weak spots and corroding solder. After each spot was flagged and jury-rigged, considering Abby's limited tools, the pair moved on down the hill.

It was a long hike to the pump house and nearing noon when they arrived. They still had quite a hike down the road to Site 3, when Abby stopped abruptly.

She sniffed the air. "Juliet, do you smell that?"

"Smoke," said Juliet.

As they reached the crossroads, Abby saw two black pickup trucks fly past, heading for the campsites. She grabbed Juliet's arm and thrust her behind her as they continued to creep close to the tree line. She'd tried to raise Meg, or anyone, really, on the walkie, but had had no luck so far.

Another truck raced past them, fishtailing as it made the turn; it was going in the opposite direction, heading towards the camp gate. Making a quick decision, Abby scooped up Juliet and ducked into the heavy scrub, waded across the nearly dry creek bed, and kept going until she reached the pump house. Retreat was often the best option.

Pausing to catch her breath, Abby pondered her choices. The smoke smell was stronger, more acrid. She was desperate to know more, what had happened, what was going on at the campsite, who . . . She looked down at Juliet, whose face was pale, eyes huge.

"Juliet. Look at me." She knelt down next to the little girl, putting her hands on her shoulders. Slowly, Juliet looked up at Abby.

"We're going to be okay, kiddo. I'll find out what's happening, I'll take care of you. I promise. We'll be okay. Now, you must listen to me and do exactly as I say. All right?"

Juliet nodded, and her breathing slowed a bit. She blinked. "Okay, Abby."

"Come on." Abby took Juliet's hand. "We're going up this hill, and we have to walk really quietly, like an Indian, remember? Don't talk, but tap my arm if you need something, okay? Like this." Abby demonstrated. She shouldered her pack and helped Juliet to her feet, and the two began climbing the hill behind the pump house, moving carefully. Bob came bounding along with them, making more noise than Abby would have wished.

They reached the cave behind the old staff buildings just as the sky opened up and a drenching rain poured down. Abby hustled Juliet inside and followed her, pausing to camouflage the opening. Juliet climbed onto Abby's lap, and the two of them huddled together, shivering, exhausted from the climb.

Finally, Abby stirred. She fumbled with her pack, pulling out the sleeping bag and spreading it against the wall of the cave, near the opening. She laid Juliet down and kissed her cheek, whispering, "Stay here, little one. I'll be right back. Bob, you too." Juliet mumbled something and rolled over, still sleeping.

Abby clicked on her flashlight and began to explore. The last time she'd been in the cave she could tell it went back much further, but she hadn't had time to check it out fully. The passage narrowed but was easily accessible and, after about 20 feet, opened into a much larger area.

She shined the light around the open space, searching for another way out in case an exit strategy was necessary. Far in the rear, to her right, was a small opening. Crouching down, she peered into the darkness. The space was narrow, but Abby thought she could navigate it without too much trouble. The real question was how far back did it go and was there another opening? In any case, it was time she got back to Juliet.

The radio crackled to life. "Ab, are you there?" Cal's voice came through, barely understandable. "Abby, pick up! Where are you?"

Abby snatched the radio off her hip and pressed the talk key. "Yes, Cal, I'm here. What's going on?"

"You need to get back, quickly. We've had a . . . um, incident and we need to contain this ASAP."

"Roger," said Abby, making her way back to the sleeping child. "Be there shortly."

She paused, back in the front of the cave, and took stock of their supplies. She sorted the blankets, tools, and canned goods, anything non-perishable, and made a large pack. Juliet, still sleeping, would be fine for a few more minutes. Abby made her way back to the larger cavern and stowed everything out of sight. Just in case.

She gently woke Juliet, who sat up immediately alert. Abby lifted her much lighter backpack and the two made their way down the hill to the road, heading back to camp, Bob trailing in their wake.

CHAPTER EIGHTEEN

The campsite was in chaos.

Noah had set up four tents close together in the field near the kitchen shelter and was barking orders at several assistants who rushed back and forth. Calypso was sitting at a table, alone, and appeared to have abdicated her responsibilities for the moment.

As Abby approached, she jerked to life. "Thank God you're here, Abby. This is a mess if ever there was one." Cal gestured towards the tents. "Noah is doing the best he can, but . . ." She took a deep breath. "Emmy's over there, Abby, she's helping Noah."

Abby visibly relaxed and whispered to Juliet, who scampered across the shelter to Millie. "Now," said Abby. "Talk to me."

"Early this morning, Lorie was on her way to the showers when she heard someone talking. She stepped off the trail, up there where it forks, and listened a bit more but the voices stopped. She couldn't make out any words, let alone recognize who was speaking, so she came on down here.

"I guess she mentioned it to Ted, but didn't say anything else and he kind of shrugged it off."

"Where is Ted, anyway?" asked Abby, looking over towards the cooking fires, hoping for coffee.

"Packing," answered Cal. "And I want you to go with him."

Abby raised her eyebrow as Cal continued, "What Lorie heard this morning was James and Candy; they blew up the commissary, Abby. Half of it, anyway. Lorie and Meg tried to stop them.

"They're in that last tent. Together. They didn't make it, Abby." Tears poured down Cal's face. "Find them. Make them pay."

Abby's head was spinning. She needed coffee—no, hell, she needed a drink. And a shower. Wait. Explosion. Dead. Meg and Lorie. Abby bit her lip. Later.

She hugged Cal and stopped to speak with Millie, giving Juliet a goodbye hug as well and admonishing her to behave and to, by all means, stay right with Millie at all times. Then she went to find Ted.

She found him in the tent he'd shared with Lorie, red-eyed and hair sticking up, gun parts and ammo scattered around. She paused, then called his name.

Ted jerked to attention, his grim face crumpling as he lurched toward Abby and broke into tears. She held him awkwardly until his outward grief dissipated, patting his shoulder, trying to comfort him. Finally, she held him at arms' length and made him look at her directly.

"Ted. We've got a job to do."

"Yes," he said, letting his breath out like a runner prepping for a race. "I'm okay now. For now. I can do this."

"Okay then," said Abby. "I'll meet you back here in 15 minutes." She walked out of the tent and down the path to her own. Someone, probably Emmy she thought, had left a fresh bucket of water and some soap and towels. She quickly sponged off and changed clothes. She refilled her pack from supplies on hand, not knowing what else was available but confident that they could find whatever they needed on this hunting trip. She'd seen the truck heading out earlier, a few hours' head start tops, so she didn't think Candy and James would be on foot. Yet.

Abby grabbed an extra knife and sheath and her .45 to complement the Mossberg and .357. A couple ammo boxes and she was ready. Ted was waiting.

The truck ran smoothly down the center of the road just outside the gates that Sandy carefully closed behind it. She disappeared silently back into the brush, ready to watch and wait as long as she was needed. She knew what was going on all right; she'd been there when James and Candy had crashed through as they escaped and she'd spent the morning making repairs.

Her grief was real, and deep. But she was a good soldier; she'd stand her post until told otherwise.

Ted and Abby drove down the road away from the camp on their grim mission. Candy and James had gotten a good two-hour lead, so the odds of catching them were very low. At this point, the exercise was futile from a practical standpoint but did allow for a certain release of tension for the hunters. In spite of the day thus far, Abby was thankful that she'd had a chance to speak with Emmy before leaving and, even more so, thankful that she was driving and not Ted.

His current state of mind was almost frightening to watch in its single-mindedness. He and Lorie had been an item, on and off, for years and had recently come to some sort of understanding the last Abby had heard. Lorie had been a friend of Abby's for almost as long as Ted had known her, yet Abby felt oddly numb at this stage.

The loss of Meg, too, she refused to contemplate. Meg had been larger than life in many respects, prickly at times, but like a marshmallow on the inside to those who knew her best. Abby roughly shoved everything out of her mind except the current job at hand.

The truck swerved as Ted suddenly grabbed her arm, and Abby stood on the brakes. "There," he pointed about 50 yards ahead to the right. Abby backed the truck and pulled to the narrow shoulder, killing the engine. They stepped out and listened.

Nothing.

That was wrong. There should have been birds, small animals in the brush, something. Just silence. It appeared as though the fugitives' truck had gone off-road and some clumsy attempt had been made to camouflage the location. In fact, Abby could see the glint of a stray ray of sunshine reflecting off the black paint.

She and Ted split up, silently, circling around to enter the treeline from opposite angles. Both had weapons at the ready, safeties off; both had experience on their side, and patience now that the quarry was within reach.

Suddenly, Candy appeared directly between them, running towards the road, screaming. "Don't shoot, don't shoot! I'm sorry, I'm so sorry, please don't shoot!"

Abby dropped to a crouch; Ted lined up his rifle sight. Candy fell to the ground, her scream cut off as she hit hard. Ted was off and running towards her as Abby took aim.

She stopped short; Ted was standing over Candy, finger on the trigger, barrel pointed at her head. She prayed Ted would move, just a hair to the left. He shifted, and Abby fired just as Candy flew through the air at Ted, a long, wicked knife blade shining in the sun.

Ted staggered backward, grazed by the blade, bleeding. Abby fired again. This time, she didn't miss. Candy crumpled to the ground, bloody and lifeless.

Abby approached silently, helping Ted to his feet. She gently pulled away his hand to examine the knife wound. He'd live. She spared a glance at Candy, dead and still. Anger. Cold, hard anger. She wasn't sorry. At all. She put a finger to her lips as Ted tried to speak, tears in his eyes. She gestured towards the open field beyond them, and held up one finger. James was still out there.

A truck door slammed.

Abby and Ted froze for a split second, then dropped to the ground. Abby whipped out her binoculars and tried to focus, searching for the road. Then she felt for her keys; safely in the pocket where she'd stashed them. She motioned for Ted to follow her and they cautiously made their way back.

A second door slammed. James was apparently either counting on Candy to stop them, or he was panicking and oblivious to the amount of noise he was making. They could hear him tromping back through the underbrush, approaching swiftly.

The footsteps stopped.

"Candy, where the hell are you? Hello? Candy!"

Ted stood upright, awkwardly bringing the rifle around to point towards James' voice. His eyes were glazed, and he began a steady gait, one foot at a time, towards James. Abby reached for him, but missed. He kept going. So did James.

The two men were face to face. James was pale and shaking as he raised his hands in a gesture of surrender. Ted shot him.

"You son of a bitch." Ted walked right past the body as it fell, back to the road.

CHAPTER NINETEEN

Back at the campsite, Abby took her long-awaited shower and tried to ignore the blackened, crumbling outer walls of the nearby commissary. She shivered a bit, even though the sun was high and the breeze calm. She'd left Ted in the capable hands of Emmy and hurried down here as soon as she could.

Ted had managed admirably on the drive back, following Abby in the second truck, but upon their return he'd immediately collapsed. Emmy was keeping an eye on him while he slept.

Brad was in charge of dinner that evening and Abby idly wondered if it would be edible. She was rather hungry, having not eaten since early that morning. Then she remembered that the funerals would be tomorrow.

Later that evening, following a decent dinner, actually, the group met in the kitchen shelter. No one else was around, too tired and subdued from the day's events to want to socialize much. Cal was there, of course, trying to pull her emotions together, and Abby and Emmy. Janey had come in from the field much earlier that day and Brad was pouring coffee. Sandy had preferred to remain on duty; Pops and Noah strolled in together and Noah took a seat next to Abby. Zoe was with Ted, who was still fitfully sleeping.

"So," Cal said, bringing the meeting to order. She took a deep breath, let it out in a rush, and quickly added, "Candy and James tried to blow up the commissary, for unknown reasons, then took off. Abby and Ted went after them; they are no longer a threat.

"Tomorrow . . ." Her voice broke, and tears filled her eyes once again. "Tomorrow at dawn we will have a service for Meg and Lorie, over near the Old Cathedral." Cal sat down abruptly and Abby reached for her hand.

Noah stood up. "Those who were injured . . . this morning . . . are all recovering well. We had a few minor burns and some scrapes, and one head injury; a slight concussion, but I don't foresee any developing problems.

"In other news, I've made very little headway on pinning down this virus but the spread has slowed and there's no real evidence of contagion.

"However, we've been monitoring any news sources that are still in operation, and it seems as though . . ." Noah paused and looked at Cal. She nodded.

"You may as well hear it," he said.

"They're estimating that a minimum of 95% of the world's population is . . . gone." He cleared his throat. "That means that there are fewer than three-and-half million people left in the world.

There was a stunned silence.

"In this area, with a prior population of just over one million, there would be almost 50,000 folks still here. However, we've been in touch with only a couple other groups, similar to ourselves, and so we know for sure that there are at least 200."

Nobody moved, nobody spoke. It was inconceivable that so many had died or, even worse, disappeared. Unreal.

"This incident occurred almost two months ago, and it seems that St. Louis, being right in the middle of the country, was hit pretty hard. Then, too, there may be others out there who are not organized or who are unable to communicate, others who are barely surviving or will be unable to do so for much longer."

Pops stood up. "I reckon it's my turn to speak my piece," he began. "We do have about 50 folks here at the camp, and it seems to me that should be our main concern. I've been studying on it for a bit the last few weeks or so, and here's what I propose.

"Calypso and I had a mighty fine talk this afternoon and, while she's going to remain in charge and be our go-to person, and Noah's going to do his level best to keep us all healthy, looks like I'm running the camp itself. Leastwise until I keel over myself which, Lord willing, won't be for quite some time.

"Anyways, here's the plan, and I'll keep it short 'cause I know you all are worn out and wanting to head to bed soon. Janey has found us a spot up on top of this here hill behind us; that's just about at the property and fence line, which won't keep out any determined varmints but there's nothing past there except fields and some more woods. Plenty of room to see something coming at us. Brad is arranging to turn it into a site for us to hunker down in, and we expect to move up there in a week or so.

"Abby, we're gonna need you to check the whole fence line, making repairs as you go if those are possible. And of course, scouting out anything nearby. I expect you might need some help, but I'll leave that up to you; there's a lot of ground to cover. Once that's done, we'll prepare to pull back. Sandy's already working on a new perimeter, and she and Janey will be in charge of that.

"We'll also be sending crews into town on a regular basis, alternatin' days, so to speak, so we can restock and reassess the whole situation.

"Any questions?" Pops looked at Cal. She shook her head. "All righty then, we'll meet over at the base of the Cathedral at 0700."

Abby, Emmy, and Noah started slowly up the hill as everyone began making their way out of the shelter and into the night. They climbed silently, mourning those who were lost, thinking about what was to come. Emmy broke off from the group to go check on Ted and relieve Zoe, and Abby and Noah seated themselves on the step outside the tent.

Exhausted, Abby leaned against Noah and he put his arm around her, gently. The two sat for a long time, each lost in their own thoughts.

As the moon rose, Abby turned to Noah and kissed him.

She took his hand and led him inside.

The day of the funerals dawned cool and crisp, a typical Midwestern October morning. The leaves were turning, the breeze was still; a heavy dew lay on the grass. The entire group, nearly 50 refugees, walked slowly in pairs and groups over to the east side of Sunnytop.

Brad and his construction crew had labored the day before to build the two coffins and dig the first graves for the small community. Everyone knew that, eventually, there would be more.

Silently, they filed past the two who had been lost, each pausing for moment in prayer or thought, perhaps resting a hand upon the new wood. Climbing to the huge rock that overlooked the meadow, they silently sat in a circle and waited.

Finally, Cal stood up. She spoke of Lorie, and told how they'd first met; she talked of Lorie's contributions to the group and ended with expressing her deepest sympathy to everyone, especially Ted.

Several others stood, in turn, and talked about Lorie. Then Ted arose and stumbled to the front of the group.

He managed. Barely.

Emmy helped him back to his seat.

Abby walked to the front of the group, all of them silent. She cleared her throat and took a deep breath. Her heart ached, especially for Cal. Meg, she knew, was probably smiling at them, encouraging them, and so she imagined Meg's voice in her head.

"Suck it up, sister! I know it's rough, hell, I invented rough—but it's all ya got now."

Abby began to talk about her old friend and mentor. Finally, it was all over.

Cal stoically led the way back down the hill, and they lowered the coffins into the ground. Meg and Lorie were gone. A cool rain began to fall.

The following week was a busy one. Immediately after the burials, eight individuals had approached Cal and stated their intention to leave. Cal directed them to Zoe, who had taken over the commissary, and the small group was outfitted for their departure.

They left on good terms, unlike James and Candy, but had declared they had not felt safe since the threats had been brought to light some time ago. And especially after the explosion itself.

Abby reluctantly accepted the nominal title of Cal's assistant, as long as she was in camp. However, following Pops' game plan, she geared up and spent the better part of that week tromping through the woods. She left Juliet in Millie's care, with strict instructions to trust the girl to no one else but Emmy. Emmy, she knew, would never let the girl wander. And there was Bob to keep an eye on things as well. Of course, the last time the dog had happily been an accomplice.

Abby's plan was to start at the new camp site, up on Purple Mountain, and work her way back over the ridge to where the old corral had once stood. From there, she'd go down the natural terraces and to the lake; it would be a slow process, as she felt it necessary to recheck some of the abandoned units along the way. She'd arranged for Emmy to bring Juliet to the lake on her third day out; she knew Juliet would be missing her and she thought better safe than sorry where the girl was concerned. And, too, she admitted to herself, she would want to see Juliet as well. And Emmy, of course. Maybe they could spare a couple hours.

As Abby stepped out of woods and the glittering water appeared, she could see a tiny figure on the dock, waving. She quickened her step, slightly fearful until she spied Emmy sitting on a picnic table under the shelter.

She jogged down the hill and scooped up Juliet, hugging her tightly. "Hey, what about me?" laughed Emmy. Abby set Juliet down and grabbed her friend, planting a kiss on her cheek for good measure. Bob, of course, got in on the action and gave Abby a few good licks, tail wagging.

The three walked onto the beach area, Abby gratefully dropping her heavy pack. She stretched out on the sand, warm from the sun; a contrast to the chilly breeze. Juliet plopped down on her lap and snuggled against her chest.

"So, Em. Tell me all the news."

"Nah, you first."

"Well," said Abby, mockingly, "The birds all seemed in fine form; the squirrels are socking away acorns like crazy. The raccoons, however, thankfully stayed out of sight." Abby shuddered. She'd been treed by a 'coon once and hadn't forgotten the terror of those glowing eyes yet. Juliet giggled.

"All right, all right, you win! Surely I can do better than that!" Emmy became serious.

"We lost five more, Abby. They just took off during the night, but they left a note. Said it was too cold, or would be, and they'd rather be indoors.

"I mean, seriously? With what? A fire in the middle of some living room?" Emmy shook her head. "Whatever. So that means there are just a few dozen of us left."

Abby mentally counted. There were ten of the core group remaining; that left just twenty additional people. She hoped the new bunker area was coming along quickly, if they lost too many more before it was finished, it might be difficult   to actually winter here as they'd planned.

She sighed.

"Okay, what else?"

"Let's see . . . the tent frames are finished, we packed the canvas up there yesterday. We're starting to dig the trenches and Janey's been setting up a couple outposts. A lot of equipment has been hauled up there too. A lot," Emmy repeated, rubbing her sore arms.

"And tomorrow, I'm taking a crew into town."

Abby started for a moment. Emmy was quite capable, of course, but Abby was afraid for her. She'd much rather Emmy stayed here, safe, until she herself was able to go. Unfortunately, she still had a good five days or so to finish this assignment.

"Great!" she said, trying to smile. "Find me some beer, will ya?" With that, she dumped Juliet off her lap and pounced on Emmy, tickling her mercilessly until she laughed so hard she began to cry. Abby held her until she calmed, and Juliet cuddled with them both, looking serious and sad and poking her thumb into her mouth.

Abby promptly plucked said thumb out of the girl's mouth and kissed the top of her head.

"All right, both of you, listen to me. Yes, this is tough, and yes, we've been through a lot already. But we have to do this—we don't have a choice. We can't give up. This is it, chickadees.

"Bad as it is, the alternatives are worse. Now, c'mon, let's have some lunch. We've all got work to do."

CHAPTER TWENTY

Abby hiked straight up the backside of Sunnytop from the lake and made camp. She'd sent Emmy and Juliet off after lunch, gratefully stowing a few treats they'd brought her. She knew she probably wouldn't see them again until she'd finished her rounds. She'd hiked around the lake before her ascent, but the fence line hadn't been disturbed and she'd seen nothing unusual; still, it was full dark before she was able to sit down and rest for a bit.

After she finished some dried beef and a package of ramen, Abby settled back against her bedroll for a smoke. She was tired. Tired from thinking and planning and worrying. Today it was just too much and, overwhelmed, she closed her eyes for a few minutes.

She remembered meeting with Cal, the initial information she'd been given. It hadn't required much consideration to join the group, it didn't sound like she'd had much choice. And besides, there certainly wasn't anything or anyone else to stop her.

She'd recruited Emmy, the one constant in her life, with the full approval of Cal and so here they were now. Hiding, scrounging, fearful. But, Abby shrugged, alive. And with some hope, at least. Things weren't really so bad. For now.

By morning, Abby had regained some of her optimism and packed up the campsite, hiking to the west. Nothing to note, as she'd expected since she was some distance inside the property line. Back along the eastern ridge and descending near the camp gates, Abby was amused that she could just barely spot Sandy on guard duty; few others would find it so easy to discern a slight movement, high in a tree.

She continued on, climbing the southern slope of Eagle. She paused halfway up for a quick handful of trail mix and a swig or two from her water bottle.

She paused again, just a few feet further, when she smelled smoke.

Dropping to the ground, Abby cautiously looked around as far as she could turn her head in both directions. She narrowed her eyes, focusing beyond and through the leafy underbrush. She heard a twig crack.

There. Up a bit higher and to her right. She slowly reached back for her .357 and pulled it forward, checking the chamber and releasing the safety. She waited, scarcely breathing.

Footsteps sounded, making more noise than warranted, but they were moving away from her. Within minutes, they faded, the source of the noise making no attempt to either engage her or to hide his presence.

Abby lay still for a few more minutes, straining to hear.

Finally, she stood up and replaced her weapon, warily checking the immediate area. When she reached the spot where the intruder had first appeared, she studied the ground for a few minutes. Two choices: follow, or continue her assignment.

Naturally, she opted to follow.

Abby first stowed her pack, camouflaged, at the base of a tree; she marked it with a tiny chink in the trunk near the ground.

She swapped out her water bottle for a full one and made sure her knife was in its sheath and double-checked her gun. Pockets full of jerky and trail mix, she started off after the intruder.

When she reached the fence line, Abby paused. She'd easily tracked him, but could see no break; ah, there it was! Cleverly hidden, but not so much that a trained woodsmen wouldn't see it. She slithered, belly down, through the opening and crouched near the chain link, waiting.

She heard nothing at first. Then, cautiously turning her head, holding her breath, footsteps. They were moving away from her. She took a quick swallow of water and started walking in the direction of the sounds.

Abby moved silently, watching the ground, the trees, and glimpses of sky. She focused on the intruder. He obviously wasn't expecting to be followed or, indeed, had any knowledge that she was nearby. Then he stopped.

Murmuring voices, low, and then nothing. Now there were two sets of footsteps, in sync with each other; the odds didn't worry Abby at all, not yet.

One hundred yards ahead, the pair stopped. So did Abby. She could hear sounds of a campsite, a match striking, a pot being set on the fire. Apparently, the men believed they were at a safe distance from the camp itself. She could hear conversation as well, although it was muted.

She made herself comfortable at the base of a tree, putting the tree itself between her and the campsite. She glanced up and saw that she could easily climb, if need be, and quickly too. Bits and pieces of the conversation began to drift toward her.

"Cal . . . nice setup . . . moving the site . . ."

"We'll show her . . . too bad . . . James . . ."

". . . Need to take them . . . soon . . . few days . . ."

"Better check in . . ."

". . . In a minute . . ."

Abby had heard enough. Silently, she began to climb the tree, just high enough for a decent view but still hidden in the leaves. It seemed as though these two were the scouts for a bigger group, an unknown entity, and had at least heard of Cal. Possibly they were the source of the threats Cal had received a month or so ago.

At any rate, Abby wasn't about to let them "check in" with anyone. This was a direct challenge with substance—the men had a plan which they were about to implement. No choice.

She looked out through the branches and analyzed the situation. Two men, average size. A shotgun propped up against a tent pole. No other weapons in sight. Abby realized, of course, that that meant little; she assumed there were more because thinking any other way could mean death.

One man, taller, presumably the one she'd followed, appeared slightly more watchful than the other. He paused every so often to stop and look around, and seemed alert. However, based on his so-called skill in the woods, Abby was confident that it was mostly for show. His companion was relaxed and unaware of his surroundings.

Abby waited, and listened.

"Hey, Jeff! What do you want for dinner?"

The taller man looked up, and Abby saw his face. She recognized him. And so would Cal. He was the dangerous one.

The one she'd shoot first.

Years ago, Cal and Jeff had been an item. A few of their friends were happy; mostly Jeff's friends. Abby had had a bad feeling about the union from the start. Things were fine for the first six months and then, suddenly and inexplicably, the two were married.

It lasted almost exactly, to the day, two years.

During that time, Jeff had managed to alienate even his own friends, scamming and conning anyone who crossed his path. He always wanted more: more money, more expensive clothes, more fancy cars. Nothing was ever enough.

At first, Cal seemed oblivious to Jeff's wheeling and dealing. Soon she began to make excuses, invent reasons. And finally, she knew. That's when the physical abuse began.

Since most of Cal's closest friends had long been absent from her life, as per Jeff's machinations, no one knew for three months. Finally, in desperation, Cal packed her bags and fled the house which was soon to be returned to the bank anyway, and ended up at Meg's.

Jeff was too composed and arrogant to go looking for her, let alone beg her to return, and Cal immediately filed for both a restraining order and a divorce. Jeff disappeared, leaving behind tens of thousands in unpaid bills, a massive load of credit card debt, and a foreclosure.

With Meg's help, and a reunion of her closest friends, Cal was able to pull out of her depression, take charge, and deal with the mess. She vowed never to be taken advantage of again, and set her mind to forgetting the entire episode.

And now Jeff was back.

Hot anger filled Abby. What he'd done to Cal, to others. How careful he'd been, how calculating. And now he was here again, to destroy, to wound.

Abby lifted the .357 and took careful aim. She waited for the slight breeze to die down; she had one shot at this, so to speak, and had to make it count.

Bang!

Jeff dropped to the ground, clutching his chest. The other man turned, slapped his hand to his side and grabbed air as he, too, went down. A neat hole appeared in his temple.

Abby shimmied to the ground and approached Jeff cautiously; the other was beyond her help and her concern. She made sure Jeff's hands were empty, and knelt down next to him. Blood soaked his jacket, but his eyes tried to focus.

"Abby," he rasped. "Should've known it would be you. Say 'hi' to Cal for me."

"Scum," said Abby. She shot him again, right between the eyes.

By nightfall, Abby had slipped back through the perimeter fence, repaired it, and reached the summit of Purple to set up her camp. There were a few more weak spots in the fence that would need her attention tomorrow, but first she had to radio Cal.

Keeping it brief and vague, as they had agreed for the purposes of radio communication, Abby let Cal know that two threats had been found and dealt with and that the breach had been sealed. She also told her that the remainder of her trip should be significantly shortened as long as the perimeter held. Cal, in turn, informed Abby that all was well and the move was going according to schedule.

Signing off, Abby set about cleaning her guns and sharpening her knife. She finished a quick dinner and a smoke and stretched out on her bedroll. She wanted to have an early start, hoping to finish the east side and move north. Working along Flagstaff and Pioneer should go quickly, merely a routine check, and then she'd be back at the main site.

She wondered at her lack of regret or, really, lack of much emotion at all when she'd killed those two men. Ha. As though

Jeff fit any definition of that, other than physically. It was her job to protect the group, just as it was for all of them. Yes, she'd been angry; justifiably so. But she would have done it anyway. Odd how this…whatever it was…changed the stakes.

Six. She'd killed half a dozen…people. Yes, human beings, regardless of their illnesses, or flaws, or evil deeds. And it had gotten easier, true, but she still felt rather sick inside. Something else to analyze, to ponder. When she had time. When the world wasn't crazy.

Abby set off just as the sun rose. She found a few minor breaks in the fence itself and a couple posts that needed to be reset. By noon she was nearing the descent between Purple and Flagstaff and decided to make a quick detour to the cave she'd found. It took a bit longer than she'd anticipated, but she was pleased. It simply meant that it would be difficult for someone else to find as well.

She climbed back up, to the top of Flagstaff, then crossed over to Tank Hill. A cursory inspection of the water tank showed everything in order. She was on schedule so far; she'd reach the main site before nightfall.

Robin Tidwell

CHAPTER TWENTY-ONE

Ted was back on duty, supervising the few girls who had remained in the camp, when Abby walked into camp. She hugged him briefly and smiled back at his own feeble, sad attempt. She saw Cal sitting nearby and touched her arm, motioning her to follow. The two walked over to the unlit campfire.

"All right," said Cal briskly. "Tell me."

"It was Jeff."

Cal's face blanched. She cleared her throat and struggled to stop the slight tremor in her hands. She cleared her throat again.

"Jeff," she repeated. "That Jeff? The same scumbag from back when? What the hell?"

Abby replayed the conversation between the two men. Jeff had known James and, presumably, Candy. Jeff was behind the explosion. And the earlier threats. And of course, Jeff was now dead. Eliminated.

Relief shone on Cal's face even as tears welled from her eyes. Abby put an arm around her shoulders and the two sat there for a few minutes, in the dark.

"Bastard," said Cal, and she rose to return to her duties.

Abby was relieved to see Emmy, all in one piece, knowing she'd gone to town the day before. The intruders had distracted her enough, but now she was eager to find out what, if anything, was happening in the outside world.

"Absolutely nothing," Emmy said after dinner when the two of them, with Juliet of course, were sitting on the steps of their tent.

"We drove in, me and Noah and two others in a second truck, and picked up the list of supplies that Cal had for us. Noah needed more drugs and things, and we found those too. It was almost too easy. No signs of any people, at all, and everything just sitting there.

"Of course, there's no electric, so the smell in some places was pretty bad. Most of the, um, rotting and all, has pretty much gone away. The smell, that is. A lot of fat vultures lurking around, though."

Abby grimaced. "Guess it'll be my turn tomorrow. Cal mentioned it tonight." She kissed Juliet on the top of the head. "Will you miss me, little one?"

"Yes," said Juliet. "You're always gone . . ." Her tiny voice trailed off.

"Fair enough," said Abby. "The day after tomorrow, we'll go out hiking, just the two of us. Will that work?"

Juliet jumped up and grabbed Abby around the neck, almost knocking them both over into the tent. "Yes!" she shouted.

Noah was nowhere to be seen, and hadn't yet returned to the tent by 9:00, so Abby allowed Juliet to sleep over. Emmy ran to let Millie know while Abby dressed the little girl in one of her own t-shirts in lieu of pajamas. She carried her down to the shower house to wash her face and brush her teeth, then she and Emmy resumed their talk, quietly, as Juliet fell asleep.

"Was it awful?" asked Emmy.

Abby shrugged. "Not really. I didn't know it was Jeff until right before I shot. And it wouldn't have made any difference; they both had to be stopped.

"New world, Em. I wish it wasn't like this, but we have to work with whatever we have. And in this case . . ." Abby was suddenly very tired. "Let's go to bed."

Abby tossed and turned throughout the night, waking periodically to check on Juliet who could sleep through a thunderstorm. Too restless to try to sleep anymore, she walked back down to the smoldering campfire and lit a cigarette. She leaned back on a log, staring at the stars as they faded into morning.

Janey was the first to arrive at the shelter and she started the fire and put on coffee. Ted ambled down in her wake and sat beside Abby.

"How are you doing, Ted?" she asked.

"I'll be fine." He tried to smile. It just wasn't working. "Lots to do, gotta keep busy. Sleep would be good, though," he admitted.

"I hear ya," said Abby. Janey handed her a steaming mug. She sipped slowly, then headed back to her tent to get ready for whatever the day might bring.

The trip to town started in almost a festive mood; everyone was glad to be getting out of camp for a bit. Janey and Abby were in the lead truck, Mark and Barbie followed in the second. They were to start at the southern end of town, working a grid pattern, searching for whatever they could find that might be useful for the coming winter. It was a bit chilly, but warming quickly, and the blue sky was clear and bright.

They drove down Highway 55, taking the last exit, and turned east on Route A. Skipping the commercial district, they concentrated on homes. It was on the second street when Janey froze.

"Choppers," she said, and pointed to the sky. They all looked up. There were six, flying in formation. "Get down!"

They dropped, wiggling underneath the truck. The choppers continued on, but two circled back directly overhead. They descended so low that dust and gravel was swirling, making it impossible to see or hear. Finally, the noise and dirt faded as the choppers rejoined the others. Janey told everyone to stay put and she crawled out, remaining crouched near the wheel well.

"They're coming back," she said. "Let's roll. I have no idea what they're looking for, but I have a feeling about this one.

"Abby, you drive. Mark, Barb, we're splitting up—take a left on Commercial and drive north. Find a warehouse or big garage and pull inside or next to it. Then take cover.

"We'll go south and see if I can tell what's going down."

The trucks spun out and turned in opposite directions. Abby drove fast but steady, as Janey leaned out and watched the sky. She caught a glimpse of Mark pulling into a parking lot near what she assumed was a mechanic's garage just as they topped the hill.

"Pull over!" yelled Janey. "Now!"

Abby yanked the wheel hard to the left as a huge fireball exploded over the intersection they'd just left behind. The truck bounced and rolled, landing on its side. The girls were flung around the cab, and Abby took a sharp knock on the head. She woozily tried to open the door but Janey pushed her back down.

"Don't move," she hissed. "Stay still, close your eyes." They could hear a chopper descending, but no one emerged. After what seemed like many long minutes, the bird rose into the air, circled once, and headed north along with the rest of the fleet.

"All right," said Janey. "Let's take a look at that cut." She dabbed it with a wet bandana. "You'll live."

"Now what?" asked Abby shakily. She was used to stalking game, following trails, and occasionally shooting at something human, but she had no real experience with the US military firing upon her. Or any army, for that matter.

"We wait. We'll give them thirty minutes in case they come back. Here, have a drink."

Abby gratefully accepted the water bottle and took a long drink. She handed Janey a cigarette and they both lit up. Within a few minutes, Abby was calmer.

"So what was that all about?"

"Not sure. Those were Super Cobras. Marines. They're generally reserved for top-secret work but, well, typically not within our borders. Holy crap."

This piece of news certainly did not help the situation. Janey checked her watch. "Okay, let's go."

They climbed out of the truck through the passenger side, landing heavily on the gravel shoulder. Up ahead they could see only a thick cloud of black smoke, slightly drifting to the east. Both girls drew their sidearms as they walked down the highway, keeping to the right in case a dive into the ditch should become necessary.

"I'm starting to get really tired of all this," muttered Abby. In spite of everything, was it really too much to ask to have a day without drama?

They tied their bandanas over their faces as they approached the smoke. It was beginning to dissipate somewhat as the wind picked up, still blowing to the east. Abby was relieved that it shouldn't affect the camp as long as the breeze didn't shift.

Catching a glimpse of what lay beyond, yet still not where the fireball had actually landed, Janey stopped short and grabbed Abby's arm.

The town was gone.

More than half of it, anyway, much more. Not a building was standing. The ruins were charred and smoking. Gone. As one, they looked to the right, down the hill where Mark and Barb had fled to the garage. Nothing. No truck, no bodies. Obliterated.

Abby sat down. Fast and hard. And stared. Janey put a hand on her shoulder. They stayed there, unmoving, for a long time. Finally, Janey pulled Abby to her feet and they returned to the truck, still on its side in the ditch. Abby tossed her water bottle and grabbed two beers out of the cooler. They sat in silence.

At last, Janey picked up her radio and fiddled with the dials. "Cal. Janey. Yes. No. Send someone. Yes. Just south of Route A. Yes." She clicked off.

The silence continued.

CHAPTER TWENTY-TWO

The black truck screeched to a halt, rousing Abby and Janey from their near-stupor. Emmy emerged and rushed to Abby, her face turning pale as she looked back to the smoking ruins of the town. She was followed by Noah with his medical bag but Abby and Janey waved him off. Brad was the last to exit the vehicle and immediately hooked up the winch, smiling at the girls. He was relieved that everyone seemed okay; dealing with blood and death just wasn't his thing.

"What about . . ." asked Noah. He gestured vaguely to the north.

"Nothing you can do for them," Janey answered briskly. "We walked. We saw it."

Within a few minutes, the truck was righted and checked over by Brad; Noah gave the tires a few kicks and the three girls gathered the loot that had spilled from the bed. A radio crackled to life, and Emmy answered. She talked to Cal for a few minutes then turned toward the rest.

"We need to go down there," she said. "Janey, it's safe, right?"

"Well, I guess. I mean, I've heard a few things about some new weapons but not like this. And not in our own country for

heaven's sake. Don't think it's nuclear but if it is, well, we're dead anyway. Close definitely counts in that department."

They started to climb into the trucks when Noah stopped Abby. "Are you okay to drive?"

Abby snorted. "Hey, Emmy—tell Noah when I'm 'not' okay to drive!"

Emmy almost laughed out loud. "Never, Noah. Abby is never 'not' okay to drive!"

The two trucks moved slowly into town, passing the spot where Mark and Barb had pulled off the road. There was nothing there, no garage, no truck, nothing. Half a mile later, after cruising down the main drag through the ever-lessening smoke, they saw the truck.

Flat as a pancake, tires melted into the pavement.

When they reached the northernmost end of the town itself, the debris began to appear. It seemed as though the tremendous explosion had tossed anything that wasn't anchored for at least a mile. What it didn't incinerate, that is.

They stopped to regroup, just before crossing under the highway to return to camp. Without exception, they were all stunned by the devastation.

"What the hell is the point of this?" raged Janey. "They have to know there are survivors—what did you tell us, Noah? Ninety-five percent loss of population? That leaves five percent of us left. What the hell?"

She stopped. She looked at the others. They all understood, even Janey. They weren't supposed to survive.

They made their way back to camp, a subdued and quiet group. They ignored the questions and immediately gathered in the command tent with Cal and the others. Abby and Janey gave their report, then Pops rose to speak.

"We're moving up top at first light. Brad tells me he's almost finished anyway and what's left can be done when we get there. Gonna be a big job, we have to truck all the supplies up there too." He glanced at Cal for confirmation and she nodded.

"Janey, you're in charge of cleaning up down here. I want everything erased—everything. All signs that we were here.

"Abby," he grinned. "You're going to get those kids up there. They go first. The little one and the teens. Those girls can help set up, under your direction, and once it's going you can pitch in with the rest of us." He looked around at everyone, in turn, emphasizing the situation.

"This is big, folks. We had an inkling, but never thought it'd come to this, not really. Cal and me, we got plans and you know most of 'em. The rest will come. Now let's go tell everyone else. Pull it together. We got a job to do."

All ten walked, together, down to the shelter to break the news. Cal began with her suspicions, the research, the conclusion that she and Pops had drawn. The questions came fast and furiously; some showed anger, most were merely bewildered. Janey filled in the events of the day and at that, everyone quieted immediately.

Pops closed the session, reiterating the instructions he'd given the leaders just a short time ago, and sent everyone off to their tents.

Abby stopped by Millie's and scooped up Juliet, hugging her tightly. The little girl had been sleeping, but she came awake instantly when Abby arrived.

"I'm so sorry, little one. We can't have our day tomorrow like I promised. Tomorrow we're moving up top. All of us."

Juliet snuggled further into Abby's lap. "It's because of bad things, isn't it?" Abby swallowed hard, at a loss for words. "That's okay. I have you to take care of me, Abby. I'm not afraid." And with that, Juliet was fast asleep again.

Abby tucked her back in and quietly left the tent, smiling sadly at Millie. The older woman stopped her and took both her hands in her own; she looked her square in the eyes and said, "Abby. She's right. She'll be okay, we'll all be okay. Even you." Millie hugged her and Abby left, making her way back along the rocky path.

CHAPTER TWENTY-THREE

By late November, it was snowing. The weather had held until then, cold and rainy, but nowhere near the freezing mark. They all routinely dressed in layers for warmth, as fires were kept deliberately small and used mainly for cooking. Supplies were running low and Abby was waiting for a break in the storm to venture out of camp.

The good news, if there was any, was that the blizzard also kept planes grounded. The surveillance pilots didn't want to go out in this stuff either; after the past month or so they probably didn't really believe anyone was still out here.

The grapevine was still lively. The camp kept in touch with a few other groups, scattered remotely around the state and into Illinois. Most were ragged, hungry, cold, and dispirited. They all said the same thing: the military was rounding up strays, those who had survived the initial epidemic. They wanted everyone in one spot, probably to study, possibly just to control. Or kill. No one talked about that. Not much anyway.

Abby made her way through the snow to Millie's tent. The sounds of coughing reached her long before she entered. Flu and pneumonia had joined forces and invaded. They'd already lost several, and Noah was running short on medicines.

Abby wasn't worried for herself; she never got sick, hadn't since she was a child. As soon as the contagion began to spread, she'd packed Juliet off to the tent she shared with Emmy and kept her there. So far, the small girl also seemed immune.

But she was concerned for Millie. The older woman was in great shape, but she was still no spring chicken. And she wasn't doing well.

As Abby ducked inside, Pops rose from Millie's side. "I think she's doing better, Abby. Take a look, what do you think?" His eyes were pleading and sad. Bob lay at the foot of her cot.

Abby knelt beside Millie's cot and took her feverish hand. Millie's eyes were open, but unseeing; she occasionally mumbled a few words in between spasms of coughing. Abby looked at Pops. He knew.

"Has Noah been by lately?"

"Just this morning, right before you got here. He gave her some morphine pills but they don't seem to be working too well . . ." His voice trailed off. "Guess I've seen a lot, Abby. Too much. This is about killin' me."

Abby awkwardly patted him on the shoulder. "I'll sit with Millie for a while, Pops. Why don't you step out for some air?"

He bit his lip for a moment, then gave a brusque nod. "All righty then. Won't be long." He stepped outside, lowering the tent flap.

Abby nearly dozed off in the dim light, but started upright when Millie spoke. It was barely a whisper, true, but she sounded coherent for the first time in days. "Shhh," said Abby,

"Don't try to talk yet." She gave the woman a sip of water. Millie broke into a coughing spasm. Abby gave her another sip.

She waved the cup away and tried again. "Where's Clarence?"

"What?" said Abby. "Oh, Pops. He'll be right back. Just stepped out for a minute."

"Help me sit up." Millie struggled to rise, but was too weak. Abby shrugged. Probably couldn't make things worse. She arranged a couple more pillows behind Millie's head and wiped her forehead with a cloth; it was surprisingly cool to the touch.

"You remember what I told you, Abby, when we moved up here?" Her words were halting and slow, barely audible, but her mind was clear. "I meant it then, and I mean it now. And you take good care of Juliet for me. That baby sure does love you." She began coughing again.

Abby glanced around frantically. This didn't sound good at all and she didn't mean the coughing. Almost everyone was coughing lately, and she almost didn't notice that anymore.

Just then, Pops appeared at the entrance, Juliet in his arms.

Noah was right behind him. Millie smiled.

Juliet jumped down and threw herself at Millie, sobbing. The dying woman patted her back and held her briefly before beginning to cough again, a wracking sound from deep inside. She held the child away from her and looked directly at her.

"Juliet, I love you like my own but I gotta move on now. Abby'll take care of you. I promise. I know you love me, but you love her too and you'll be safe with her, for always." She kissed Juliet and handed her to Abby, then looked up at Noah.

"Doc, you remember what you promised me?" Noah smiled faintly and nodded. "You know," Millie went on, "I don't believe those deathbed confessions are always from the one dyin'." And she winked.

"I'm awful tired now. Clarence, are you there? Can't seem to see too well all of a sudden." Pops knelt down and took Millie's hand, gripping it tightly.

"I'm here, darlin'."

Noah lightly touched Abby's arm and the two of them, Juliet crying in Abby's arms, stepped outside.

Within a few minutes, Pops left the tent too. "She's gone."

CHAPTER TWENTY-FOUR

Christmas was approaching. There hadn't been any snow for over a week, but the wind was bitter and the sun seemed to have disappeared permanently. Abby, on fire duty today, had had to trudge even farther afield than usual to bring in her quota. She'd barely given Christmas a passing thought until Juliet said something.

"Abby?"

"Yes, little one?"

"Will Santa know how to find me?"

Abby paused. Santa hadn't figured prominently in her childhood; neither, really, had Christmas itself. Her aunt celebrated nothing and, indeed, had rarely even smiled and certainly never indulged in any type of frivolity.

"Well . . . um, sure, of course he can find you. Doesn't Santa know everything?"

Juliet did not appear to be convinced.

"Abby, of course Santa knows! And I'm sure he'll be here, right on schedule!" Emmy stepped in, saving the day. At least for the time being. Abby shot her a look. "Come on, honey, I'll help you write him a letter. And we'll have to find a sock for you to hang up, so he can fill it."

Juliet giggled. "You don't hang up a sock, Emmy, you hang up a stocking!" The two went over to Emmy's bunk and began their project. Juliet was smart as a whip. Emmy had been teaching her letters and numbers and she could write a few short words already.

That evening after dinner, when Juliet was playing games with some of the teens, Abby pounced on Emmy. "Okay, smart one, how are we going to pull this off?"

Emmy smiled secretively. "Oh, I have a few tricks up my sleeve. And so does Noah and Ted and Pops and a few of the girls." At that, she flounced out of the tent and made her way over to Cal's. Well, flouncing was not entirely accurate. It was difficult to manage that with four layers of clothing and while ducking one's head against the wind. But she did leave, with a small, mysterious smile.

Abby stretched out on her bed. It was chilly, but at least there was no wind. This Christmas thing might be out of her sphere, but there were a few things she could probably manage. She made mental notes, but felt herself drifting off time and time again. Bob was on the cot with her, which provided some additional warmth if one could stand his dog breath.

Noah ducked inside, shivering. He pulled off his gloves and rubbed his hands together, standing over the brazier. "Damn, I think it's getting colder."

Abby sat up. "How's Zoe doing?" A few days after Millie died, Brad and Zoe had announced that they were having a baby. The bitter cold certainly wasn't helping matters, but Zoe had been terribly sick for the past week.

Noah shrugged. "Not a lot I can do up here. A hospital would be the best place for her. She still can't keep anything down except a little water." He yawned. "I need to get some sleep, one of these days."

"Here, let me help," said Abby. She moved over to Noah's bunk and unlaced his boots; she handed him a fresh pair of socks and hung up his coat and scarf to dry. Abby turned her back as Noah changed into his sleeping gear. No one wore pajamas anymore, or even just sweatpants, it was too cold in spite of the small bit of warmth in the center of the tent.

"Abby," said Noah. "We need to talk." He reached for her hand to pull her down beside him.

"Not now," said Abby with a look of panic in her eyes. "You said you needed to sleep." She kissed him on the forehead. "So go to sleep!"

Noah sighed and laid down. Within minutes, he was sound asleep and Abby breathed easier. It's not that she didn't want to talk to Noah, it was that Noah wanted more than conversation. And Abby wasn't sure that she herself wanted more than that. True, there had been that night they spent together after the commissary explosion...but Abby knew the reason behind that. Death.

They buried Zoe on a clear, cold day, the day before Christmas Eve. She'd lost the baby, a tiny boy, and bled to death. Brad was handling it well, but Noah continually beat himself up over what he believed to be his own inadequacies in saving her.

Of course it wasn't his fault; they all knew that. Lack of equipment and supplies were to blame. They were even running low on basic medicines. Clothing and blankets were ample, but food was likely going to have to be rationed before spring arrived. Abby had had her doubts anyway about anyone trying to care for and raise a newborn, considering their current predicament.

After the burial, Brad remained beside Zoe's grave for a time; Noah took off into the woods. Emmy and Juliet returned to their tent to practice reading, but Abby went to see Cal.

Cal sat alone, knees drawn up, shivering. She'd lost weight since Meg's death but Abby figured they were all probably thinner at this point. The two sat in silence for a while, lost in their own thoughts. Abby patiently waited for Cal to speak.

"Maybe we'd have been better off staying put and taking our chances, Abby."

"I don't think so, Cal. Pops is still keeping in touch with other groups, and the news isn't good at all. Not sure how much is rumor, but . . ." She shrugged.

Cal deliberately shook off her melancholia. She straightened up and swung her legs off the cot. "So, are you ready for this big Christmas deal tomorrow?"

Abby frowned. "Beats me. I seem to have been kept in the dark about it. I do have something for Juliet, but I'm a little worried about all her Santa Claus talk."

"Nah," said Cal. "Don't worry. I'm sure everything'll be fine." She winked at Abby and pulled on her coat and gloves. They strolled back to the fire to join the others, telling stories of Zoe in the old days, before this unthinkable mess had gotten so out of hand.

Christmas Eve dawned crisp and bright; at least there was no snow, although the air held some promise. Juliet was beside herself with excitement, bouncing from tent to fire to cooking shelter and back, over and over again.

Emmy insisted they not let her lie down for a nap, rightly believing that this would have her up until all hours, waiting for Santa. Abby was dubious. She was also exhausted from chasing Juliet, but at least it kept them warm. She'd already wrapped Juliet's gift with a piece of old newspaper she'd snagged from the woodlot where they kept all the fire equipment and supplies.

At last, dinner was finished, cleanup complete, and everyone gathered around the campfire to sing carols. Juliet was visibly drooping when Abby finally carried her back to the tent and helped her get ready for bed. She saw the sock that Emmy had hung near Juliet's cot and sighed.

The girls had just gone to bed when Noah returned. He clumped inside, shaking snow from his hooded parka and Abby jumped up to help him.

"Where have you been?" Abby hissed. She didn't want to wake Juliet, and Emmy appeared to be sleeping as well. Or was pretending to do so.

"Out. What's it matter to you, anyway?" Noah was sober, thankfully, but completely uncooperative.

"It matters to all of us, Noah. You should know that, in spite of . . ." Abby's voice trailed off. "Besides, I do care."

Noah laughed harshly. "Right. Sure."

"Noah." Abby reached up and took his face in her hands. She kissed him lightly.

"Abby, stop." He grabbed her hands. "I'm not playing here, I love you. We don't know how much time we have, but it's all or nothing for me." He stared down into her green eyes. "Tell me you will."

"What? Tell you I will what?" Abby pulled away. "Noah, I care about you. I do. But I'm not—I'm not going to be with you. I can't. Not now. Not until . . ."

"Until we're safe? That's not going to happen, Abby. So it's never." He turned his back on her, sat down, and began to unlace his boots.

"Good night, Abby. Merry Christmas."

Abby awoke on Christmas morning as a small weight was flung onto her chest. "Abby, wake up! It's Christmas! Santa was here!" She groggily rubbed her eyes and tried to stretch, but the weight was persistent.

"Juliet, get off me!" The child obliged, grinning. "What on earth are you talking about?" Abby sat up and swung her legs over the side of the bunk.

Juliet's small sock had been replaced with one of Emmy's larger ones and was bulging mysteriously; the brazier in the middle of the tent was glowing. There were all kinds and sizes and shapes of packages lying around a tiny evergreen, balanced precariously at the foot of Juliet's cot. The tree was decorated with bird feathers and pinecones and even, on closer inspection, a few necklaces and earrings scrounged from deep within backpacks and duffle bags.

Abby was astounded.

Juliet jumped about, clearly unable to decide what to do first. She finally settled for pulling Abby up and over to the small tree, pointing.

"Look, Abby, look! Isn't it pretty? And look at Bob!" The shepherd had a huge red bow tied around his neck and was trying to look dignified.

Emmy ducked through the tent flaps and grinned. "And you had doubts about Santa," she teased.

Abby threw up her hands. "I need coffee!"

A crew carried the tree out to place it near the fire pit, along with Juliet's gifts. Breakfast was eaten while watching the little girl open her presents. For once, everyone was smiling and talking; it was really quite festive. Juliet held up every gift and thanked the giver; she was beside herself with joy, scampering around, digging into the pile, chattering like a squirrel.

Finally she was finished, and Abby scooped her up to return her to the tent for a brief rest before Ted served their Christmas dinner.

She sat Juliet down on her cot and handed her one last package. It was flat, rectangular in shape, and a bit heavy. Carefully, Juliet opened her gift. It was a knife, just like Abby's but smaller, for little hands.

Juliet looked up solemnly. Abby nodded and smiled. The little girl cautiously withdrew the knife from its leather sheath and gently put her finger on the blade.

"Yes," said Abby. "It's very sharp." She showed Juliet how to fasten the sheath onto her calf; it was a little long for such short legs, but Juliet would grow into it quickly enough. She took it off then, and laid it on her pillow.

Throwing herself into Abby's arms, she whispered, "Thank you, Abby. I love you!" Obediently, she lay down on her cot, but just then there was a knock at the doorway.

Pops entered and smiled at the little girl. He was holding something behind his back. Abby withdrew to let them have a few minutes and went over to tidy her own bunk and finish getting ready for the day.

The old man sat down next to Juliet and put his arm around her. "These are for you, sweetheart. Grammy made them before…before." He handed her a pair of bright, cherry red mittens, on a string to keep them from getting lost.

Juliet clutched them to her chest as tears formed in her big, blue eyes. She sniffled. Pops looked rather teary himself, but simply hugged the little girl tightly and kissed the top of her head. He gave a Abby a hug as well, before he left, and whispered, "Thank you. And merry Christmas."

All crews had the day off today; truthfully, there wasn't a lot to do in the dead of winter except guard duty—and Sandy remained on the job, seemingly wanting only to be alone and useful. No one had seen much of her these last few weeks, except Cal, with whom she was bunking when in the campsite.

Firewood, of course, was a priority, and the cooks were always busy. Ted tried to rotate anyone who was interested but their numbers overall were diminishing. They'd lost Millie and then Zoe, and five others to the flu in just the last few weeks. From over 60 people gathered initially, just 23 remained.

But today was Christmas, a day of festivity. While they mourned those who had died, they celebrated those who lived.

CHAPTER TWENTY-FIVE

Spring came at last, along with many changes.

While the core group remained in the camp, nearly half of the others decided—after much discussion—to move back to the metropolitan area. Cal and Noah both tried to discourage this, making them aware of the consequences; Janey was more concerned about their potential status as informers.

The die cast, a family of four plus one couple elected to move closer to the town where, they assumed, supplies would be easier to obtain. While Abby tried to make it clear that the town no longer existed, they assured everyone that there were still homes and maybe even stores that would aid their survival. No one was thrilled with wintering in the outdoors, but some were certainly less hardy and that was a heavy factor.

That afternoon, several hours later, Sandy came into camp with news. Radios had not been in use for some time, as they could be traced and tracked via GPS. She met with Cal, alone, then Pops arrived. Soon everyone had gathered at the fire pit.

Cal wasted no time. "Mike and Susan and the kids, and Jim and Janice were all taken . . ." She looked at Pops. He nodded.

189

"They were all captured by—by US Marine personnel about 45 minutes after they left the gates.

"Sandy followed them, under my direction, to make sure they made it safely away. In spite of precautions taken, at some point they must have believed that there was little danger. Sandy said they acted as though they were simply on an outing and weren't paying full attention when the choppers landed.

"In light of this, everyone will remain in camp but for certain assignments, no exceptions. We have believed our cover here to be sufficient, but will be working on improving that and making other necessary changes."

Cal sat down and waited for questions, but there were none. Everyone was calm and resigned, they knew the stakes. If not prior to this, certainly now. Pops milled around the group, speaking a few words to each. Brad was beside himself, wanting to avenge the families or at the very least do something besides sit around . . . he was too valuable to the entire group to go on any assignments, and he knew it.

Abby sat down beside Cal. "Okay, what's up?"

Cal looked around and said, in a low voice, "I need you to do some scouting. Outside the camp. Come by my tent later." She got up to leave, but paused to speak briefly with Noah.

Eventually, everyone returned to their tents, some glancing anxiously upward. Abby tucked in Juliet and left her with Emmy while she made her way to Cal's. She was a little surprised to see Noah and Pops there as well, but Noah brushed past her on his way out without a word. Their friendship had been rather strained since Christmas Eve.

"Abby," said Cal. "We've decided to send you outside for an extended mission. We need to know what's going on; specifically, who is doing what and where.

"This will be short-term, and you'll have the radio for any emergency. You'll leave in the morning and we expect you back within two weeks. Unless something happens."

Cal reached into her pocket and handed Abby a single capsule. "From Noah. If you need it." They looked at each other for a long moment.

"Got it," said Abby, breaking the spell.

"Here, Abby." Pops handed her a sheet of paper. "Look this over, get the gist, memorize what you can. We'll talk more after dinner." He squeezed her shoulder and smiled. Abby walked outside into the sunshine, shivering just a bit.

She spent the afternoon packing, checking her weapons, sharpening her knife. She read over the paper that Pops had given her, quickly memorizing it. It was standard reconnaissance, with the added twist of intel gathering. Where, if any, there were troops stationed; whether or not they were mobile or stationary. What was their purpose and how aware were they of the presence of those in the camp. Not too difficult.

Not easy.

After dinner, Abby worked with Juliet until the little girl's bedtime, helping her whittle a large stick. She was making something for Pops, a surprise. Just as Abby was tucking her in, she jumped up with a shriek—Noah suddenly appeared.

He gave Juliet a good-night kiss, then turned to Abby. He looked directly at her for the first time in many weeks, then turned away. "Be careful, Abby," was all he said.

Abby did not respond. She walked over to Cal's tent and slipped inside.

"The fact that they were caught so close to the gates is a definite cause for concern. Abby, we need to find out what's going on, but I don't want you going too far out—or in, as the case may be. In other words, make sure we're secure here, but learn what you can. And, if all else fails . . ."

Cal's voice trailed off. She didn't want Abby to go, she didn't want any of this to actually be happening, but there you have it. It was necessary, all of it. They'd been too long without real news, without knowing the status of Co-opCom, the biological disaster, anything at all. Sitting around and wondering when you were going to be captured for whatever reason just wasn't working out—they needed to be safe, and they needed information.

Abby stood to leave and hugged Cal. They clung together for long minutes, finally stepping back and trying not to show their fears. Abby cleared her throat, but couldn't speak. She stepped outside to meet Emmy at the fire pit.

The girls sat together, in silence, for a long time. Emmy put her arm around Abby's shoulders. A light mist began to fall.

At last, Abby arose pulling Emmy with her. They walked back to their tent, arm in arm, still silent.

Morning came, damp and cool. The sun was just beginning to rise when Abby kissed a still-sleeping Juliet goodbye and walked outside. Bob started to crawl out from under Juliet's bunk; she told him to stay. She paused at Noah's bunk, but kept going. Nothing good would come from waking him, nothing but false hope, perhaps.

Emmy and Cal met her outside, with a mug of coffee of course. Cal gave her a few last-minute instructions and then she was off to learn whatever she could about the enemy. If, indeed, there was an enemy.

Abby walked on the side of the road leading out of the camp, under the canopy of trees that were just beginning to show tiny leaves. Not much cover, but some. She kept an eye on the sky, just in case. When she reached the gates, Sandy appeared.

"See you soon, Ab. Take care." Sandy tried to smile, and almost managed. She squeezed Abby's hand and retreated into the brush.

There was more cover here, and more shade. Looked like it was going to be warmer than usual today. Abby continued down the road until she reached a pair of old grain bins set almost directly at the edge of the pavement. She ducked between them and paused to get her bearings and decide on a route.

She took a drink from her water bottle and began to climb, heading east. She knew there'd been a few more houses built in the area in the last couple of years, but was pretty sure most were south of the camp. As she neared the top of the hill, she slowed her pace, watching the birds for any signs of nearby humans. Or whatever.

The birds continued to sing and occasionally she could hear small animals in the brush. The sun was climbing and the day was warming. Up ahead, Abby could see a faint outline of a roof. She swung the Mossberg off her shoulder and clicked off the safety, holding the gun in a ready position. Silently, one step at a time, she approached the small frame house. The door was ajar.

She slowly circled the yard, keeping inside the trees, but heard no sounds coming from the house. A few quick strides and she was up against an outer wall, near the corner of the front porch. Shifting the shotgun to her left hand, she drew the .357 with her right and warily walked up the steps.

Still no sounds. Abby kicked open the front door and jumped to the side, back against the wall. Nothing. Cautiously, she began to step inside and noticed a rifle lying on the floor.

What used to be human hands were still clutching the butt of the gun, and what used to be, possibly, a man, was lying next to it.

She quickly took in the small room and the hallway leading to the back of the house. Nothing. A couch was set against the south wall and on it rested the remains of more people, residents of the home she assumed; it appeared to be a woman and two young children.

If Abby had to guess, she'd say the man had died from defending his family against…something. Or perhaps they'd all died from contracting VADER. Impossible to be sure, since there wasn't a great deal left to work with. At any rate, violence itself could probably be ruled out.

Quickly and thoroughly, Abby checked the rest of house. Two bedrooms, a bath, a kitchen. That was all. No one else. Since the door had been left open, the inside was in pretty bad shape but, far as Abby could tell, no humans had been here. Just animals, wandering, nesting, making messes. Even the fridge door was hanging open, and most of the cabinets.

Abby began loading up what could be useful, canned goods mostly, and building a pile on the front porch. She'd holstered her sidearm and set the Mossberg down on the kitchen table, along with her heavy backpack.

She took the first load out to the woods beyond the clearing, along with the shotgun, and quickly created a cache for the supplies. Just one more trip finished the job and she went back inside to search for other items.

In the first bedroom, she discovered two boxes of shotgun shells and in the second, some clothing she thought would fit Juliet. Lord knows it had been hard enough to keep the girl warm over the winter with too-large clothing and shoes. These would keep, as long as the animals didn't get into them before Abby could return.

She made one more trip to her cache, then loaded up and started walking. She wanted be much farther away from that scene before she stopped for lunch because, although she'd done her job efficiently, the whole thing was too depressing and brought to the forefront the entire situation.

She climbed the next hill before stopping and ate a quick sandwich. After a smoke, she fieldstripped her cigarette and stretched out for a few minutes. As the crow flies, she'd only traveled about half a mile; up and down hills and hacking through the brush, however, translated to twice that in measurement and double again for effort.

Abby began to walk again and came to a wide, open area. She skirted it to the north, since that would be her general direction anyway, and looked up. Still nothing, just a clear blue sky with a few puffy white clouds.

Moving slightly northeast, Abby removed her jacket and tied it around her waist. She was halfway to Marble Springs Road by mid-afternoon and had still encountered no one, either friend or enemy.

Due east from her position was Patterson Road, Marble Springs was still slightly to the northeast where it dipped south. Pausing for a moment, Abby moved toward Patterson. She knew there were a few homes scattered along that road and fervently hoped they were entirely unoccupied, by the living or the dead.

First, however, she had to cross the wide, cleared strip where the power lines had been set. Scanning the skies, she saw nothing. Running wasn't going to be easy, given how loaded down she was, but it was obviously the quickest route back to safety. Taking another look upward and a deep breath, she ran in a straight line for the trees a hundred yards away.

Then she heard it. The distinct whine of the same choppers that had flattened the town last fall. She ducked and rolled, coming to her feet just inside the forest.

Abby calmed her breathing and moved back into the shadows.

As she watched, hidden, the six choppers flew down the length of the utility easement in formation. None slowed or broke rank and, thankfully, they continued south.

Abby turned and broke into a long, fast stride, wanting to put as much distance between the choppers and her as quickly as possible. Focused on the sound of the blades, she nearly blundered into a barn before getting herself under control.

Stopping short, she yanked out her gun and clicked off the safety in one motion. She froze, barely breathing. Nothing. She moved stealthily to the side of the barn and crept around the corner. Still nothing.

As she rounded the front, she could see what remained of a house. Flattened and burned, just like the town. She breathed easier, deciding she was alone.

Abby consulted her map; another house was located directly south of her, but neither of these were actually on Patterson itself. She decided to make camp between the two, as the second needed to be checked as well. She figured it would be a quick jaunt in the morning as, more than likely, that house was in the same condition.

Morning proved her right, so she continued up Patterson, keeping well out of sight, until she reached Marble Springs. By her calculations, she was directly east of the old infirmary where they'd originally set up a site; about a mile and a half in a straight line, just over two if one accounted for the hills.

No more demolished homes, and no more human remains, left Abby in a slightly more cheerful mood than the previous day. So far, so good. She was missing Emmy and Juliet; she didn't allow herself to think of Noah at all.

By early afternoon she had re-crossed the power line easement with no signs of choppers and had covered nearly two miles. She stopped for a sandwich and refilled her water bottle from a small spring. Rabbits and birds were everywhere, showing her that, if there were people around, they weren't much into hunting. Knowing the area well, she doubted that last part.

Abby turned north toward the road. There were few homes along Marble Springs, but they needed to be checked. No signs of anyone in the woods meant they were either holed up, or gone. She stopped near dusk, several hundred yards from the road, and made a cold camp. It wasn't miserable, but still a bit chilly at night this early in the spring.

The rain began before the sun rose. At first a trickle, it quickly turned into a downpour. Even Abby, with her excellent vision, was having trouble seeing more than a few yards around her in spite of the tree cover.

She decided to wait it out and spent a few minutes reinforcing the branches she'd woven overhead. She dreaded the forced stop, knowing she'd have too much time to think.

The good news was that those choppers, if they came back in this deluge at all, wouldn't be able to see any better than she could. Unless they were using infrared.

Damn. Nevertheless, she started a small fire to heat some soup and try to take off the chill a bit from her wet clothes, gambling on the chance that no one would send out aircraft in this weather.

Suddenly, she remembered the capsule that Cal had given her. She pulled it out and looked at, idly wondering how Noah had obtained it. Wondering, too, what he had thought of Cal's plan in case of Abby's capture. She wasn't too worried about Noah, or Juliet; she knew Emmy would take of the little girl. She just didn't want to think about things, period.

By late afternoon the rain had stopped. Abby changed into dry clothes, doused her small fire, and prepared to hike up to the road. She planned to leave her pack and her shelter, taking only the water bottle and her weapons.

She found three homes, all on the north side of the road. Two were demolished, one abandoned. She wondered why one remained standing, but decided that wasn't important. There were no signs of life, and no signs of any recent occupation.

Somewhat tired and dispirited, Abby returned to her camp. The sun was out, but setting, when she heard the choppers again.

Under heavy cover in the woods, Abby could see nothing, but she could hear them all right. She shuddered. Something about those sleek black machines, as well as their firepower, gave her the creeps.

As the sound faded, she relaxed and finally drifted off to sleep.

CHAPTER TWENTY-SIX

Over the next three days, Abby covered almost four miles and checked half a dozen houses. The county was simply deserted. The most noteworthy thing she'd discovered was the family in the first house, so very near to the camp. The rest of the homes were either demolished or empty.

The weather held until nearly the end of the first week, when the temperature dropped to the mid-30s. A few flurries fell, but the skies cleared quickly. Abby didn't dare build a fire, even under shelter, as she'd been hearing those choppers every day now. She shivered through the night, and was up and moving along with the sun.

Now she was moving south and, encountering nothing but a second utility easement, reached Rice Road within just a few days. She looked longingly towards the east where the campsite was just over the next ridge, but kept going.

That night, she slept poorly, waking from unspeakable nightmares that her subconscious refused to allow her to remember. She was left with a vague feeling of unease that lasted until the following night.

She camped on Cardiac Hill, near the site of the old camp corral. It was tempting to call down for Emmy to come visit, or to just backtrack a bit and go over the top of Purple to the campsite—but she wasn't finished yet. Rice Road had had more of a population than the other places she'd been and there might even be someone around.

With a sigh, Abby curled up in her bedroll and drifted off, sleeping soundly for the first time in more than a week.

After breakfast, Abby loaded her pack and shouldered the Mossberg, anxious to finish and get back to camp. She hiked down a faint trail, still visible after all these years, that came around well behind the lake and should end very near the road.

As she hacked her way through some scrub cedar, she heard the choppers again. Hunkering down, becoming still, she listened. They seemed to be a bit north, hovering. Abby bit her lip. They could very well be right over the campsite which, as camouflaged as it was, wouldn't bear close scrutiny.

There was nothing she could do. Nothing. It would take half a day or more to climb back up there under optimal conditions and by then, well . . . it would all be over. If indeed the choppers were there, watching and waiting.

Abby shook her head to clear the images that formed. Keep going, she told herself. Do your job, then go back. Unless you hear something. Surely someone would get word to her . . . if it was hopeless.

Finally, the sounded faded.

When Abby reached the edge of the woods, she faced a dilemma: too much open space. Whether she went left or right or straight ahead, she had to cross at least a hundred yards or more of field and road.

She had three choices, none of them particularly good. She could make camp here and wait. She could go to the east, then south across the road; take it in two steps instead of a mad dash over a longer distance. Or she could make a run for it.

She chose the latter.

She heard the choppers, again, just as she crossed the pavement, and dove into the woods, coming up with her .357 in hand. She pulled back into the shadows even more, watching the sky.

They hovered, descending, for a mere minute, then took off, flying northeast. Back to St. Louis, Abby thought. That's where they needed to go, to find information. Not here. Nothing here but the group up at the camp. And that, she knew, was who they were looking for.

She followed Rice Road, staying in the woods, until the woods ran out. That's where she camped for the night, another cold camp, but the weather was fine and so she endured. She relaxed a bit, having a supper of jerky and dried fruit. Made the last of her coffee too, drinking it cold, but needing a jolt to her brain to counteract the stress of the day.

All right, Abby, she told herself. Think. You've found nothing yet, no people, few homes standing. Yet the choppers keep coming.

The question was why.

Noah had said that 95% of the population had succumbed to VADER and there were only about 150,000 left in the St. Louis area. That covered a lot of territory, but they were a good 50 miles south of the city center. Abby wracked her brain trying to recall the population of the county here. Maybe 200,000 before? A few more?

She figured perhaps 10,000 survived. Maybe. Subtracting the numbers in the bombed town, there would be even fewer. Mike and his group, however, had been taken. Not killed. So there could be other survivors, held somewhere? Abby didn't know.

And she certainly didn't know why. Since the US Marines were the ones doing the hunting, it couldn't be good. At all.

She lit another smoke and drained the last of her coffee, making a face at the taste.

She was heading back in the morning. There was nothing to be done here, no groups had been reported anywhere near them and the county was so decimated that surely no one was left. There were few homes standing, a couple outbuildings, but Abby had seen absolutely nothing to suggest anyone hiding out in the woods.

The only thing left was to discover where everyone had gone, and why. And for that, she needed to go back, first thing in the morning. She cleaned her guns and reloaded, sharpened her knife. She was ready.

Abby traveled northeast again, bypassing Sandy Creek, until she reached a wide, open field. True, the weeds were growing unchecked, but the footing was precarious and the cover nonexistent.

She opted to swing to her left, near Lake Atwood, and avoid the field altogether. The tree canopy wasn't much, but it was better than nothing. She'd heard no choppers all morning and was heartened by that absence.

By noon she'd reached the far side of the lake and chose the most direct route: straight up and over Sunnytop. By dinnertime, she was back at the campsite and reporting to Cal and Pops.

Abby gave a verbal report, then pulled out a sketchbook and drew a rough outline of her trek. She pinpointed the pertinent findings, made notes, and handed the whole package over to Pops.

Worn out, she went to find Emmy and Juliet who, after a too-brief greeting several hours earlier, she hadn't seen in almost two weeks.

Juliet clung to Abby, and Emmy hovered nearby. After dinner, the three retired to their tent; Noah appeared to be out. Emmy shook her head at Abby's questioning look.

Finally, Abby convinced Juliet that yes, she'd still be here in the morning, and yes, it was bedtime. She tucked her in and she and Emmy wrapped up together in a quilt and sat on the tent steps, whispering so as not to wake Juliet.

After breakfast, the entire group met. Cal informed everyone that Abby had returned safely and that there was no immediate danger in the area. However, she cautioned, there were still choppers flying over on what appeared to be regular missions. She finished by assuring them that there were, indeed, plans to gather more detailed intel.

"So," Cal said, "In the meantime, everyone needs to stay close to our base camp here, and undercover at all times. We're safe enough if we don't go wandering off, and we have the bunkers as well. Not comfortable, but safe. For now."

Pops spoke up. "What Cal's trying to tell you all is that these choppers seem to be rounding up folks that haven't come into the city yet. The point is that we don't know why. So unless you want to take your chances, keep low."

The meeting was over and Emmy and Juliet went off to their lessons; Cal summoned Janey and Abby to her tent.

Noah was already there.

"Here's the deal," Cal started off immediately. "We want Abby and Janey to go up north, at least as far as Arnold; farther if you can manage it. We need to know what's going on up there. And everywhere," she added.

Janey was ready. "C'mon, Abby, it'll be fun!"

In spite of herself, Abby laughed. "This is your idea of fun? I'm a lot more at home in the woods than on some secret spy mission—Cal, are you sure about this?"

Cal shrugged. "Who better to send? With Janey's military training and your background...unless you'd rather Emmy go?"

"No," said Abby immediately. "No. Of course I'll go, but I've only just gotten back."

"No problem," said Pops. "We kinda figured as much, so you two leave the day after tomorrow. Noah, give 'em the list."

Noah handed a sheet of paper to Abby. "Besides what Cal and Pops have asked, this is some information that I need about the bio agent as well as a list of drugs that I'd like you to, um, acquire." He gave a small, fleeting smile.

"But, under no circumstances do I want either of you to risk yourselves for any of this. It's not as important as—as what Cal's asking. If you have any questions, you know where to find me." He gave Abby an inscrutable look and walked out.

Abby and Janey pored over the list, then took mental notes while Pops and Cal gave them some additional instructions. It was nearly noon when they were dismissed. As the girls left Cal's tent, they divided up the list of supplies they'd need and agreed to meet the next evening for a last-minute assessment.

Abby grabbed a sandwich and slowly walked back to the tent, thinking. Juliet came in just a few minutes later, running to Abby and jumping on her cot.

"Abby, what do you want to do today? Can we practice my shooting? I'm not sleepy, really! Can I skip my nap?"

"Of course, little one," said Abby, distractedly. "Why don't you get your case out and show me how much you remember about taking it apart, cleaning it, and putting it back together again?"

Juliet obediently pulled out the gun case and set about laying down a cloth and disassembling the Glock. "Look, Abby, see!"

"Very nice, Juliet, keep going." Abby was making a list of supplies and, at the same time, wondering how to break the news of her trip to Juliet.

"All cleaned!"

Abby inspected the .22 carefully. "Perfect," she said, and went back to her list, rubbing her forehead in thought.

"Okay, Abby, see!"

Abby frowned and picked up the Glock. "Where did you get that, Juliet?"

"It's a Mini-G5. Janey gave it to me. So my gun won't make a lot of noise. She said that was the safest, so I could practice."

That, thought Abby, and so when you fire it no one will be able to pinpoint your location. She made a mental note to thank Janey herself and was annoyed with herself for not thinking of it. "Come on, little one, let's head out. And remember, we have to stay under cover and can't go too far."

"I remember. And Pops showed me how to hide, too, just in case."

Abby resisted the temptation to ask, "Just in case what?" She knew what, but wasn't sure she wanted to hear Juliet's interpretation.

The two had a nice time, out in the woods, Bob staying close by as usual. Juliet had indeed learned how to conceal herself and did a pretty good job for a four-year-old. Abby gave her a few pointers, but spent most of her time naming targets for Juliet to shoot. And the little girl was accurate at least half of the time, no mean feat considering the distance of some of those targets. They went over Abby's hand signals for the field, too, and Juliet remembered them perfectly.

After dinner, Abby gave Juliet her bath and then sat her down to tell her that she'd be leaving again. The small child handled it well, tearing up but not having a tantrum. She was remarkably well behaved for one so young, especially so for one who had survived so much trauma.

Abby, however, nearly came undone when Juliet threw her arms around her neck and whispered, "I love you, Abby. Please come back to us."

Surreptitiously wiping her eyes, Abby walked back to the fire pit not really paying attention, and sat down.

"Oh, sorry!" She jumped up from Noah's side. "I didn't realize you were here."

Noah sighed. "It's all right, Abby, you aren't bothering me. We probably need to talk, anyway."

Abby stiffened. She didn't want to talk, not to Noah. "Really, I can't stay; I need to start putting together supplies for the trip . . . and I really need to go find Janey . . . or Emmy. I need to—"

Noah reached up and pulled her back down. "Slow down. I can see that 'anyone but Noah' is your theme tonight, but please . . . just give me a few minutes."

"Fine." Abby tried to relax, but gave up quickly. "Go ahead."

"Abby, I—" He stopped when he saw the look on her face. "Never mind. I'll skip that part. Look, I don't want you to go on this mission. For a lot of reasons. It's too dangerous. We don't know what's going on. You could be taken prisoner—"

"I thought that's what the capsule was for," interrupted Abby.

"Well, yes. But I don't think there's anything to gain, really. I mean, we're okay here, we just need to stay put, keep doing what we're doing."

"Noah, you know that's not right. You know we can't just sit and wait. If we did that, it would just be a matter of time before they come for us. At the very least, we can learn how better to be safe, stay safe; how to protect everyone."

He slumped in defeat.

"Besides, we might be able to find out how to actually defeat them," rang out Janey's voice. She sat down beside Abby, who smiled a bit.

"You always did want to pick a fight," she told Janey, who lightly punched her in the shoulder. That, for Janey, was agreement.

Noah rolled his eyes. "See, that's just what I was afraid of—you two, there's no telling."

"No sweat, Doc. We can handle it. We'll come back with all the info and stuff you asked for, and maybe more besides!"

Janey was confident, you had to give her that. And well-trained, thanks to the USMC. Who they seemed to be up against. Abby pondered some more, lost in thought. She didn't notice that Noah had left.

"So," said Janey, "As long as we're here, how's the list coming?"

"It's coming," said Abby. "In the morning I'll check in at the commissary with Ted and get what we need."

"I assume we're going to head pretty straight north?"

"Yes," answered Abby, "Barring any er, obstacles."

"Ha. Bring 'em on!"

Robin Tidwell

CHAPTER TWENTY-SEVEN

The whole camp saw the girls off on their venture early Thursday morning. Noah watched as they disappeared down the side of the hill and Juliet ran to him.

"It's okay, Dr. Noah," she said. "Abby'll come back. She promised."

Noah smiled down at her and tugged on her blond braid, just like Abby's. His eyes were unaccountably stinging and he brushed a quick hand across them. He scooped up Juliet and took her to breakfast.

Abby and Janey followed the creek and paused at the gates to say goodbye to Sandy. She greeted them with her customary restraint and nodded solemnly as they left. She had her doubts that they'd make it back, but it wasn't her place to say so. Meg had given her the job of guarding those gates when they first arrived, and here she'd stay, keeping her mouth shut and her eyes open.

Twelve miles via the highway, nearly 20 cross-country, they could reach Arnold by nightfall if everything went according to plan. Both girls were loaded down with weapons, ammo, and foodstuffs, and extra clothing, including a set each of Thinsulate, in case of inclement weather. April in Missouri could be very fickle; snowfall was not unheard of. They were grateful they'd collected enough supplies before the town had been bombed.

They passed the old stone quarry just off Highway M, skirting the edge, and made a mad dash across the highway right after a group of choppers flew over. They stopped under some heavy cover for a brief rest before continuing on, slightly to the east now.

As the sun climbed, so did the temperature. Abby had noticed that the choppers were flying lower now, and she mentioned it to Janey, who simply shrugged. They both knew the reason, there was no use talking about it.

Based on what she'd seen the previous week, Abby thought travel would be more difficult when they reached the outskirts of Arnold, so she and Janey stopped earlier than planned. Abby set up camp in what they believed was a well-protected glade with a heavy canopy, and Janey volunteered to do a little reconnaissance.

Within an hour she'd returned, pale and shaking. The town was gone.

Janey sat down heavily and Abby handed her a beer. Warm, of course, but palatable. After a few minutes, she was more composed.

"It's gone, Abby, just like the other one. I thought . . . I mean, I guessed. I don't know! What are they doing?"

Abby shook her head. "Beats me. But that's what we're here to find out."

The girls made a quick change of plans over their cold dinner; no fires now or any time soon, they were too close to what used to be civilization. They figured they were as safe as could be, at the moment, so they'd both get some sleep for a few hours and set off at midnight, hoping to get through most of the city limits by sunrise.

Of course, from here on in there wasn't going to be much rural property, just more homes and businesses . . . or maybe not. But ruins, at least, afforded more protection than open space. There was no question of turning back. They came for information, and they were going to get it.

The night was cloudy, which was a bonus. No moonlight to illuminate the pair as they stealthily maneuvered through the edge of town. Janey took the lead here, in suburbia; or what was left of it.

They crept through the devastated town, keeping in the shadows, ducking and hiding in ruins at strange or unexpected sounds. No choppers were sighted, or heard. Or any humans whatsoever.

Before sunrise, the two were nearly to Highway 141. They found an abandoned house, still more or less standing, and hunkered down in the basement. Sharing some jerky and a can of peaches, Janey and Abby fell asleep, exhausted.

Morning brought the sound of choppers.

Janey wondered aloud why they didn't seem to be using infrared to hunt for them; she speculated that it might have something to do with the heretofore unknown weapon that was being used to devastate the countryside, or possibly with VADER itself.

"So long as they don't," said Abby, "And we're careful, I don't suppose it really makes any difference. Besides, we have more things to decide and discuss.

"For instance, I propose that we split up."

Abby listened for some time to Janey's tirade. Finally, she calmed down a bit. "All right, all right. I'm listening. I won't like it, but I'm listening."

"I want to head over to Babler. We'll need some kind of base camp up this direction, there's no way we can get the info we need in just a day or two. And we'll hardly be able to duck and cover for much longer. Surely once we get to the city there have to be people."

Janey thought for a few minutes. "So, you want us to set up 30-some miles from the city center and do what? It'll take us a couple days, probably, to sneak in and out."

"Yeah, but we can hide better in the woods—surely they've rounded up any survivors that far out, and there wasn't really anything to bomb. Better odds, really; hard telling what we'll run into around here."

"I see your point . . . kind of . . . but I still don't like us splitting up. Cal was pretty specific about that." Janey began tapping her fingers and then got up and paced, thinking out loud.

"You take the woods, I'm in the city . . . it'll take me a couple days to get downtown. You can probably manage in a bit less to get to the park.

"I don't know, Abby, it's not like we'd be within shouting distance. What about Emmenegger? It's a lot closer."

"True." Abby thought for a few minutes. "But it's also smack in the middle of the county. And Babler has more hiding places, it's ten times as big.

"Besides, not sure I like the idea of being right on the river. Just one more thing to watch."

"Fine," said Janey. "I assume you have a plan?"

"Of course," said Abby.

As soon as it was dark, the girls left their shelter and hugged briefly before separating. Janey moved to the east, to the river; she was planning to be in the city limits, about 8 miles north, well before sunrise.

Abby decided to strike off cross-country, knowing the area well, and intended to stay as much in the woods as possible. Knowing St. Louisans' penchant for green space, this was entirely doable.

As the moon rose, she was crossing Highway 30, very near to where she'd stopped on her way to get Emmy late last summer. She made a face at the memory and hoped that someone had at least removed the bodies from the convenience store before it was bombed. If it had been bombed. No time to check, even if she wanted to do so.

When she got to the Meramec, she stopped for a rest. Not loving the water, Abby was still an adequate swimmer. Fortunately, this early in the year, the river was shallow in many places; she just had to pick the right spot.

She had sat down near the shore, well back in the trees of course, and watched the water. No signs of life, but no signs of death, either. And no traffic in the middle of the night, on the water or in the sky.

Waiting until the moon passed into a cluster of clouds, Abby held her Mossberg high and stepped off the bank. She moved slowly but steadily, going deeper within minutes. Continuous movement stopped her from sinking into the mud and she kept going. Exhausted, she pulled herself up on the other side and crawled into the brush. She idly wondered how Janey was faring.

Just a few more miles to go to the park boundaries; Abby knew that, normally, she could hike that distance within a couple hours or less. Things were far from normal. She looked at sky, then at her watch. Just past midnight. She stood up and stretched and hoisted her pack onto her back.

Before sunrise, Abby had skirted the edge of Wildwood and entered the park. She knew the spot she was aiming for, right in the middle. Good cover, a spring, a few rocky outcroppings and some small crevasses; no limestone caves like those further south, but plenty of hiding places.

She'd seen more intact homes on her trip up here, but few commercial buildings. She imagined that those responsible for this . . . round up . . . had planned, at the very least, to flush out survivors with a definite lack of supplies. But she was confident that she could find whatever they needed.

Abby stowed her gear under an outcropping and wedged herself in with it. She pulled a few low-hanging branches down in front and ate a handful of trail mix, then leaned back and closed her eyes. She sniffed the air. Something didn't smell quite right, but she didn't think it was anything particularly dangerous. She slept.

Abby discovered the source of the smell upon awakening. The forest around her was more bare than usual at this time of year. Where some trees should have been fully leafed out, there were merely buds; those that should have been budding were still bare.

Fire. At some point, probably last fall, the park had burned. Or someone had burned it on purpose. Abby thought the former was more likely, as survivors hiding out here wouldn't necessarily have had the skills to do so. Accidents did happen.

Abby took in her surroundings carefully. Further down the ridge she could see a stand of evergreens, apparently unscathed. Furthermore, if she inched out from under the rock just a tad, she could see an almost clear delineation between the undamaged and burned areas.

Well. That changed things, and slightly in her favor. She could stay close to the rocks and make her way over to the more lush area, over by those trees, and make camp. Hopefully any hollows or crevasses were near enough, in case she needed to get even more out of view.

She left her pack behind and moved along the rock wall behind her, keeping low in the event of a flyover. She reached the spruce trees within minutes, pleased to note how thickly they were grouped together. This would do nicely.

She scanned the area around her and discovered, just to the east, another outcropping similar to where she'd left her gear. Perfect!

Abby began by weaving together some of the lower branches; the job was invisible from the outside but would keep out all but the heaviest downpour. She swept up some of the older, dead needles on which to set her bedroll and cleared a space for a small fire. As long as it was under the tree and the flames kept very low, she should be safe from both fire and visibility.

She fetched her supplies and finished setting up the small camp. Easily found the spring she remembered from past visits. After breakfast . . . or lunch, at this point, since they'd effectively reversed the day/night correlation, Abby went in search of a better hiding place.

She found it quickly, just up the slope from her camp, and it was better than she'd hoped. Situated just behind a large rock, which blended into the backdrop of the opening, was a small crack. Larger than it first appeared, it proved just wide enough for Abby to enter.

Inside, there wasn't much space and, additionally, no secondary exit. But it would work for both herself and Janey, when she arrived.

Now, all she had to do was wait for Janey.

CHAPTER TWENTY-EIGHT

It had been three days, or nights rather, since the girls had split up. Realistically, Janey could be there by morning or within a day or so. Longer than that, Abby would come into the city itself. They'd planned the route for the most part, but it would be easy to miss each other in the dark. Nighttime was the only option now for travel.

She tried not to think about what would happen if Janey was taken prisoner.

Abby spent her time going over Noah's list of medicines and supplies and thinking about their situation. Not hers and Noah's, oh Lord, she tried to avoid that subject even with herself. But overall, what in the world was going on?

Cal had warned her; warned all of them. VADER was released, supposedly during a trial in a remote area, but it got out of hand or, most probably, someone was pulling a fast one. Not the right expression, Abby knew, but apt. Regardless, Ultratron was probably involved in a lot more than the creation of the virus.

Sixty people had gathered at the camp. The core group, as well as a few friends and some families. All but twenty were

217

gone now, some of them dead. Other groups had survived this . . . plague . . . but none had been heard from for months.

Some of those who had left were captured by USMC personnel. USMC choppers blew up the town. Their current predicament appeared to be engineered by the government. The US Government, specifically. Or rather, Co-opCom itself. There was no real US remaining.

And Cal had worked for them.

Abby shook off her thoughts. Ridiculous. If she was going to follow that train of thought, she could extend it to Noah: he'd said he was working on the cause and effect of VADER, but had made zero progress. Of course, he hadn't had all the equipment and lab space to properly work at it, but still…he hadn't reported any thoughts or theories either, not for a long time. And what about all those blood samples he'd collected from everyone?

Enough.

Why would anyone, let's say Co-OpCom since everything seemed to point that direction, release this thing? Abby mulled it all over, and over again.

Of course she believed, as did many, that the current administration was a joke. Amateurs. But this virus or whatever didn't target only a certain political segment, it was pretty indiscriminate. She remembered those she'd lost. Nope, that wasn't it. But a smaller population would be easier to control. Perhaps those being taken alive were also being subjected to some kind of mind-altering techniques?

Again, enough. She wished Janey would hurry up. Near midnight on the fifth day, Janey appeared.

Abby had been stalling for several hours, knowing it was time to go, hoping it wasn't necessary. The enemy sure wasn't going to get two women, staggering around in the dark, if she could help it.

Janey sprawled out under the trees and stared up at the canopy. "Oh, my God," she said. "That was a trip." She'd covered the 30 or so miles from downtown in just over a day, traveling around the clock. "Not too difficult," she told Abby, "Lots of hiding places where there's a higher population. Or used to be."

Abby built a small fire and offered Janey a smoke. Janey reciprocated by pulling two bottles from her pack. "I got your back, huh?" Abby smiled, and they began dissecting information. "The big news," began Janey, "Is the reason they aren't using infrared is because that virus-thingy-whatchamacallit has rendered it useless on anyone who was exposed. Which basically means all of us. And no, I don't know why, maybe Noah could figure that out or something.

"But the bigger news is the reason they don't fly at night."

Abby waited.

"It's not in their contract."

"Contract? They're Marines, for crying out loud. They have the choppers; Sandy saw uniforms." Abby was thinking furiously.

"Nope," said Janey. "Mercenaries. I got inside, Abby. I heard them. Humph. Marines." She shook her head. "Didn't really ever believe my peeps would go that way, and it turns out I'm right.

"As for Sandy, she wouldn't know military if it snuck up and smacked her on the butt. I know," she grinned. "I tried."

"So," said Abby, slowly, "They use military aircraft, dress in some kind of uniform, but have limits on what they will and will not do. And someone is paying them to take out entire towns and people too?"

"Not 'someone'," Janey corrected. "We are. The United States Government."

So it was true. At least the government involvement. They'd all suspected, been sure of it even, but now it was put out there plain and simple.

"Why?" asked Abby.

"C'mon, Ab. Think. Haven't we, as a country, been going downhill for years? Especially this last decade? Heading toward 'one world' government?

"Look at all the bullshit regulations, the freedoms being taken away. Look at the kinds of so-called wars we've been involved in, the overstepping of every branch in the good ol' US. Ignoring the Constitution, stomping on everyone who disagrees . . . oh good Lord, I could go on and on!"

Abby knew. She'd come to just this same conclusion the other day. She was more than familiar with the difficulties in obtaining basic necessities, the nonsensical ordinances, the contradictory executive orders, taxation. Amateur hour, right? Power-hungry sons of bitches.

"I get it," she said quietly. "Knew it for a long time, just never thought it'd go so far.

"So now what do we do?"

"Fight back," said Janey. "Duh."

In spite of Janey's arduous trip to the base camp, the girls talked until nearly dawn, pausing only for a quick bite of dinner. Or breakfast. Whatever they were calling it now.

Janey had gone to the old theater downtown which had been turned into a concentration camp of sorts. This is where those captured were being held while awaiting indoctrination.

She'd seen no one familiar and, again, the guards were only hired help. No US military were to be seen, anywhere.

"How on earth," said Abby, "can they afford this? Weren't we something like trillions in debt, or whatever number comes after that?"

"Yeah," Janey said. "Remember all those stories of 'missing' campaign donations? That's the most likely scenario. Ol' Whatshisname planned pretty well when he pulled that electoral change and took three more terms.

"So we got the 'who' and the 'why,' and even the 'how.' Well, more or less. Bigger brains than mine will have to figure out how to counter that. But, Abby, we need more intel. We need to go back in there."

"Yes," said Abby. "But first, I need some sleep." Janey didn't argue that point at all. In fact, she was out cold before Abby could bank the small fire and crawl into her own bedroll.

They'd been gone from the main camp down south for almost a week and, while no one was expecting them for at least another ten days or so, Janey had brought additional information that Cal needed to know. Plus, there was the matter of Noah's list.

The plan was to leave in the early evening and head into St. Louis. Once there, they'd split up again, Abby in search of supplies and Janey to make the attempt to infiltrate at least a barracks, maybe higher. Like she had said, most of the good rumors were circulated among the troops and most had at least a grain of truth.

The girls spent the afternoon readying their weapons and packing light for the trip. Most of what they'd brought would be cached in the rocks. They removed all traces of their presence from the base camp; at least it would fool most people.

The pair entered the downtown area just before sunset. Janey had observed a curfew for all the soldiers and the few civilians who were apparently still free. Abby had plans to mingle with those people, while Janey was going to attempt to enter the barracks, bluffing her way inside.

Abby had a slight change of plans. Instead of stepping into a situation about which she knew so little, she instead hid in the shadows as much as possible. She chose one couple to follow, eavesdropping as they strolled.

"Did you see those new recruits?"

"Which ones, soldiers or civvies?"

"The soldiers, of course! Half the time those civvies are so brain-dead when they join up that they're just no fun at all." She sighed, aggrieved as though this were a personal affront designed to make her life miserable.

Her companion laughed. "Join up? That's a good one!"

"Yeah, it's a good thing we just get rid of most of them."

Abby's finger tightened slightly on the trigger of her .357. "They're so useless. But we have to be nice . . . at least in public."

"Ah, yes. We must be tolerant, after all."

"Of course. They were really just raised wrong, you know. They can't help it if their self-esteem isn't high, like ours, or if they believe in God and those other myths. It's our job to teach them."

"So tell me about those new soldiers."

"Well, the president himself brought them over."

"Over? From where?"

"Oh, I don't know. Someplace foreign. Doesn't matter. I'm not sure what they'll be doing, but I'm sure he made the right choice—he always does. He's just so . . . involved . . . and compassionate. If it weren't for him, why, I might've had to actually have a job and all.

"You know, before everything happened. But I still had everything I wanted. Didn't have to lift a finger! And my neighbors, those poor schmucks, had those 9-5s every single day!"

The pair laughed again at this supposed witticism. Abby grimaced. She followed them for a couple more blocks, until their inane chatter was about to drive her over the edge. Then she slipped inside a darkened doorway.

The only useful thing she'd heard was about the new recruits from overseas, and that was precious little. She stayed put for a few minutes, contemplating her next move.

Up ahead and across the street, she noticed what appeared to be a restaurant. It looked as though it was open, too, and lights and muted music spilled out the door. She crept closer, then decided to boldly enter and find a spot to sit down. Taking a deep breath, she made her move.

"Ma'am! I'm sorry, you'll have to leave that at the door." He gestured toward the shotgun. "You must have just gotten back in town. We changed the rules last week, after that incident . . . oh, you probably haven't heard if you were gone.

"One of the soldiers made a comment that was believed to be intolerant, and another one shot him. Blew his head right off, and let me tell you it was quite a mess!" The doorman babbled on as Abby reluctantly handed over the Mossberg.

"Huh," she said. "What was it all about?"

"Well," the doorman answered conspiratorially, "he wondered what we were all really doing here, and why we had to, you know, get rid of so many people. He even questioned the president!" The man was clearly horrified, as well as delusional, thought Abby.

She tried to look serious. "Oh, no, that's terrible. I can't imagine!" And she couldn't. At all.

"So you see why I have to hold it until you leave. Can't have anything upsetting our diners, you know. Not again."

"Of course," said Abby. "Where shall I sit?"

"Oh, here, where are my manners? Come with me, please. And in case you haven't been here before, just ignore the prices on the menu. Everything is free here; we're subsidized, you know."

Abby kept her face neutral and sat down, facing the door, back to the wall. There was good reason she felt so outnumbered and unprepared. Relax, she told herself. Eat, and listen. If anyone talks to you, smile and nod.

The doorman, or maître d', or waiter, whoever he was, took her order and she sat back and waited. It didn't take long for various bits and pieces of conversation to drift her way.

She took mental notes, and barely noticed as the waiter brought her dinner. She looked up when she realized he appeared to be waiting for something.

"Yes?" she said.

"Oh, good, you have time to talk! I was hoping you did. I mean, you seemed lost in thought and all. It's just so dull around here, I thought you might have some news, or could tell me something interesting you might have seen."

Abby was briefly at a loss. He certainly was a Chatty Cathy.

Maybe that wasn't so bad.

"How could you be bored, with all these people here?" She waved vaguely at the crowd.

"Oh, you know. They never notice me except to complain about something."

"What's to complain about? The food is wonderful." Abby dug into her beef stroganoff; it was almost as good as Ted's. "And you seem like a nice enough kid."

"Probably this," he said, holding out a withered hand. "We're all supposed to be equal, you know, the same. And everyone's supposed to like each other. All the time." He rolled his eyes. "Yeah, right. They still call each other names, even use the 'R' word. Especially around me."

"What's your name?" Abby asked him.

"Henry. And I'm 20 years old and I live with my mom." He sounded rehearsed, and then it struck Abby: Henry was mentally challenged and he looked much younger, probably because of his disability.

"But I'm not always gonna live with Mom. They say I can go to medical school and be a doctor someday, because no one is dumb and everyone can learn. They said they'd help me and everything, so I can do it, just like anybody."

"I see," said Abby carefully. Either Henry had bigger problems than she'd thought, or all these people were delusional as well. She knew the trends well, having been a high school coach, but now it was blatant. Not so long ago, some kids were deemed 'challenged' and time and money were spent disproportionately on their educations, everyone with a brain knowing it was a waste.

Now, it seemed, everyone was going to be truly "equal." Whatever that meant. All the same. No one was stupid, or dumb, they just needed training in spite of any handicaps. Right, thought Abby. That'll work.

"You should know that. Anyone can do anything now! We're all the same. You just have to put your name on a list, and it happens. And we don't have to pay for anything, do we? It's great. I don't even have to work, but I do 'cause it's fun.

My mom doesn't work. She watches TV a lot. And gets her nails done. But they're so pretty. And we have a nice house, a really big one.

"You're pretty like my mom. What's your name, anyway?"

"Susan," said Abby, without thinking.

"Oh, I like that name. I knew a Susan once. Before I came to work here. She was brought into the hospital where I used to work, you know, from out there somewhere." Henry waved his arms, pointing vaguely.

"She wasn't like everyone here. She was different. I liked her. But then they took her away."

Abby thought furiously. Susan, huh? From "out there?" Couldn't be. Yes, it certainly could.

"So, which hospital was this, Henry?"

"Oh, come on, you're teasing me! The other Susan did that too! It's the only hospital, St. Mary's." At that, Henry clapped his hand over his mouth and looked around surreptitiously. "We're not supposed to say that! You won't tell on me, will you Susan? We're not supposed to use any relig-religious words like that!"

Abby put a hand on his arm. "Of course I won't tell, Henry. Now, I've really got to be going. Have to check in you know, since I just got back from my mission." She stood up and thanked the boy again, then walked out the door.

She let go a sigh of relief as she found a deserted doorway and sat down on the steps. St. Mary's. Not too far. That would be her next stop.

CHAPTER TWENTY-NINE

As Abby walked the dark and increasingly deserted streets, she thought about some of the things Henry had said and some things she'd overheard from other diners.

Sounded as though this new society—the best description she could come up with for now—valued everyone equally, certainly not a bad thing. Abby believed that everyone had value, for one reason or another. But to encourage someone like Henry to be a doctor? Ridiculous!

Some of the diners had been talking about how they had "plenty of time" before it was their turn. Abby wondered what that was about . . . their turns for what?

One of the women who, Abby now remembered, had looked paler than the others, had been having an animated conversation with her partner about a recent abortion. The woman had glanced at Henry a few times and Abby had caught something along the lines of, "Thank God I didn't have to put up with something like that!"

Abby shook her head. They claimed everyone was the same, yet wanted to get rid of certain individuals; they got everything for free, yet anything they happened to earn was put into the common pot—paying, she suspected, for those fancy weapons, choppers, and mercenaries. She wondered what would happen when the money ran out.

She had planned to cut through Forest Park, but it seemed as though "they" had necessitated a change in those plans: the perimeter was fenced off, with barbed wire. And sniper towers.

She moved slowly around the edges, keeping to the shadows. A few blocks past the park and she had arrived at the old hospital. Ducking behind a hedge across the street, she waited and watched.

The St. Mary's sign out front had been covered with a white tarp, upon which the newly handwritten lettering stood out: Citizens Medical Services. She could also see a lengthy line going into the doorway of the east entrance.

Abby was about to enter the queue when a heavily armed guard appeared and, using the butt of his rifle, began hassling an older man. It was then that she realized everyone in line was older, perhaps 60 at minimum. She would have stood out in such a group, but what in the world was going on?

The line began to move. Some were crying, some looked resigned, a few were laughing like they were attending a party. Abby was pretty sure it was no party. She moved down the street, still keeping in the shadows, and stopped to get a view of the west entrance.

This side, too, had a line, a shorter one; women only. Most were obviously pregnant, some didn't appear to be in that condition; maybe they were friends? The mood was festive. Abby frowned.

She really needed to get inside. Besides, Susan might still be in there.

There were pedestrian bridges from both parking garages, on either side of the main building, to the first floor. Six more floors rose above that. An elevator tower on the east side garage was as high as the roofline, but the distance between the two buildings was a good 25 feet.

She shrugged. Looks like the only way in was to blend into one of the already-formed lines, then try to leave the area once she was through the doors. It was such a cliché, it might actually work.

Abby crossed the street and stood in the back of the line. She was sure she knew why these women were there but, having zero experience with babies or small children, had no idea how she would fake pregnancy. Many of her fellow standees, however, seemed like normal females waiting for . . . something. So she waited along with them.

A young woman accidentally bumped Abby's arm. "Oh, sorry," she said, smiling. Abby smiled back.

"Not a problem."

"Isn't this exciting?" asked the stranger, a petite girl about the same age as Abby.

"Um, yeah," said Abby.

"Are you okay? Having second thoughts?"

"No, not really." Abby was thinking about her plan. Nope, no second thoughts there.

"Oh, good, 'cause it's real easy. This is my third time. I must be really fertile or something!" Several women nearby giggled; Abby felt sick.

"See, they think we just don't know anything about birth control, or we can't afford it. So they gave us this clinic." She was on a roll now. Many others chimed in:

"You tell it, sister!"

"Whoop, whoop!"

"We just don't like using that stuff—it's a real pain, ain't it, ladies? And this way we don't have to worry; get knocked up, get rid of those extra cells—it's not really a baby anyway, am I right?"

"You bet!"

"Right on!"

"Say it loud and proud!"

"We can do what we want, when we want. My sugar daddies aren't gonna be no baby daddies!"

Fortunately, the line began to move and Abby was spared a scene-causing sock to the woman's jaw. She still felt sick, but managed to choke it back down and consider her plan further.

Once through the doors, she'd grab an unattended white coat and a stethoscope—they always had those in the movies, right? And start exploring. Shouldn't be too hard . . . maybe.

Finally, it was her turn inside. "Name?" asked a bored voice. "Um, Susan. Susan Smith." Abby inwardly grimaced. Really? That's the best she could come up with?

The official didn't seem to notice. "Sign here."

The girl who'd been in line with her was next. "Well, hello there Tasha, back again?"

Huh, Abby thought. Didn't need to ask that one's name.

While Tasha chatted with the official, Abby took a chance and slipped into an empty room. They obviously weren't expecting anyone to stray, it seemed that all these women were perfectly fine with the choices they'd made.

There was a second door in the room that Abby had entered; she opened it cautiously. A closet. With the requisite white jacket hanging on a hook. Perfect. She put it on and carefully opened the door to the hallway. The guard was still chatting with Tasha, flirting, actually, and Abby stepped out boldly, striding down the hallway towards the lobby of the hospital.

As she crossed the open space and walked past the empty fountain in the center, she noticed a similar scene at the head of the line of older people. One stepped forward, gave her name, and a doctor appeared and escorted her to the elevator.

There were guards, too, armed and standing at attention.

"Name?"

"Frank Sanders." The elderly man was weeping, but making every attempt to stand up straight. His eyes were fixed on something in the distance.

"Wait here for the doctor. Next?"

Without thinking, Abby approached. "Come with me," she said. The man followed her obediently. They stepped into the elevator; there was a guard inside as well, and he pushed a button. The car descended rapidly.

Abby escorted the man through the open elevator doors and down a hallway. There were few people in sight, and sounds of crying could be heard from behind some of the closed doors. Abby stopped at a room where the door was ajar; it was empty. They stepped inside and she motioned for the man to sit.

"Tell me what's going on here."

The old man blinked. Then again. Abby knelt down in front of him and took his hands. "Please. Talk to me."

He cleared his throat. His hands shook. "You must be new here. I was in the death line."

Abby had suspected, but Frank confirmed it. "What the hell?" She jumped to her feet.

"Shhh." Frank pointed up, to the ceiling. Abby doubted there was anyone listening or watching, but she lowered her voice.

Frank blew his nose noisily and cleared his throat again. "I'm seventy years old. It's my turn. Should have gone before now, but I managed to avoid it. I might be a little slow at getting around, but I'm in good health. No reason for this. No reason at all.

"But that's why I'm here. And everyone else in that line. When you turn 60, you're supposed to come in voluntarily. But sometimes, when they get bored, they do a round up. Like cattle," he said indignantly.

Abby was stunned. There had been talk, sure, before the "incident" as they were beginning to call it, but she'd pretty much ignored the rumors. There were a lot of rumors, after all. Many people had passed this one along but she'd dismissed most of them as fear-mongering whackos. Huh. Probably better not make that mistake again.

"Tell me more, Frank."

And Frank did. Much more. More than Abby thought she could handle.

First he told her, after so many folks had dropped dead, they rounded up all those still living. They started cognitive testing, physicals, took blood samples. Then the questioning began. They wanted to know who was missing.

Most of the bodies, Frank knew, had been disposed of by the government; some, he claimed, had merely disappeared. Abby could corroborate that, at least. But she was pretty sure Frank was an observant guy, and still had all his marbles. She kept listening, taking mental notes.

When people came up still missing, he went on, they started using those bombs on the outlying suburbs; then they moved out into the country, taking out the smaller towns. Whenever they found someone alive, if it wasn't too much trouble, they brought them in. For testing.

Most people didn't have jobs anymore, unless they worked for or were recruited by Co-OpCom. He himself dealt in the black market, which was thriving, because being over 55 disqualified you from benefits. He sniffed. Like he would accept anything from them . . .

So that's how he'd survived so long. He didn't need their handouts, he kept to himself, but eventually they came for him. And here he was.

"Now," said Frank. "I told you everything I know. I'm ready for my shot." He rolled up his sleeve, and sat there, stoic until the end.

Abby was aghast. "Frank, I'm not here to kill you. I'm on your side."

"But you're a doctor! You might not be as evil as they are, but you work for them!"

"No, Frank, I don't. I'm . . . I'm undercover. Black market. I came here from . . . down south."

Frank's eyes widened. Abby hoped she'd done the right thing in telling him the truth. Then he smiled.

"Well, then," he said, rolling down his sleeve and straightening his collar. "How can I help?"

Abby began to pace. She needed to think. Frank could certainly be useful—he had already given her a lot of information. But what could she do for him in return? She'd spared his life, in a way; at least he had thought so at first. But they both knew that wasn't entirely true. So now she had Frank to watch after, and she wasn't sure she was up to the job. In his own words, after all, he'd said he moved slowly—that might not be good enough to get him out alive.

"Do you know anything about the hospital? How to get around, where the testing is taking place? Anything?"

"Of course," said Frank. "I conducted a lot of business here, up until a few days ago. Why do you want to go to the testing floor?"

Abby wasn't very forthcoming. "I just need to check on something. Someone."

"Fair enough," said Frank. "There are some parts of the building that aren't being used, but I can get us in and all the way up. Just stick with me.

"And lose that coat. You're not a doc anymore."

The two of them left the room. They saw no one except the elevator guard and they walked right past him as though they had every reason to be there. Frank held open the stairwell door for Abby. "After you, my dear."

He was right, thought Abby. He was rather slow. She was at their first stop, the third floor, and Frank was just leaving the first. She tried to be patient.

They exited the stairwell and Frank motioned for her to follow. They paused at the nurses' station, where a large woman waved Frank on and went immediately back to her paperwork. He opened a door marked "maintenance" and shut it quickly behind them, then pulled the light cord.

Just past the door was a panel. Frank expertly removed the screws with a tool he took from his back pocket. "They didn't frisk me very well when they brought me in," he said with a brief smile.

The opening he uncovered was fairly small, but it revealed a larger duct. Frank apologized. "We have to get past the fourth floor this way. No friends on four. Just move carefully, but it's a lot better insulated than you'd think."

Abby went first, so Frank could move the panel back into place. She was surprised to see there were screws on this side as well, obviously altered from the original. Then again, Frank was full of surprises.

It took a good 45 minutes to crawl up two floors. While the ducts were slanted a great deal, they crossed back and forth many times; Frank, predictably, was much slower than Abby and she took the opportunity to catch her breath.

Frank listened near the panel for a few minutes before deeming it safe and removing the screws. Both were happy to finally to be upright, on their feet. He replaced the panel and checked outside the maintenance room door. Then he took Abby's arm and they strolled out.

A nurse at this station waved them on as well, and Abby relaxed slightly. Just one more floor. They climbed the stairs, Frank lagging a bit again, and came out on the seventh floor. This floor wasn't nearly as quiet. Abby could hear moans from behind almost every door and screams coming from at least one room.

When they reached the nurses' station, however, this one all but ignored them. She slammed a clipboard down on the counter and Abby jumped. Before she could react further, Frank grabbed her arm and yanked her into a nearby room. Apparently he could move faster than he'd let on.

She started to speak, but Frank clamped his hand over her mouth as footsteps approached. She shook him off, but remained silent. After a few minutes, Frank whispered, "Okay. Who's the friend you're looking for?"

"I didn't say that," Abby retorted. "I said 'something.'"

"No one comes up here unless they're desperate, young lady.

Now give me a name."

"Susan Murphy."

"Stay put," said Frank, and he slipped out the door.

He was back within minutes, and gestured for her to follow. They walked down the hall just a few feet, and he held the door for her. Susan was lying in the bed.

Abby looked at Frank questioningly and he nodded. He moved over to a chair near the door and Abby walked to the bed.

Surely this couldn't be Susan. Her flaming red hair was dull and thin; she was so emaciated and hooked up to so many tubes that she was barely recognizable. Abby took her hand and stood there, silently, tears welling up.

Suddenly, Susan's eyes flew open. "Mike?" she croaked.

Abby bit her lip. She shook her head. There was nothing she could do here for Susan, and she had no idea where Mike was . . . or if he was even alive.

Susan shed no tears, but shook her head side to side, very slowly. She was obviously in pain. Abby turned to Frank to ask what the hell what was going on here, but he put a finger to his lips.

"Abby." At least Susan recognized her. "Get out." Abby felt Susan squeeze her hand, barely, and she knew. She leaned down and brushed the woman's hair off her forehead and kissed her cheek.

"Goodbye," she whispered.

Frank and Abby retraced their steps, but this time stopped on the first floor. They made a mad dash out the door to the parking garage, and didn't stop until they were safely hidden between two SUVs. Yes, indeed, Frank could move fast when he wanted to do so.

"Now what?" asked Abby.

"Now," said Frank, "We go back to my place."

CHAPTER THIRTY

Fortunately, Frank lived quite near the hospital in a high-rise building, but only on the second floor. No need to unlock the door, he explained, as the goons who brought him in didn't allow him to lock it in the first place. Why bother? He wasn't supposed to come back. He did, however, lock it behind them, but left the bright red death notice intact on the outside.

Frank seemed to have discovered a new lease on life since he learned that Abby didn't intend to kill him. He even, he showed her, had a hiding place in case of just such an event as he'd experienced. Of course, he added abashedly, he'd been taken by surprise and hadn't had a chance to get inside it.

"Now," he said. "Tell me everything."

"Nope," Abby responded. "You first."

"Well, you remember that last war? About 25 years ago?" Abby nodded. She'd been a toddler, but she remembered the talk of the day and of course she'd studied it in school. "I was in that," Frank continued. "Overseas. My wife and I both made it through, then retired here and thought we'd never leave. Of course, I saw the whole thing coming. Early on, too. We lived up in North County and things were changing might fast. Just went from bad to worse."

237

"After Evelyn died, I moved down here. And when things really got bad, I started trading. Black market, like I told you. Not so much guns and ammo, although I have my own personal stash. Mostly food. And favors."

Frank looked at Abby. "Now, young lady, it's your turn." Abby hesitated. She wasn't sure how much to tell Frank.

"I was warned by a friend on the inside, so to speak. She put together a group and we went into hiding. Now I'm here to get information."

"Huh. That's pretty basic, but good for you, girl, on keeping things close to the vest." Frank studied her face for a few minutes. "Are you here alone?"

"Yes," said Abby.

"No, you aren't. But you're not a bad liar either." Frank smiled. "So what's your next step?"

A bit reluctantly, Abby pulled out Noah's list and handed it to Frank. He scanned it quickly, then gave it back.

"So, you have a doc in your group, huh? Tell you what, I'm gonna get a little shut-eye and you keep watch. Wake me up in a couple hours." He crawled into the hidden space and within minutes Abby could hear light snoring.

With that racket, Frank wouldn't stay hidden for very long.

Abby made herself comfortable and looked around the room. It was a small apartment, a studio, and simply furnished. She grabbed a bottle of water out of the fridge and sat down in a comfortable chair near the window. The curtains were drawn but for a crack, and so she watched and waited.

Around 4:00 a.m., she woke Frank who was instantly ready to start his day. He made coffee and poured a bowl of cereal while Abby stretched out in the hideout, then he said, "I'm going out for a bit, so I'll be closing this up. You'll be perfectly fine. No one comes around during the day, not from the government anyway. And if any friends stop by, they'll see the notice and figure I've been caught. But I'll lock the door anyway."

Before Abby could protest, he was closing her into the tiny space. Lovely, she thought. Locked up by a psychotic old man who had seemed so normal. Well, maybe not. She decided, since last night and all, that she probably could trust him; regardless, she may as well take advantage of this and get some sleep. She'd been going all day and most of the night and, no matter how this all ended, she'd need to sleep.

In no time at all, Abby was out like a light.

She awoke several hours later to a sound she couldn't at first identify. Within minutes, Frank appeared as he unscrewed the panel to the hideout. As she crawled out and stretched, relieved to see the old man, he handed her a cup of coffee. Walking over to the small dinette, Abby noticed a package.

"Yep," said Frank. "I took another trip over to the hospital and got your stuff. Least I could do, really."

Abby was so grateful that she almost hugged him. She'd had no real idea what Noah needed and certainly was in a quandary over how to obtain it. She stuffed the package into her small pack.

The two sat and talked for a bit before Frank began yawning. Abby insisted he sleep for a while. She went back to the chair by the window, thinking about all the things she'd learned and hoping that Janey had been as successful. She replayed her conversation with Frank, too, as she considered what it all might mean to the rest of the group.

Suddenly, the door to the apartment was thrust open. Abby jumped up but wasn't quite quick enough. Two soldiers grabbed her arms and pinned them behind her before she could think to even draw her knife.

Determined to remain silent and not give them any satisfaction whatsoever, Abby felt herself being dragged into the hallway. She hoped Frank had heard the commotion—how could he have not—and would do . . . something. She didn't know what.

The men roughly placed a dark sack over her head and shoved her into an idling car. She soon gave up trying to memorize the turns and stops, hoping that wherever they were taking her wasn't too far. And then another thought occurred to her.

What if Frank himself had blown the whistle?

At last the engine was killed and two doors opened. Abby was yanked from the car and, with a soldier on either side, half-dragged up a set of steps and into a building. A quick elevator ride and a march down a long corridor, and she was flung into what certainly felt like a concrete cell. A door slammed.

Her hood was pulled off, gently, and as Abby blinked, readjusting to light, a voice said, "Hey, Ab. What took you so long?"

It was Janey. Abby guessed neither of them would be at the rendezvous this evening.

"Can't believe they nailed you, Ab. Me, I wandered a bit before I found the barracks. One of them, anyway. Hung around for a while, then went into the dining hall. Good dinner, I'll say that for 'em!

"Anyway, got to playing cards with a few and then this big guy walks up to me starts asking questions. Then a few more of his big-guy friends joined in." She sniffed. "Amateurs."

Abby got it. Janey had taken them all on, foolishly perhaps, although she was sure some of the troops had gotten a thrashing. "So," said Janey, "After the MPs broke it up, they started questioning me. Don't look at me like that, Abby, I did fine! But apparently, since they couldn't find my file, they brought me here.

"And," she added, "Someone put two and two together and now you get to join the party. Any ideas on how they found you?"

Abby thought of Frank. Yeah, she had some ideas all right.

But she wasn't talking about them yet.

"I think, instead of how we ended up here, we should be finding a way out."

"Can't be done," said Janey. "Zero exits here except that solid steel door, and miles of concrete everywhere. Our only chance is to slip past the guards or shoot them. And there are a lot of 'em."

"Yep," said Abby. "And I'll bet they took your ammo too, huh?"

Janey looked aggrieved. "Wish I still had those grenades."

Abby felt something on her leg. Hard. She jerked up her pants leg and pulled out her knife. They missed this? Really? She hadn't thought about it in the confusion of her capture—she wasn't military, never had been. And these guys missed it?

Janey's jaw dropped. "Not very thorough, are they?"

"Here." Abby handed the sheath to Janey. "You keep it. You know hand-to-hand combat, you're trained. For me, it's a last resort and anyway, the knife's mostly for skinning animals."

"Yeah," said Janey, "I'll skin me a few animals all right." She strapped it onto her leg. "Okay, here's what I learned the last couple days."

There were around 1500 soldiers in the area, Janey told Abby, under a Colonel Barton. Few were actual US military, mostly the young ones. She'd done some digging on this Colonel Barton but had found little information. They were all being well-paid, though. And most weren't US citizens at all.

Contracts were specific: no night flights, strict maximum hours on duty, all the benefits. And no limitations, no Geneva Convention rules, nothing. If you got caught, you were on your own.

"Just like we are," said Janey. She went on for another hour or so about weapons, training, and numbers.

"The reason for their presence is a show of force. Keep the people in line. Smaller population makes it easier to control, unless someone goes off the grid; they're betting that no one will. It's simple: you toe the line, you get everything you need and some of what you want, for the right price. Behave yourself, do whatever they want, and you're fine. One wrong move, and it's all over.

"Your turn."

Abby told Janey about Henry and the lines at the hospital. Then she talked about Frank. She left out the part about her capture.

Janey fell silent.

"I can't live like that," Abby ventured after a brief time.

"Yeah, no kidding," Janey said.

There was a clanking sound and the door came open. Two guards entered the room, heavily armed, and grabbed Abby; two more dragged Janey out into the corridor. Abby was dropped onto the floor and the guards left, slamming and locking the door again.

Fast movers, thought Abby as she rubbed her bruised hip. Damn. She scooted over into a corner to get as comfortable as possible and . . . wait. She wondered where they'd taken Janey.

And if they were bringing her back.

CHAPTER THIRTY-ONE

Abby didn't have long to wonder. Within two hours, Janey, or what was left of her, was deposited back in the cell. She was barely recognizable.

Deep bruises covered every inch of exposed skin and, considering the rags that were all that remained of her clothing, there were a lot of those bruises. Blood trickled slowly from her ears and her mouth. Her breathing was raspy and labored.

Abby crouched next to her. "Janey," she whispered. There was no water, nothing she could do for her. She touched her hand, gently.

Janey opened one eye, barely, just a slit. "Capsule," she croaked. Abby hesitated. "Dying . . . told nothing. Now . . . please."

Abby dug through Janey's pockets, finally finding the capsule that Noah had given her. Still, she paused. With surprising strength, Janey grabbed her arm, jolting Abby back to the moment.

She bit her lip and, reluctantly, placed the capsule in Janey's mouth. "Thanks . . . don't . . . give up . . . Ab." And Janey bit down, hard.

And that was all.

Abby released Janey's hand. The door clanged open again and Abby whirled around, crouched, ready to spring. Two guards entered and stood to either side of the doorway. An older man, in uniform, pins and ribbons and badges on his chest, entered; he was accompanied by two other soldiers, not regular troopers but of some rank.

"My dear," said Frank. "The colonel wishes to speak with you. You will please come with us."

Abby couldn't find her voice. So it was Frank, all this time. And she—and Janey! Abby was too angry to even sputter. She jumped to her feet, prompting an unholstering of weapons, and stomped out the door. Frank took her arm as they strolled down the corridor.

"Do not try to escape." He squeezed her arm painfully.

The six of them rode to the top of the building, crowded into the elevator. At least Abby had figured out where she was being held. The Federal Building, downtown. Made sense. As much as anything.

Her mind was spinning. Escape. Frank. The colonel? What did he want with her? She could guess, certainly. The same thing they'd come in search of: information.

Well, he wasn't going to get it. She surreptitiously felt the inside pocket of her jeans. Yes, it was still there. Noah's capsule.

A guard opened a door to a small reception area. The two guards remained outside, the two ranking officers followed Abby and Frank inside. They stood at attention while Frank led Abby into the inner office. It was empty.

Frank pulled off his hat and loosened his tie. "Quick," he told Abby. "Don't have much time." He handed her a knife; the same one she'd given Janey.

She blinked. "But . . . what?" she stuttered. "What?"

"Damn, girl, come on!" Frank was already removing one his maintenance panels. "Get inside!"

He pushed her along, crawling in with her, and replaced the panel. Taking the lead, Frank began to move. A whole lot faster than Abby'd seen him go before. They came to a cross-pipe which descended to the left and Frank tumbled down it, Abby right behind him.

They landed with a thud or, rather, a series of thuds, onto a pile of trash. As they brushed themselves off, Frank held up a hand, motioning Abby to silence. Then he relaxed, and strode confidently over to small window set high in the wall. It opened easily; Abby suspected this wasn't the first time Frank had been down here.

With few difficulties, they climbed outside into the darkness. Abby was nearly bursting with questions by the time they arrived at Frank's apartment building. Instead of going up the stairs to his place, though, Frank led her around back. He boosted her onto the dumpster and clambered up behind her, pulling down the fire escape ladder.

Up they went, then through a conveniently open window. An elderly woman greeted them with, "It's about time. I almost gave up on you two."

Frank walked directly to a closet without greeting the woman and disappeared. Abby stood in the middle of the room, awkwardly waiting for him to reappear.

"Well, Frank was right. You are a pretty thing. In spite of the dirt," she laughed. "Here, come on over to the sink and get yourself cleaned up."

With nothing else to do for the moment, Abby did. She felt a little better. And by then, Frank had returned.

He handed her the Mossberg. It had been in his hideout when Abby was taken in, and the guards had shown no interest in her pack near the kitchen table. He gave her that, too.

"Couldn't get your sidearm back, but I pulled this out of my stash." Abby looked carefully at the Beretta. It looked new. "Ammo's in the side pocket of your pack."

"Does she have time to eat something, Frank?" The old woman was pulling some cans out of the cabinet and had slapped a skillet on the stove.

"Nope, sorry. Been here long enough. Now, Abby, do you know where you're going?"

Abby nodded. "I'm heading west. But . . . aren't you coming, Frank?"

"Nah," he said. "I'm staying put. I'll be okay. Besides, when you come back, I'll be right here, ready for whatever trouble you get yourself into." He winked.

Frank helped Abby through the window and watched as she started down the alley. He was tired. Too much running for an old man. He wondered if he'd ever see her again. Damn, that had been fun!

It was full dark now, which suited Abby just fine. She had over twenty miles to travel, and that was a straight shot. She had no doubt that she'd have to make a few detours along the way and that, by the time the sun rose, she'd better be under cover.

She kept a sharp eye out, in spite of the limited visibility, and listened carefully as she walked. Soon she was able to tune out anything extraneous but still remain alert.

She tried to think, to plan, but so many things had happened too quickly and she finally gave up. And walked.

Abby stopped near dawn at an abandoned barn near what used to be Maryville University. She crawled into a shadowy corner and leaned back against her pack after trolling through a side pocket and finding a couple sandwiches. Frank's lady friend must have put them in there. She drained one of her water bottles as well, and made a mental note to replenish that just before she fell into a deep sleep.

The sun was already well to the west when Abby awoke. Shocked that she had slept for so long, she wished desperately that she had some coffee. Since she had some time before sunset, she pulled out her knife and her whetstone and sharpened the blade.

Next, she disassembled and cleaned the shotgun and reloaded and, finally, examined her new Beretta. Frank had done well, indeed.

Ready to go but waiting until dark, rested, fed, and prepared, Abby was at last able to go back over the events of the last few days.

First, there was the devastation…the physical loss of civilization. Surely, all those people couldn't simply be dead . . . gone . . . vanished. But they were. Along with their homes, their possessions. And those who'd somehow escaped VADER, the survival difficulties afterwards—they were in the city. And most, it appeared, were at least content with the status quo. She'd met no one who wasn't.

Abby thought of Henry, the man/boy who'd waited on her in that restaurant. She wondered what would become of him, with his disabilities and yet his impossible plans for the future. Surely he wouldn't survive; she was positive that much worse was coming and he'd be an early casualty. An easy target.

The hospital. That was simply appalling. Unreal. Yet it had been almost a festive atmosphere, at least on the west side. The other line? All of those older people were alone—that's what struck her. No one to see them off, no families? Of course, the families had perhaps been dead since last summer. Still, it was strange.

And that led to Frank. She'd saved him from the death line, he'd risked his life for her. At least three times. He could have left the city with her but he chose to stay, to help people like that woman who'd made her the sandwiches; someone who probably had avoided the death line as long as he, somehow. And she knew, if he stayed alive, he'd be there to help her again if she came back.

Janey.

No, she couldn't think about that yet. She knew she would, yes, but not until she was a lot safer than she was now. Maybe back at the base camp. Maybe when she'd returned to the others. Maybe.

Abby stood up and stretched, shouldered her pack and the shotgun, and set off down the darkening road, senses alert to the sounds of the night.

Abby retrieved her supplies from the base camp and checked her watch. It was just past midnight; she could get in another six hours of travel. She headed due south, cross-country, avoiding most of the roads.

She was just north of Cedar Hill, just past daylight, when she had to stop. She was worn out and needed to find a spring and get some rest. This was farm country, so the cover was minimal; the town itself had likely been demolished, as had so many others. She saw a frame house up ahead, mostly standing but leaning as though a strong wind had come through recently. Or perhaps due simply to age and lack of maintenance for many months.

At any rate, Abby was grateful for the shelter; patrols could fly over at any time. She was even more grateful when she discovered an old cistern in the yard, and hoped it would still churn up water.

She worked the rusty handle, not too optimistic, but very soon the handle became harder to turn and suddenly a gush of water came pouring out. She kept at it until the water ran clear, then set an old bucket under the spout to catch what she could.

After stowing her gear on the sagging porch, Abby collapsed just inside the door of what used to be a kitchen. It had been ransacked by animals and there was a huge mess but she really didn't care. She cleared a spot for her bedroll and fell asleep immediately.

She was awakened by rain as the strong wind blew the drops through the swinging door. Shaking her head to clear the bad dreams that had plagued her all night or, rather, all day, she sat up and took stock.

Remembering what Janey had told her, she figured it was safe to start off now. She didn't care about rain, and so far there was no thunder or lightning—always a consideration when walking in the woods. She checked her weapons and stowed her bedroll in the pack and set off, angling east.

Barring anything unforeseen, she should be at the camp just after sunset. Now that her mission was near completion, Abby could allow herself to think about Emmy and Juliet and the others. And Noah.

As Abby approached the base of Purple, she could feel eyes watching and was sure there were guns following her movement. She'd missed Sandy up at the main gate but assumed she'd simply been camouflaged better than usual.

She heard a click as she reached the base of the trail that lead upward, and froze. Realizing in a split second that it was merely a safety being clicked on, Abby was practically knocked over when Emmy ran out and grabbed her.

"Oh, Abby! Thank goodness you're back!" Four more people came out of the trees, holstering weapons and smiling. The group made their way to the site, Emmy clinging to Abby's arm and chattering. No one could have missed hearing their arrival.

Cal and Pops emerged from the command tent and Noah arrived, Juliet on his shoulders. Before the questions could begin in earnest, Cal directed Abby to her tent. She did allow Juliet to come along, which was a moot point; Juliet wasn't going anywhere without Abby.

Abby gave her report; she told them about the hospital, the lines, Frank, her capture and rescue. She talked about the soldiers, the mercenaries, and she passed along what she had deduced about upcoming plans as well as the things that happened last summer and those that were going on now.

"And Janey?" Cal asked gently.

Taking a deep breath, Abby told them about Janey's capture, and her death.

It was close to midnight when Abby finished, but she wasn't tired yet. She was used to staying up all night so, after tucking in Juliet, she and Emmy sat on the tent steps and talked well into the night. Abby still hadn't seen more than a passing glimpse of Noah. And no sign of Sandy, either.

Ted and his remaining crew—just two now—cooked breakfast and the entire group lingered over coffee to discuss the new information. No one was inclined to leave after hearing the news Abby had brought.

Before long though, it was business as usual: the fire crew gathered and stored, Emmy worked the commissary, Brad kept up on repairs with his three helpers. Cal and Pops mediated the occasional disagreement and Noah treated a few minor injuries. He had thanked Abby for procuring the requested supplies, but he moved to a vacant tent where he could also run a pharmacy of sorts as well as treat patients when needed.

Abby made a few nighttime trips into town, gathering anything needed by the camp that could still be scrounged. There wasn't much left, truthfully. Others had been there, although she never saw anyone. Once in a while, Emmy came with her. Mostly she spent time with Juliet, practicing marksmanship or teaching her about the woods. The little girl had a birthday coming up and was very excited about turning five.

CHAPTER THIRTY-TWO

On the morning of her big day, Juliet pounced on Abby who, still half-asleep, mumbled something and half-heartedly pushed her off. Juliet came right back and put her nose up to Abby's and stared at her, cross-eyed, until Abby sat up.

"Okay, okay," said Abby, laughing. "Happy birthday! And don't cross your eyes, they'll get stuck that way and then you'll look goofy all the time!"

"What? Will they really? That would be cool, Abby!"

"No, it wouldn't little one, you'd never be able to hit your target then."

"Oh," said Juliet. "Then I guess I wouldn't want that. 'Cause I do love to shoot. Bam, bam!"

Abby sighed. "All right, settle down. Go get . . . never mind, I see you're already dressed. Did you do that yourself?"

"Of course, Abby. Only babies can't dress themselves, and I'm five now! I can do anything!"

"Well, then, let me get dressed too and find some coffee. Then we'll see what's what."

After breakfast, Abby took Juliet to a special spot that she hadn't been to in years. Naturally, Bob accompanied them although he was beginning to show signs of aging and moved much more slowly. Way back at the top of Indian Hill, just over the crest, was a small spring. It bubbled up from the limestone and fed into a small, shallow pool. The old trail was completely overgrown and the pool itself was heavily sheltered by the trees, especially now, in the middle of summer. It was cool and quiet, except for a few birds high up in the trees.

Juliet was delighted. She sat down on a rock where the sun barely touched and dipped her fingers in the water. She giggled at her reflection. Abby leaned the Mossberg up against a tree and joined her.

"Abby, can I put my feet in the water?"

"Of course you can. In fact, you can wade in it and even float. Come here." She took off Juliet's boots and socks, and her own, and held the little girl's hand. "Come on!"

They stepped into the pool and Juliet squealed at the feel of the icy cold water. Soon she was splashing Abby, who splashed her right back, and before long they'd both landed fully in the water. Abby took Juliet into deeper water and showed her how to float on her back and how to dog paddle.

"But," she warned, "You are never, ever to come here by yourself. Playing in the water is fun, but it can also be dangerous."

Glancing at her watch, Abby finally called a time-out and dried Juliet off, handing her some clean clothes. They sat under a tall pine, on a carpet of needles, and ate the picnic lunch that Ted had packed for them.

Afterwards, they stretched out under the tree to rest a bit. Juliet claimed she wasn't sleepy at all, because she was five now, and only babies took naps. Within minutes of this speech, she was out like a light.

Abby was having a hard time keeping her eyes open as well. All those backwards days and nights were mixing up her internal clock; she was never quite sure when she was supposed to be sleeping. To keep herself awake, she began to go over a mental checklist she'd made in case of emergency.

She'd left a few things in the cave behind the old office; and she had a cache outside of camp, up the hill past the grain bins. She'd plan to get away in a few days to check on both, and move the latter down to the cave as well. She'd take a few things with her, too, like some extra ammo especially.

Finally, she stirred, and woke Juliet. "Can't we swim some more, Abby?"

"No, little one, we have to get back for your birthday dinner."

Juliet clapped a hand over her mouth. "I almost forgot! And Ted said he was making me something special! Come on, Abby, hurry up!"

Abby laughed and put on her pack, taking Juliet's hand. They walked back along the tops of the hills as the sun began to set.

Over the next few month, Abby made several trips to the cave. She'd acquired a decent stash of blankets, cooking equipment, ammo, and had started a stack of firewood. It was a long process, carrying everything up the hill into the cave and then moving it through the narrow crevasse into the larger space. But it was well hidden. And most of the things she scavenged from the farmhouse up the hill or in town.

One morning, just as the last of the leaves were falling, Bob failed to get up and greet them. Juliet cried inconsolably for some time, and even Abby was seen to brush away a tear or two. They had a funeral, for Juliet's sake, and buried him near the others.

Christmas came again and, while Juliet was almost as excited as the year before, the rest of them were weary of hiding. Living in fear took its toll that winter, especially during a blizzard in late January.

The sun had been out for several days, temperatures had warmed, and everyone was hoping— although knowing it was highly unlikely— that spring was on its way. Abby awoke that morning feeling the change in pressure and she noted the lowering sky. By noon, it was snowing heavily and the wind was picking up.

It snowed all day and all night, and well into the next day. In all, 24 inches fell. Everything was buried, and the only good thing was that the snow provided a bit of insulation. The wind was still bitter, but had slowed considerably.

They found the bodies two days later. The young couple had gone for a walk in the snow, just as it began, but had apparently gotten turned around and been unable to find their way back. Cal had refused pleas for a search, and they all knew they really couldn't risk losing anyone else. So they waited until the storm stopped.

Grave digging was hard work when the ground was frozen, so they did the best they could, in shifts. Everyone pitched in and helped, but Brad took on the brunt of the work. He'd become solitary and gruff since Zoe had died last year, and tried to work off his pain and anger in physical labor.

Soon it was actually spring, and Abby decided she needed to make a trip back to the city. She was curious as to how Henry was faring and she wanted to check on Frank. Besides, since the winter hiatus was over, choppers could be seen more frequently now and they needed to know what was happening.

Cal reluctantly gave permission and Abby went to find Juliet and break the news. Surprisingly, it was Emmy who most strenuously objected.

"No! I've just gotten used to you being here, and now you're leaving again? It was bad enough, a few nights here and there . . ."

"Emmy, relax. I won't be gone long this time. Promise. I know exactly where I'm going and what I'm doing—and even who I'm going to see when I'm there.

"Besides," she joked, "Since I'm going alone, I have to come back or it'd be a wasted trip."

"No," said Emmy again. "You aren't going alone, at least. I'm going with you."

They argued back and forth for a while, and Abby finally threw up her hands. "Fine! But only if Pops agrees to watch Juliet while we're gone."

Juliet brightened at this. She loved Pops. But mostly, she just looked sad.

Abby and Emmy went to see Cal. She was absolutely against the idea of both of them going to St. Louis, until Pops stepped into the discussion.

"Well, now, Cal. I don't see the harm. They can look after each other, if need be, even if they can't manage to look after themselves sometimes." He winked. "I'll be happy to take care of Juliet, and she'll be happy too. So there ya go."

Cal was slightly mollified. "All right. But you both better come back. I'm giving you one week—that's it. After that, I'll come looking for you myself, and that's a promise." She stomped off to the fire pit.

They decided to leave that night. No point in stalling. They could put Juliet to bed in Pops' tent first, then hit the road. So to speak. They began to pack, to check weapons, and Emmy made a trip to the commissary. Juliet helped. She knew she'd miss them both, but she was looking forward to staying with Pops, too.

Abby made a big bed on the floor of the tent and the three of them laid down and told stories and whispered until they all dozed off. Juliet was still taking the occasional nap, and the other two needed some sleep before they left.

After dinner Emmy walked Juliet to Pops' tent and Abby went to see Noah. They hadn't been alone in ages, and Abby still wanted to keep it that way. Noah was resigned, but had eventually become able to be civil, friendly even, most of the time.

Abby, however, was rather short with him when they did encounter each other. This time she went straight to the point. "Do you have another one of those capsules?"

"Hello, Abby, how are you? I'm fine, thanks for asking. I heard you're taking a trip this evening. With Emmy." He seemed almost jealous, but Abby thought she was probably imagining that.

"Yes, sorry. Glad you're fine and all that. And yes, we are. So do you have any?"

Noah sighed. "Yes, I do. Hang on a sec." He rummaged through a case under his cot. He stood up with a capsule in each hand.

"This one's yours, and this one's Emmy's." He handed them to her. "Go ahead, put yours in your pocket."

"Why? Aren't they the same thing?" What, did he have an especially heinous death for her in mind? She'd seen the effects on Janey; it seemed as though she'd simply gone to sleep.

"Of course," he smiled. "I just want to make sure you have it."

Ah, he did know her pretty well. She shrugged. It would be cold day in hell before she'd use it anyway. Then again, she remembered Janey....

"Well, happy trails, Abby."

"Um, thanks. See ya." She turned and left.

The girls stopped at the gate to visit with Sandy for a bit. She often preferred to remain here instead of coming back to the site each night, and had quite a nice camp set up for herself. Abby wondered if even she would have been able to find it, it was so well-hidden.

Sandy appeared to be weathering their enforced exile well, but she'd always been something of a loner, following Meg around on the fringes but seeming content with that. She watched them walk down the road, wondering if they'd be back. And when.

Abby and Emmy had no trouble at all walking to Arnold and were there well before sunrise. They holed up in an old café, near the back where there were still two walls standing. They ate sandwiches and, unbelievably, found a few cans of Pepsi, undamaged. Hadn't had that for a long time now.

They laid out their bedrolls, side by side, and drifted into sleep. The late afternoon was chilly and Abby awoke to find Emmy had scooted over next to her while she slept. It was hard to get up into the cold, but Abby roused her friend and soon they were on their way again.

This leg of the journey was a bit farther and the closer they got, the more careful they had to be. The sun was nearly breaking the horizon, across the river, when they reached Frank's apartment building. Abby knew, of course, that Frank couldn't have gone back to his own place, but she was hoping that his lady friend might still be here and know his whereabouts.

The dumpster was still there, in the alley, and Abby motioned for Emmy to wait there while she climbed the fire escape. She hoped the old woman was an early riser.

259

She peered into the window; there was one small lamp lit, and a figure standing at the sink. Abby concentrated and focused. Then she tapped on the glass.

The figure turned and approached slowly and Abby could see that yes, it was Frank's friend, but she didn't appear frightened or even startled. She opened the window and smiled and Abby climbed inside.

She froze as she heard a click.

"I've had you covered since you were halfway up the ladder, young lady. Come on in and have some breakfast."

It was Frank. Alive and in one piece, as far as she could tell. Abby was so happy she hugged him. Then she hugged the old woman as well. She leaned out the window slightly and whistled, and soon Emmy had joined them.

Introductions were made all around. The woman's name was Clarice, and she and Frank were, obviously, good friends. She'd been hiding him since last year. Surprisingly, the authorities had left her alone.

"Well," she said. "Ol' Frank here, they owe him some favors. Even if they can't exactly find him." She laughed.

"Now," interrupted Frank. "What are you girls up to?"

Abby explained that they'd come into the city to check on him . . . and on Henry. They wanted to see if things had changed and what, if anything, was happening. And they had another list from Noah, if that was possible.

"Well," said Frank. "I can fill you in on most of it. And I reckon I can get you the stuff on that list. But who's this Henry?" Abby told him. "Ah. I don't know any details, mind, but there was a round up about six months ago. All the ones they considered damaged and a drain to society. Sounds like your Henry was probably one of them, especially if he was out and about and even working, like you said."

Abby slumped down in her chair. Damn.

"But here, give me your list. I'll slip on over to the hospital tonight and see what I can find. Clarice, why don't you fix these two young women a bite to eat before they hit the hideout?"

Clarice complied, happily, and Emmy went to help her. Frank raised his eyebrow questioningly and nodded towards Emmy.

Abby sighed. She still wasn't happy about Emmy putting herself in danger like this, but what could she do? So she merely said, "She got tired of my leaving all the time."

"Well, she seems a little different from you, Abby. Can't put my finger on it, but are you sure you won't have to be playing nursemaid?" Frank's eyes went wide and he froze. Emmy was standing behind him, holding a razor-sharp knife to his throat.

"Are you still worried, Frank?" she asked sweetly. Abby grinned. It had been awhile since she'd needed to be tough and fast, but Emmy hadn't forgotten a thing.

Emmy released Frank and walked over to Abby. She put an arm around her and perched on the side of the chair. "As long as I'm doing all the work and you're just sitting here, why don't you tell Frank about those two times—two—that I saved your sorry butt?" And she flounced back into the kitchen.

So Abby did. She told Frank how she and Emmy had known each other for twenty years and how they'd been close the whole time. How they'd gotten in a few scrapes as kids and then, as they grew older, found themselves in even more serious situations. And yes, Emmy had indeed saved her butt. Twice.

CHAPTER THIRTY-THREE

When the girls awoke, the late afternoon sun was streaming into the apartment. They crawled out of the hideout and stretched and Clarice, who was cooking, pointed them in the direction of the bathroom. Frank was nowhere to be seen.

After showering, Abby and Emmy felt much better. They checked their weapons and stowed everything back in the hole, just in case there were visitors. Clarice kept nervously watching the door; apparently, Frank had been gone for some time now.

Finally, just as Clarice was beginning to pace, Frank returned. She gave him a long hug, but said nothing, and began to set dinner on the table. Frank handed Abby the package he'd obtained for Noah.

"All right," said Frank. "Let's talk about what's going on here.

"As I said, a lot of people they consider damaged were taken in. To the death line, just to be clear. Seems they got over that whole death penalty debate pretty quick. Of course, they already were killing babies and the punishment for theft or almost any other petty crime was shooting on sight, so what can you expect?

"Jury trials? Ha. Those went out a long time ago. No one wanted to serve unless they were paid. Don't know what they'd use money for, the government keeps giving everything out for free.

"Anyway, I expect you want to go looking for this Henry boy, but you be careful. I got a couple of jackets here that you can wear, help you blend into the military, but you better leave that Mossberg here. I'll give you a couple of assault rifles too. That's what they use, fully automatic too. A police force. Can you believe it?"

That was a rhetorical question. They could all believe a lot at this point.

"So, the baby-killing lines keep getting longer, if anything; they pay you not to have kids, you see, but if you ask me, they're cutting their own throats with that one. So, what? People keep dying, but there are no new soldiers for their cause? Maybe they have something else in mind." He shrugged. "Doesn't make sense.

"But they're still using mercenaries. Not sure where they're coming from, or how they're being paid. Of course, the whole economy is a mystery. Must've had a lot of gold stockpiled somewhere when all this went down.

"The good news is that they aren't hunting people down anymore; leastways, not out in the country. Oh, they do flyovers now and again, but unless they see something particular, they aren't going in.

"And they've got things under control here. Most of the citizens are so indoctrinated by now, or afraid, that they turn themselves in when they hit 60. There are a few of us old coots still running around," he admitted, "But they don't really pay us much attention. Long as we're not using up resources, or so they think."

It was a lot to take in at once. Abby was relieved at the news about forays by the military and hoped that was the case.

She still intended to scout around a bit tonight and try to confirm this. And to see what became of Henry, if she could.

"Well, enough of my blather," said Frank. "Let's get you two ready to go." He got the jackets and the assault rifles, pronounced them as ready as ever, and he and Clarice hugged both girls before they left.

"See you in a bit," he told them. "And don't be late!" He laughed as he closed the window.

Abby and Emmy climbed down the fire escape to the dumpster and moved east, farther into the city. Abby avoided going past St. Mary's; she couldn't deal with seeing that again.

She found the restaurant where she'd met Henry a year ago and they walked inside. A different young man was at the desk and a heavily armed security guard was monitoring a metal detector; a second was frisking those who walked through it. The young man made note of their dress and waved them around the security checkpoint, seating them nearby.

"We don't get many soldiers in here." He was friendly enough, but the smile didn't reach his eyes. Abby wondered if he was as enamored of this new regime as he seemed to be. Of course, he was actually working as opposed to the majority of the citizens, based on what Frank had told them.

"I've been here before, thought I'd bring my friend," Abby said casually. "I used to talk to Henry."

The young man stiffened. "Here are your menus." He left abruptly.

The two girls didn't talk much; mostly, they were listening to the conversations around them. The waiter returned, took their orders, and left again without saying much at all. He looked around nervously while he was at the table.

It was a party atmosphere. Everyone was chattering about new stuff they'd purchased with government vouchers; mock debates about religion bounced back and forth. Wine flowed freely. No conversational topic was off-limits it seemed. Women discussed their latest abortions as though they'd simply made appointments for a manicure; men good-naturedly argued about video games. Cursing was constant. Abby felt as though she was in a roomful of young teenagers but no, these people were rapidly closing in on middle age—and eventually the death line.

Emmy finally flagged down the waiter, who'd been deliberately ignoring them, and asked directions to the restroom. He pointed. She walked through the room to the back, and the conversations diminished to whispers. Abby tensed, waiting.

As Emmy disappeared through a doorway, the buzz grew louder again but Abby was the target of many surreptitious looks. No one made a move, in fact, people seemed glued to both their chairs and the eyes of their dinner companions whenever she glanced their way.

Her hand crept toward her knife. She knew if she drew her gun or made any move at all toward the rifle she could well cause a panic. And that would draw even more attention to them.

She breathed a sigh of relief as Emmy returned, but her return brought even more looks and a few outright glares.

"Finish up," Abby said under her breath, "we need to get out of here."

They ate their dinner, casually sat back and finished their drinks then, just as nonchalantly, stood up to leave. The waiter came by as they were leaving the table and brushed up against Emmy, then hurried on his way to the back of the restaurant.

Once outside, the girls continued a leisurely stroll down the street until they came to an abandoned office building. Abby jimmied the door and they went inside, sitting on the cool granite floor, out of sight.

"What was that all about?" asked Abby.

Emmy pulled out the note the boy had given her. "I assume he wants us to come to the back of that restaurant at 11:00. Pretty simple. No cloak and dagger stuff here." She tossed the note to Abby. "What do you think?"

Abby looked at the piece of paper. "What do you mean, what do I think? I think that's what it says, yes, but I'm not so sure we should follow directions."

"But we should. I mean, I should. You can stay back and be a lookout, in case something goes wrong. When I went back to the restroom, Abby, everyone in the kitchen stopped talking. I mean, just stopped, mid-sentence, whatever."

"Yeah," said Abby, "But they did that in the dining room too."

"But," said Emmy, "When I came back out, they were back to normal—a few of them even smiled at me."

"Probably plotting your torture," said Abby.

"Oh, come on! Where's your sense of adventure? Besides," she added, "We might find out something about that Henry kid." Abby pondered. What Emmy had said was true, of course.

On the other hand, she'd been cooped up for a long time and maybe her excitement was getting the better of her judgment. After a few minutes, she decided to go with Emmy's intuition.

"All right. But let me point out that it might well be your funeral. Or mine."

"In that case," said Emmy, her eyes sparkling, "We'll have to make it count!"

The girls easily found the alley leading to the restaurant, and waited some distance off until the appointed hour. At that time, Emmy crept forward, keeping to the shadows, while Abby hung back a bit.

Three men came out the back door and surrounded Emmy. At least, Abby assumed they were men; it was hard to tell. They were dressed alike, dark clothing, and their faces were covered.

"So," said the tallest one, rather built like a linebacker, "You and your friend wanted to know about Henry, huh? Where are you from? Who are you? We know you aren't real soldiers."

Emmy tossed her head, her brown braid snapping the air. "Who are you?" she demanded. "I know you aren't just cooks." One of them took a threatening step toward her, but Emmy stood her ground.

Abby was ready to jump in, but she waited a moment to see what Emmy was up to. Lord help her, the girl had guts.

"You need to come with us," said another one.

"Nope," said Emmy. "Not happening. Not until you answer some questions."

"You are the one who needs to answer questions. And Henry'll know which ones to ask. And he'll know if you're lying." The tallest one had spoken again but Abby was jolted for a moment. Had he mentioned Henry? Henry was alive?

Before Emmy could continue the conversation, another man stepped out of the shadows.

"It's all right, Abby. You can come out now," said Henry.

Henry was not only alive, he was a key player in the rather newly formed resistance. In fact, he explained to Abby, he'd been undercover when he'd first met her, gathering intel and adding to his organization.

"Still wondering about that doctor training?" he asked with a smile. "It's true, I still have this." He held up his malformed hand. "That's not a ruse. But I shoot best with the other one. And, as you saw, I'm a very good actor. Perhaps I missed my calling. Or perhaps not."

"Now," he said. "On to business. What brings you back to our fair city?"

Abby and Emmy exchanged glances. Well, Emmy's intuition hadn't failed yet, so Abby began to talk. Still, she was careful. It could still be a trap.

She told Henry that there was a group of them, living further south, and that they'd been there since all this happened. They'd only ventured to the city a couple times, and she was vague about what they'd done and who had actually come with her. She told him what they knew about Co-opCom and the things going on here; she figured, no matter which side Henry was really on, he'd know that already.

"Good!" said Henry. "I like that. A little information, but not too much. Nothing really incriminating anyway. I suppose we could torture you, but it's really not our style. We usually leave that sort of thing to our so-called president and his henchmen.

"Relax," he added, catching sight of Abby's brief look of both stubbornness and alarm. "I'm kidding. Have to have some fun around here once in a while!" Just then, a small boy toddled into the room and jumped into his lap. Henry tousled his hair and called, "Jennifer! Your son has escaped again!"

A young woman with hair black as night and bronze skin strode into the room. "Ha! My son? More like yours, since he has to be in the middle of the action all the time . . . hello, I'm

Jennifer." She smiled at the girls. "My husband would have you believe he's a big, tough rebellion leader, but he's really a marshmallow."

Abby was rapidly beginning to question her judgment, but Emmy just grinned.

"Come along, Samuel, Daddy's working." And Jennifer left the room, child in tow.

"So," said Henry. "If no one is tired, we'll get to work. I assume you travel at night? Good. We can get started. Come with me."

Abby and Emmy followed Henry down a dark, damp corridor. The few overhead bulbs barely cast any light, until they came to a large room dominated by a conference table. The walls were nearly covered with maps and charts.

Henry walked directly to a map showing the city and county streets in detail and began with military installations. "Here, here, and here are barracks and minor command centers. North, south, and west. The east side, is of course, bordered by the Mississippi and it's covered by two barges, plus a few lesser craft with better maneuverability.

"Here," he said, smacking the center of the map directly on the Clayton courthouse, "Is the main command post. That's where the top dog lives, works, and makes our lives miserable."

"Colonel Barton." And Henry told them all about this mysterious figure.

Colonel Barton, it seemed, had never been an actual colonel; indeed, he had never held any military rank nor been in the armed services. Ever. At all. But he was ambitious, and he had money and influence. A finger in every pie, so to speak, and once a powerful lobbyist. Back when lobbyists actually lobbied, that is. In the last few years, there was no real skill involved as long as one had plenty of dollars to throw around. And Colonel Barton did. He was rewarded, of course, by rising quickly through the ranks of Co-opCom.

He was also lazy, Henry continued, as well as a bully. He had well-paid men who surrounded him and catered to his every whim, and he had other well-paid men who did his dirty work. And the troops themselves were hired help, Henry added.

Abby nodded. This she knew. Colonel Barton, however, was uncharted territory. "And you have a plan?" she asked.

"Yes," said Henry. "We take him out. When the head is removed, the body dies.

"Of course, he's just one part of this mess. We have been in touch with others, other cities, mostly in the southern states, and they are with us. First, of course, they all have their own Colonel Bartons to deal with, but eventually . . ."

"Eventually what?" Emmy said. "And when is 'eventually'?"

"We start in the cities. We begin by weakening their forces. Then we strike, here and elsewhere. A coordinated effort.

"But we need more time, time to recruit. We've already started taking steps to meet the goal, but it takes time."

"I see," said Abby. "And you want us?"

"Of course," said Henry. "But not here. And not yet. As I said, we've started working. There's a lot to be done. The rumors have begun, and now we wait. It won't take long for the regular troops to begin deserting, once the message is passed around. The colonel won't be safe from his own troops then; in fact, if we're lucky, they'll take him out themselves."

"What's the message? What can you possibly spread around that anyone would care about? From what I've seen, and from what Abby's told us, anything goes here. Anything. It's not like you can say he's a cross-dresser or has a mistress." Emmy did want to know, but she was also thinking that gossip was certainly a lame way to stage a revolution.

"Why, his money, naturally," said Henry with a tight smile. "If he has no more money, he can't pay anyone either below him or above him. If the troops believe their paychecks aren't coming in, they'll be leaving in droves. Or better yet, someone will be upset enough to assassinate him."

Abby thought about this for a minute. It was possible that, at the very least, it could even out the numbers. And, too, perhaps allow the resistance to acquire or take control of more weaponry, even aircraft.

She mentioned this to Henry, and he snapped his fingers.

Two men entered the room. "Report, please," he said.

"We currently have 50 operatives, sir. We have infiltrated C barracks. Reports indicate that there is some unrest in the lower ranks."

The second man spoke, "We have been unsuccessful at acquiring any aircraft, sir, but we have secured and emptied two ammo lockers."

"Thank you," said Henry. "That will be all."

"All right," said Abby, after the pair had left the room. "What do you want from us?"

"At the moment, nothing," said Henry. "I simply want you to be aware, and to be ready if your services should be needed. We want a contact outside the city, someone who won't be compromised; someone, or several someones, who are on our side and are willing to lend assistance as it becomes needed."

Abby and Emmy exchanged a look. Emmy nodded and Abby spoke again, "We're in. What's the next step?"

Henry smiled. "I was sure you'd say yes. Jennifer!"

Jennifer came into the room with a large clipboard. "I'll be your contact. Now, let's decide on a place to meet, and how to best communicate. Oh, and Henry? Your son is getting into trouble again. I can feel it. You'd better go check on him!"

Henry shrugged. "As you may know, in Native American families the squaw is always the boss . . . Jennifer has never moved past that concept." His wife threw a crumpled piece of paper at his retreating back and he laughed and ducked.

"Well," said Jennifer. "At least we are politically correct in one aspect of our lives.

CHAPTER THIRTY-FOUR

"Now," she continued. "I have several young boys, teens, who will act as runners. They are trustworthy, but I want you to meet them and decide for yourself." She gave a low whistle and the three boys appeared.

"Samuel, Thomas, Jeffrey—I wish for you to meet Abby and Emmy." The boys offered their hands, then quickly stepped back and stood at attention. "When you see these young men, they will be your contacts. No one else.

"You may leave." And the boys did.

"We allow nothing written on paper to leave this room, for security reasons. If this room is breached, our cause is likely beyond repair. I wanted you to meet these boys so you will recognize them when the need arises, and they, you.

"When you are needed, one of them will travel south to a location the three of us agree upon. You will be signaled."

Emmy looked confused but, given Jennifer's race, Abby understood immediately. "Three puffs."

"Yes," said Jennifer. "I thought you might know." She smiled. "You have been trained, yes?"

"New Mexico," answered Abby.

Finally, Emmy caught on, "Oh, got it! Smoke signals! Like the Old West."

"Or the New West," said Jennifer. "We must make do with what we have, after all.

"Now, when you see the signal, you will meet. Let's move over here to the map. I do not wish you give away the location of your group—if we don't know, we can't tell anyone either deliberately or . . . accidentally."

Abby studied the maps, both geological and a standard street map. "There," she pointed. The spot was more rural than urban, but Abby assumed she was faster in the woods than the boys were; if there was trouble, they would need to get there quickly to set the signal fire.

"Very good," said Jennifer, marking the location. "Now that we have your cooperation and assistance, is there anyone here in the city that you may know, or know of, who may be willing to join us?"

Abby immediately thought of Frank. His participation could certainly be a bonus to Henry and Jennifer and their followers, but it was a serious risk for Frank. However, she also knew that he was always up for a chance to jump into the thick of things.

"Yes. I know someone. He has . . . connections. Especially at St. Mary's." Jennifer raised her brow questioningly. "I'll speak to him when we leave here; how will I get word back to you?"

Jennifer thought for a moment. "I will send Thomas with you. When you are within four blocks of the person's home, leave Thomas. When you have an answer, you can go back and tell him. He will return to us with the information.

"Such a sad story. They are brothers, you know. Very close. Their parents survived VADER only to be captured by the government six months ago. The boys came to us for help.

Jeffrey just turned thirteen a few weeks ago." She shook her head sadly. "Now they are our sons too."

After saying their goodbyes, Abby and Emmy set off towards Clarice's apartment to talk to Frank. Thomas trailed behind them a short distance. As arranged, when the girls stopped, so did Thomas; Emmy turned to speak to him and he had melted into the shadows. The girls continued down the street.

Into the alley, back up the fire escape, they crawled through the window. Clarice was nowhere in sight, still asleep, but Frank was waiting and watching.

Abby told him about Henry's group and their plans to overthrow the current government or, at the very least, disrupt it enough to make things more bearable for those who still possessed common sense. She didn't go into detail, yet, but made it clear that it involved an element of danger. At the same time, she emphasized how Frank's connections could be of great help.

Naturally, Frank was immediately interested. Said he hadn't felt this useful in years. He told her to go ahead and set up a contact; in fact, he wanted to start out right away and go meet these people himself.

Abby considered all the angles before she spoke. "Emmy, take Frank to meet Thomas. We won't be giving anything away as far as Henry is concerned; Frank is the one taking the risk."

Frank looked positively gleeful as he and Emmy climbed out the window. Abby moved to the chair near the front of the apartment and watched as they went down the street, keeping to the shadows.

She must have dozed off, because she awoke with a start to the sounds of Emmy and Clarice in the kitchen. Frank was nowhere in sight. Abby walked into the kitchen and sat down at the table. "Where's Frank?"

"Oh," said Emmy, "Thomas took him right away, and they went to Henry's place. The boy said he'd bring him back before sunrise." She glanced out the window. "Should be any time now."

Just then, the window creaked open and Frank appeared. Smiling, hair tousled, shirt rumpled, he jumped inside. "Feeling spry today!" he announced. "Whew, that is some plan your Henry has, and a nice setup too! Breakfast? Great, I'm starving!

"So," Frank continued around a mouthful of pancakes, "Since Thomas knows where I live, and he's the only one, he'll be my runner. And girls, Henry said they'd arranged to keep you informed of what's going on, right?"

Abby and Emmy nodded, exchanging looks. "So, I figure at this point you two could use some sleep. Just crawl on back there in the hidey-hole. I'll help Clarice finish the dishes and then I'm gonna spend me some quality time with her for a bit." He winked, and Clarice lightly slapped him with the dishtowel; she actually giggled.

The girls made haste to crawl into the hideout and pull the panel closed.

Abby and Emmy left the city as darkness descended. This time they went due south to Jefferson Barracks and then followed the Mississippi. They could see the moon glinting off one of the gunboats Henry had told them about, so they kept well off the shore until they reached Cliff Cave. There, the trees nearly met the water line.

They soon reached the rural part of the area, just south of Arnold and kept going until they found a small copse of trees very near the riverbank. They slept fitfully, both waking on and off, but finding nothing alarming.

Abby gave up sleeping just before noon and decided to do some exploring. She left Emmy snoozing soundly under the trees, and set off toward a cluster of outbuildings.

No people, no bodies; no animals either. She wondered why that was and what had become of all the farm animals. Wandered off? Rounded up? Sure, there were mostly grain farms around here, but it was rare for any farmer not to have a cow, a few chickens, donkeys, something. Weird.

An old-fashioned frame garage still stood, double doors slightly ajar. Abby cautiously approached and used the barrel of her Mossberg to ease them open. Nothing emerged, thankfully. She peered inside.

A mini-van, of all things. The back end was raised, and the van was fully packed. Some family getting ready to flee, no doubt, but interrupted by . . . what? Never mind, she told herself, didn't matter. Keep going, don't think about it.

Abby rifled through a few boxes, finding nothing of interest, then she noticed the suitcases. Pulling one out, she discovered it was packed with clothing that obviously had belonged to a little girl. Some pink dresses, flowered shorts and tops, a few pairs of jeans. She held up a dress and looked at the tag.

It said a size six, but she wasn't sure. How did little girls' sizes run anyway? Well, it looked like it would fit—and if it would fit, most of the rest should too, right? Juliet might not be excited about dresses, but Abby took one of them anyway…just in case. She did grab the jeans and tops, though, all of them.

Feeling momentarily sad for the little girl who wasn't going to need these anymore, she nevertheless put those emotions on the back burner and focused on the task at hand.

When she returned to the stand of trees, Emmy was awake. They shared some cold fried chicken that Clarice had sent with them and drank cold instant coffee. Blech, thought Abby, making a face.

Then it was time to talk.

"Well," said Emmy. "That was an interesting trip!"

"Yeah," said Abby. "I'm still flummoxed over the whole Henry thing. I mean, seriously Em, you should have seen him at the restaurant! He must have majored in theater, I dunno . . . but Frank was really on fire, wasn't he? When we left?"

Emmy giggled. "Quality time!"

Abby smiled, then became serious. "So now we wait."

"Yep," said Emmy. "But then what? I mean, suppose we see the signal. And come on up to the meeting spot. Then what? Even if all of us, well, most of us, were to come, we couldn't be much help in a fight."

"I don't think that's what Henry meant. I think he wanted us to know what was going on, in case any of them had to make a run for it or in case there was something specific he needed from us.

"I'm not sure what, either," Abby said. "But I guess we'll find out if the time comes."

"And if it doesn't," added Emmy, "We'll know he failed."

It was nearly dark and time to hit the road. The girls were back at the camp several hours before daylight and dropped wearily into their cots. Soon everyone else would be awake and they wanted to try to get back on schedule. Abby's last thought before sleep claimed her was to wonder why Sandy hadn't shown herself at the gates.

CHAPTER THIRTY-FIVE

Life went on at the camp, although basic supplies were harder to come by and fear still permeated the daylight hours. Abby and Emmy had reported to Cal, including the plans Henry and his group had made, and for the time being nothing had really changed.

Juliet was overjoyed to see Abby, and Emmy as well, and was thrilled with her new clothes. The dress, however, brought a more subdued response.

"I'll save this for special things," she told Abby.

As it turned out, Sandy hadn't been at the gates to greet them. For the first time, she'd been unable to continue her duties. She was very ill.

Noah suspected cancer, but without the right equipment and facilities, he could do little but treat her symptoms. A loner most of her life, Sandy insisted on lying near the fire pit to "be around people" as she put it. She knew she was dying and didn't want to miss anything.

Cal didn't replace her at the gates. There was no need, at this point; hadn't been, really, for some time now. As the summer wore on and became hotter and hotter, Juliet helped a crew build a shelter for Sandy.

Sandy became a fixture at the fire pit, seldom talking, always watching and listening in spite of her obvious pain. Someone was always there, and Juliet especially liked to sit beside her, telling her stories and trying to distract the dying woman.

Summer seemed never-ending that year. Emmy and Abby watched for signals that never came; Brad wandered aimlessly, often having to be reminded to stay close by and under cover. Juliet turned six, a bittersweet day for the little girl as she tirelessly watched over Sandy, who grew weaker and slept more each day.

In early September, just over two years since they'd arrived, Sandy died.

Fortunately, Juliet was still asleep when Cal found her. The strong woman who'd been through so much, had shepherded her group for two years, didn't shed a tear. She simply closed Sandy's eyes gently and whispered, "Goodbye, my friend." She went to rouse Noah, and then Abby.

They buried Sandy over on the back of the hill, with the others who had died before. Juliet took it very hard, which surprised Abby. She hadn't been this upset when Millie had died, but then, Abby reconsidered, she had been a bit younger. And she'd spent quite a lot of time with Sandy near the end.

Abby made a point of spending more time with Juliet over the next few days and weeks. And then she spied the signal, midmorning, on a clear October day.

She took Juliet to Pops, explaining on the way that she'd have to leave for a few days. The little girl was resigned. Abby notified Cal and ran to find Emmy. They were almost ready to leave when Brad showed up at their tent.

"Cal says I should go along. She thinks it'll be good for me or something."

Abby looked at Emmy; she shrugged. "Why not?"

"Great!" said Brad. "Finally I can get out of here for a while! Be right back."

And he was. And they left the camp, heading north.

The meeting place was near Fenton at a deserted shopping center that had, somehow, withstood the bombs. Mostly. Samuel was waiting when they arrived early that evening, hidden just inside the shattered glass doors of the old Walmart.

He started when he saw Brad, but was soon won over by Brad's enthusiasm. Which, in Abby's opinion, was just a little off- kilter and somehow not quite the real Brad. She pushed it out of her mind, thinking that maybe the enforced inactivity had been playing tricks on her as well, and they sat down to hear what Samuel had to tell them.

All was well, he said hastily, before they could begin to ask questions, the revolt was picking up steam and things were on schedule. There had been more mercenary defections as rumors spread, and no new influx of troops, but the numbers hadn't decreased as much as they'd expected.

However, he said, Henry was working on some new plans; none of which, Samuel stated, he knew about yet. But there was one thing.

It was Frank.

He'd been taken in two days ago, to the death line. And this time, there was no Abby there to save him.

Frank was gone.

"I'm sorry. I know he was a friend." Emmy put her arm around Abby and held her. Samuel continued to talk, but Abby heard nothing except Brad's interested questions and the boy's eager responses, a nonsensical noise that overwhelmed her as she tried to comprehend what she'd just heard.

Finally, Emmy pulled her to her feet and took her outside. In the cool night air, Abby began to regain some equilibrium. She took a few deep breaths. I can do this, she thought; I can get past this, just like all the rest of it. I have to.

The girls went back inside. Brad jumped to his feet. "Hey, there you are! Samuel and I were just talking a little. You okay, Ab?" Abby nodded and sat down.

Emmy just glared at him. "You might be a little more sensitive, Brad," she said tartly. "It's not all about you."

Brad was taken aback. He looked a little remorseful, but only for a minute. "Um, sorry . . . but hey, I was thinking, how about if I go into the city with Samuel? I mean, you two can get back by yourselves okay, right? And it'll give me something to do besides just hang around . . ." His voice trailed off. Emmy was glaring at him again. "What?"

"Seriously? You're checking to see if we can get back okay without you? Humph." Emmy was really getting tired of Brad's moods; it had worn thin back at camp and now he was over the top again.

"Fine." Abby spoke up. "He's right. It'll give him something to do. That's if it's okay with Samuel." She turned to the boy. He nodded.

"Thank you, Samuel, for bringing us the news about Frank. I appreciate the trouble you went to for us. Give Henry and Jennifer our best, and let them know we're still available, whenever they need us." She turned to go.

Brad grabbed her in a big bear hug and swung her around. "Brad! Put me down!" In spite of herself, Abby smiled. This was the Brad she remembered. More or less.

"Thanks, Abby! I'll see you soon, I'm sure. Be careful out there." Brad reached out and grabbed Emmy. "Come on, Em, don't be mad. Here, give me a smooch!"

He pinned Emmy's arms behind her and bent her over backwards with a long, lingering kiss. He finally released her and she came up sputtering and swinging. He ducked, then followed Samuel out the door. The boy was shaking his head as only teenagers can do.

Emmy was still sputtering when she and Abby left a few minutes later for the long hike back to the camp.

Months passed, winter arrived; Christmas came and went but even Juliet was unenthused. They seemed to be in a holding pattern. Those remaining in the camp, Cal, Pops, Juliet, Abby and Emmy, Noah and Ted, plus just one other family group of three, continued on with their day-to-day chores simply because that's all there was to do.

Juliet was the only real diversion, and there were almost arguments over who was going to conduct her schooling each day. The little girl was nearly seven years old now. If things were different, she'd be finishing up first grade now. As it stood, she was learning things that much older students were struggling with—if there were even any schools still operating.

Science was her favorite, with Dr. Noah. She learned the names of plants and animals and even got to do simple experiments. She caught on quickly and wasn't afraid to try anything. Emmy still worked with her on reading and spelling and writing. She liked that too, but not quite as much.

Pops taught her math. She'd mastered addition and subtraction already, even long columns of figures. Pops liked to brag about her abilities with numbers. She was okay with that; she sure loved Pops!

And she liked cooking with Ted. He was fun. He let her make combinations of things however she liked—but he made her eat them too. Sometimes they weren't very good. Cal would have been the obvious choice to teach Juliet history, but Cal was more silent and withdrawn than ever.

Abby wanted to either take her out in the woods for a long hike, or shake her, she wasn't sure which would do the most good. Between Emmy and Juliet, she didn't have much time to spare but she tried to be with Cal in the evenings as much as possible. They told stories of the old days, back when everything was fun. And everyone was alive.

It seemed to help. A little.

Then one day, the smoke appeared, far to the north.

It was noon when Emmy came running to tell Abby. They both knew that smoke at noon meant that someone had traveled during daylight hours, hazardous at best. That, in turn, meant it was very serious. Something big had happened.

The girls geared up and paused at Cal's tent to let her know they were leaving. Pops promised to tell her; he and Juliet were having a math lesson. Juliet seemed very grown-up when she hugged them both, showing much restraint this time. She told Abby, "I know that you'll come back. You always come back to me." She smiled and skipped back inside to her schoolwork.

They reached the meeting place by dinnertime, but no one was there. The remains of the fire used to send the signal was still warm. They went back inside quickly.

Emmy heard it first. They quickly followed the sound deeper into the store; moving cautiously, they came upon a young boy moaning softly in his sleep.

It was Thomas. Frank's connection. The kid couldn't have been more than 15, although he looked much younger. He was heavily bandaged but the blood was beginning to soak through. Emmy felt his forehead. He was burning up.

The girls worked as a team. Emmy gently tried to wake him while Abby went in search of first aid supplies. Yes, she had some with her but for crying out loud, this was a Walmart; surely there was something still lying around on a shelf. She grabbed what was left, damned little, and returned within minutes.

They unwrapped the bandages, tossing them in a corner, and cleaned the wounds. Knives and guns; who would use them on a child? Abby knew. She set her jaw and kept going. Using most of their water, they made Thomas comfortable and at some point he awoke. He tried to run, but then he recognized them and slumped back onto the pallet Emmy had arranged.

She coaxed him into swallowing some medicine for the fever and pain, as well as some soup. Cold, yes, but better than nothing. He was still very pale and his skin was dry. He seemed to have fallen asleep again.

All they could do was wait, and hope.

Six hours later, Thomas stirred. He opened his eyes and smiled at Emmy and Abby. Emmy gave him more medicine and some water; he was able to hold the bottle himself, which they took as a sign of improvement.

Then he shook his head, and began to speak. They had to strain to hear his soft voice as the tale unwound.

Henry had coordinated with the other groups around the country, and they'd all decided the time was right to strike. The mercenary troops had dwindled to half their original numbers, but the guards surrounding Colonel Barton were still ever-present.

Thomas and Samuel had served as lookouts, but Jeffrey had stayed behind with Jennifer and her son. He was protecting them, Thomas said. Abby and Emmy exchanged glances. More than likely, Henry had refused to send a thirteen-year-old into battle, but it was a moot point now.

They'd actually disabled the gunboats, and they'd taken out the northern and western barracks. The southern one proved much tougher. That was where Samuel had been. With Brad.

Thomas cleared his throat. Spittle ran down his chin. It was tinged red. Without showing any alarm, Emmy gently wiped it off. "Samuel tried to fight. He wasn't supposed to. Brad saved him. One of the men told me later. They both died." Thomas' eyes closed then, and his breathing became ragged. Emmy lowered her head and her shoulders began to shake.

Suddenly, Thomas' body jerked and his eyes flew open. "Have to . . . tell you the . . . rest." More blood ran down his chin, soaking his t-shirt.

"Shhh," said Emmy. "It's okay, go to sleep for a while." "No," the boy said. "Abby?" He gripped her arm with surprising strength. "Listen."

"Go ahead," she told him. "I'm here."

"They're all gone. All of them. Jennifer. The baby. My brothers.

"Everyone . . . gone . . ."

The girls covered him, and left. No burial was possible, there was concrete everywhere. And they had to leave. It was a miracle that Thomas had been able to make it all this way, injured as he was. Abby wondered who had bandaged him and suspected it was Clarice. Maybe she was still alive. They had no way of knowing, unless they went into the city; obviously the battle had gone down recently, probably earlier today.

Go north? Or south?

CHAPTER THIRTY-SIX

They went north, of course. The sun was just peeking over the smoky horizon when Abby and Emmy climbed through Clarice's window. The old woman was sitting in the chair, Frank's chair, waiting and watching.

"I knew you'd come," she said, not turning, still staring out the window at the remains of the city. "Did that boy die?"

The girls went to her, settling on the floor at her feet. "Yes," said Emmy.

They sat in silence for some time, then Clarice spoke again. "I tried to fix him up, but there was something broke on the inside. He wouldn't stay, said he had to send you a signal. And he left. Such a young boy." Tears rolled down her wrinkled cheeks.

Abby picked up a pair of field glasses from the windowsill. She looked out toward the Arch. Still standing. She panned as far in either direction as she could, taking it all in, bit by bit.

A loud boom shook the building. Abby nearly dropped the glasses, and Emmy jumped to her feet.

"We have to go, now!"

Clarice refused to budge. "I'm staying right here. Frank's gone, everyone is gone. Nothing to run to. You girls get on out of here. My time is up, that's all there is to it.

"Go on now, hurry!"

Emmy kissed her cheek and ran after Abby who was holding the window open. She went out and tumbled down the fire escape; Abby took one look back at Clarice, still in the chair, still watching, and dove through the window herself. The girls hit the ground running.

After their initial dash, Abby and Emmy found their stride and continued running at a steady pace. The booms became more frequent, but not louder. Not yet. Within an hour they were running through Affton, a whole lot less worried about encountering any people than they were about the explosions that were creeping closer.

"Abby, stop!" called Emmy, bent over, panting. She held a hand to her side. "I have to walk for a minute." They continued on, looking over their shoulders, walking rapidly.

Boom! A building not 300 yards behind them collapsed into rubble. Boom!

"Come on," yelled Abby, grabbing Emmy's arm. "Run!" And they did, the pain in Emmy's side forgotten as adrenaline kicked in. They veered off to the west; Abby remembered a cemetery nearby. Surely they wouldn't aim for that—no one there to kill, anyway and, even if they did, well, it was a good place to be she guessed.

She boosted Emmy over the stone wall and they both collapsed on the other side, exhausted and scared out of their wits. They clung together, shaking, as the explosions continued all around.

Finally, the noise stopped but the ringing in their ears did not. It was a good hour before the dust began to settle and either one of them could hear anything at all.

Abby pulled Emmy to her feet and they began to walk. There was nothing to run from, for now, and visibility was low from the combination of smoke and dust. Abby thought they must be near Grant's Farm and she remembered, from years past, that there was a pond near the entrance. She hoped that memory was correct.

They crossed Gravois Road; it was buckled and warped, almost melted. On the other side of that, beyond a split rail fence that was somehow mostly intact, was the pond.

The girls limped through the fence to the edge of the woods. Suddenly, Emmy burst into laughter. It was quite near hysteria, so Abby waited a moment before asking, "What's so funny about this, Em?" She was a little annoyed, actually.

Emmy pointed at Abby. "Your face!" Abby reached up and swiped at her cheek. It was hard to tell, since her hands were so filthy, but apparently she looked as silly as Emmy did. She hadn't actually looked at her for quite some time, they were both too intent on running away.

They washed up in the pond, after filling all their water bottles, and lay down under the trees. They fell asleep within minutes, and would have continued well into late afternoon, if it weren't for an inquisitive squirrel.

Abby woke up swinging but stopped abruptly when she saw the furry culprit. Feeling rather foolish, she woke Emmy and they shared some jerky and trail mix and discussed their predicament.

They were at least 12 miles from the camp. Maybe more. It was just two o'clock, so sunset was quite a few hours off. Abby didn't think there would be an issue with being spotted and wanted to leave right away. Emmy was hesitant. Abby made a decision.

She left Emmy resting under the trees and walked south about three miles. She wanted to climb up on the 55 interchange and see if she could get a good look at the area. It was the highest point nearby that she could think of. She could certainly see the buildings around her had been flattened, but she wasn't thinking straight. She climbed up the embankment and turned to the north, searching the skyline.

Except it wasn't there.

Abby rubbed her eyes. She blinked. It was gone. The entire city of St. Louis, and most of the suburbs. Gone. Flat. Even the Arch. She turned slowly around, still searching. Nothing.

Then Abby cried.

She cried for hours, it seemed, until she could cry no more. She cried for herself, for Emmy and Juliet; she cried for Deb and Sam and Cal and Meg, all those who'd died and yes, those still surviving.

Emotionally wrung out, Abby lay curled up on the pavement for a long time. At last, as the smoke drifted off across the river, she forced herself to get up and return to Emmy. Her eyes were red and scorched, her hair stunk, she was filthy from head to toe. But she was still alive.

She led Emmy out of the ruins and back home. Yes, she could call it home now. It always had been, of a sort, and now, after nearly three years and with nothing left to return to, it was the only home they had.

As they reached the 55 interchange, Emmy wanted to take a look so they climbed to the top. Just then, a formation of choppers flew overhead, banked, and turned back to the east. The girls watched as they disappeared.

One was different.

Colonel Barton, Abby presumed. Flying away to lick his wounds. The question, of course, was would he return? And when? Abby shook her head to clear her thoughts and focus on the task of getting home.

They began to walk, easily, without fear. The sun wouldn't be setting for hours and they'd stop then, relax a bit, and finish the journey in the morning. Abby and Emmy linked arms and trudged onward.

When they arrived at the site, Cal herself was waiting at the bottom of the hill.

"I thought I'd meet you here. As long as you were gone, I knew it couldn't be good news.

"We saw the smoke yesterday," she added.

"They blew up the whole city, Cal," Abby said wearily. "We were there. We ran." She really didn't want to relive that, but she owed Cal a full report. As full as she could manage.

"Henry's resistance failed. Well, maybe not failed, not entirely. The troops pulled out. We saw them leave, and there's nothing for them to come back to anyway."

Emmy shrugged. She had nothing to add. Nothing. She might not ever want to talk about it.

"All right," said Cal. "Let's go on up. We'll have to make plans."

They held a memorial service for Brad, as well as the others who'd died in the rebellion. Abby talked about Henry and Frank and Thomas and Samuel. Cal said a few words, and it was over. They lingered around the fire afterwards, milling aimlessly, speaking quietly.

At last, Pops asked everyone to take a seat.

"Here's the deal," he began. "It seems that we are truly alone now, at least in this immediate area. It also appears, from what Abby and Emmy told us, that this same area is now secure, or at least from government interference.

"So I'm asking now if any one you want to strike out on your own? Maybe start rebuilding . . . something. I don't have any real ideas, just letting you know that the danger seems to have passed and that there are options. We don't necessarily have to continue as we are, but we sure can. Nothing says we have to make changes, I'm just throwing that option out there.

"But," he cautioned. "Just because ol' Colonel Whatshisname has taken his flunkies away, doesn't mean he won't be back."

Noah cleared his throat. "I'd like to add that the danger from VADER has passed. We haven't known, of course, much about this...disease, for lack of a better word, and even though there are still a lot of questions, I can say that no one is at any risk from it."

Martin stood up, as did his wife and daughter. They were the last of the families who had joined them at the beginning. He looked around at each of them, before he spoke.

"We've been thinking about this for a while, wondering if things would ever change, if we were going to be up here forever . . . or until we died.

"My wife and I have been talking. We'd like to maybe take a look around the area . . . not far, necessarily. Maybe find us a house that's still standing, have a little garden. Maybe even see if there are any other people around here somewhere.

"Not," he hastily added, "That we're tired of you all or anything." That brought a laugh, and Martin blushed. "Come on, you know what I'm talking about!"

He turned to Cal, "Cousin, we're forever in your debt, and we're very, very grateful for all you've done. Everyone," he clarified. "But I'm ready to see what else is out there and my family agrees."

Cal smiled for the first time in a long while. "Martin, I'm sure we can all appreciate what you're saying. But please don't forget that you and your family were all a big part of this, a big reason we have survived. And I think many of us feel the same way you do.

"For myself, I like it here. I have no desire to go exploring, but I think I'll move down off this hill. My knees are starting to ache from the climb and I'd like to see some open sky.

"Abby, I'm sure you can point Martin toward some suitable homes; you've done the most exploring outside camp."

Abby gave a quick nod. She knew where she was headed, along with Emmy and Juliet. But she wasn't saying. She wasn't entirely convinced, as Cal was, that the danger had passed.

The others were noncommittal. Ted was restless and thought he might take a hike into the city, to see what he could see; Noah suggested going with him. He could always use more supplies, if he could find anything usable. He announced, too, that he'd be staying somewhere nearby in case anyone had need of medical care. Martin agreed that he and his family would not be leaving the immediate area.

Then there was Pops.

"Well, I'm glad everyone has been doing some thinking. It all sounds good. As for me, I'm gonna stick around here. Lived here all my life, and I'm too old to make many changes. Well, any more than I've made in the last few years!

"So, I'm hanging with Cal. We've kinda gotten used to each other. Abby, you haven't said much—and Em, what about you? I'm assuming Juliet will go with you two; but I'd sure miss seeing her on a regular basis and all."

Juliet, sitting on Abby's lap of course, piped up, "I'm going with Abby! And Emmy . . ."

"Well," said Abby, "We haven't really talked about it, what with everything else going on . . ."

"Yeah," Emmy added, "We need to figure out some things." She exchanged glances with Abby. "We don't need to decide right away."

"That's right," said Pops. "I'm thinking that we should all make our plans, talk to each other, get our bearings. It'll be enough to be able to move around and get used to not watching the sky all the time and having to duck!

"How about tomorrow we get some maps out here and Abby can give us all some pointers? And we can talk about divvying up the supplies we have here and breaking camp. I figure it'll take us a few months or so to find our spots and get moved and all."

Cal spoke up. "Pops, and everyone, I know we're all anxious to move on and out and whatnot, but winter's not that far off—just a few months, really. Maybe we should sit tight and plan on spring?"

"I was kind of hoping to get us settled before then," said Martin. "That way we could get a fresh start come spring. Of course, there's no harm in talking a little more; Cal, you might have a point."

"Let's adjourn until tomorrow, then," said Pops. "We'll start looking and planning then and see what comes up."

CHAPTER THIRTY-SEVEN

Fall was soon upon them and winter followed closely behind. The first snowfall came early, mid-October, and swept in from all sides. The meadow where they'd initially set up the camp site was buried in drifts.

Nestled against the hill, the old infirmary was warm and cozy. All of them had moved in there shortly before the snow arrived, except for Martin and his family. They'd gone up behind the camp, off Marble Springs Road where Abby had showed them several intact homes and barns.

It was a lot easier now, especially since one of the first things they'd done was get the trucks back in running condition. Martin had taken one, and there were three sitting out back. Gasoline was available at one of the convenience stores in town; it took Pops the better part of a day to rig up the pumps. They took advantage of that, and filled up every acceptable container they could find.

Ted and Noah were gone at the moment. They'd already made one successful trip into St. Louis, confirming that the city and suburbs were a total loss. They'd brought back some supplies as well as food, even some treats no one had seen in months or years.

This last time, they'd left just before the snow hit; no one expected to see them until the weather cleared.

The winter dragged on and November came. They tried to keep busy; fortunately it wasn't very cold, but the snow kept coming. Ted and Noah still hadn't returned by early December. Still, the adults tried to be cheerful for Juliet's sake, although she seemed to be handling things better than anyone else.

There was a warm spell in early December. Surely, now, Ted and Noah would return. Days passed, and still nothing. Abby was more worried than she let on, or so she thought.

"You miss him, don't you?" asked Emmy.

"Who?" said Abby.

Emmy rolled her eyes. "Yeah, right. Whatever." She gave Abby a sad smile and went on with her work which, at the moment, was trying to keep the old woodstove going. Abby had been pacing from window to window.

Juliet came running in. "Is it Christmas yet?" she asked, for the umpteenth time.

Abby sighed and reminded her about the calendar on the wall in their living area. "Oh, right!" She skipped off to the other room. Abby joined her.

They'd put up a tree earlier that week. Juliet had even convinced Cal to come with them to find one. Naturally, cedar trees were plentiful and they'd had a nice choice. Juliet had saved all the decorations from her first Christmas here, and had carefully decorated the little tree. She'd already hung a sock, too; she used one of Pops', because, she told everyone, it was the biggest.

Two more days, thought Abby. Then, if the weather held, she'd go looking for them. And that's when she heard the truck.

She opened the door and Juliet ran out. They both stopped dead in their tracks and gawked. It was one of the black trucks, all right, but it was decked out in greenery and tinsel. Two Santa Clauses stepped out. Two? It even gave Juliet pause.

For about three seconds.

Then she ran to Noah and jumped into his arms. "Where have you been?" she demanded. "And Ted, what took you so long?" She squirmed around in Noah's arms to look at Ted. Then she jumped down, landing in a snow bank.

"Humph," said the little girl. "Everyone knows there aren't two Santas." And she flounced back inside.

The two men looked crushed. Abby laughed at the looks on their faces, in spite of herself. "Come on in, you two. Everyone will be so glad you're back!" She smiled shyly at Noah. "Hurry up, it's cold out here!"

Cal decided they should have Christmas the next day. "Does that mean Santa comes tonight?" asked Juliet. Everyone assured her that it did. "I mean the real Santa," she declared. Yes, yes. He'd come that night.

"Well," she said. "Okay then."

Dinner that night was festive. Ted and Noah kept them all entertained with stories of their trip, from one escapade to the next. They'd even seen another group of people, off in the distance, but there were no incidents and they mostly ignored each other except for a few half-hearted waves.

Juliet was sent to bed at her regular time, protesting every step of the way. When Emmy went to make sure she'd brushed her teeth, Noah pulled Abby aside.

"We need to talk."

"Noah, really, I . . ."

"Not that," he said impatiently. "I don't want anyone to hear this but you. Tomorrow morning? After Juliet opens her presents?"

"All right," Abby said, reluctantly.

"Merry Christmas," said Noah, kissing her cheek and quickly turning away.

Juliet was thrilled with all her gifts; this year, the adults even managed to exchange a few small presents. It was a lot easier to make merry when you weren't worried about hiding and trying to keep basic needs met. And shivering in the outdoors all winter long.

After breakfast, Abby went with Noah on the promised walk. Emmy saw them leave, but said nothing.

They walked over near the Cathedral, where they'd had the first funerals three and a half years ago. They sat down on the large rock at the base of the hill. The sun was warm, the breeze still for the moment; temperatures still, however, remained chilly. "Abby, we didn't just see a group of people, like us, wandering around scavenging."

Abby immediately became tense. Her hands shook, but she tucked them under her arms before Noah could mention anything. "And? Come on, Noah. Don't drag this out. Are they back?"

"Yes."

Abby bit her lip. "All right, tell me everything."

Noah and Ted were just about ready to head back to the camp when the snowstorm hit. They'd holed in up north, near the old barracks or, rather, where it used to be. He said they had a good time, just shooting the breeze, found a deck of cards and played some poker. They felt pretty safe, even though they knew everyone would be worried.

When the snow stopped and the sun came out, they'd planned to dig their way south and head home. As they emerged from the shelter, they heard the choppers. They ducked back inside, hoping the truck wouldn't be noticed; they hadn't taken any precautions, believing they were pretty much alone.

As night fell, they came back outside and camouflaged the truck and then made their way toward the city center.

Noah smiled briefly at the memory; Ted had sure enjoyed playing commando. He recalled thinking at the time that it was kind of fun.

"Anyway," he continued after his brief pause. "There were soldiers everywhere, mercenaries I suppose. And some higher-up guy that everyone deferred to—he had a different chopper, some emblem on it.

"The next day, that one flew off across the river but the rest stayed behind. With all the men. They'd rebuilt the north barracks, not very well, but it was holding. Seemed like they were here for the long haul, oh, maybe a few hundred or so.

"And that's what I needed to tell you."

Abby had stopped shaking and was thinking furiously. So, Colonel Barton was back. And his men, or at least some of them. For how long? Noah seemed to think it was somewhat permanent.

She wondered why he'd bombed the whole city, if he was coming back. Of course! To stop the rebels, yes, but talk about overkill…there must have been some inkling that things were not going well. Why did they bomb the whole county? Or rather, several counties? Population control. Only certain persons were allowed to live and breathe in this new society, particularly those who did what they were told and never thought for themselves at all.

And that most certainly did not include Abby, or Cal, or any of them down here.

"We have to tell Cal," Abby said.

"I know. But I wanted to tell you first. Cal's not . . . she's pretty fragile, Abby. I know you've seen it. I'm not sure how this'll all go over with her. We've all been through a lot, but she thinks she's responsible . . . for us, for not stopping VADER, for a lot of things out of her control.

"She's slipping, Abby, and this could send her over the edge. I worried, especially about you and Juliet. And Emmy," he added.

"I picked up some meds while I was up there this time. For Cal. I think it will help, but I might need to convince her."

Abby had only been half-listening. She was thinking of her cave . . . she'd have to slip away and go up there, check supplies, bring in some more as well. She wondered, too, about other areas of the country—had they been bombed into submission as well? Was Co-opCom intent on destroying everything, starting over? Or not?

"What? Cal?" Oh yes, she'd noticed Cal's behavior lately . . . even more so her attitude and demeanor. "I'll talk to her, Noah. I'll see what I can do." She got up from the rock to walk back.

"One more thing, Abby. We may all need to hide again. In fact, I'm sure of it. And I think we should split up this time, make it harder for them."

Abby smiled. "I know," she said. "I'm ready." Noah looked at her carefully, but she was done talking.

They went back to the others.

Ted outdid himself on Christmas dinner. Abby had shot a turkey the week before, and he and Noah had brought plenty of food from the city. Even working with canned goods, Ted was a master chef.

After dinner, Juliet played with her new toys; however, she seemed a lot more interested in the tin soldiers than in the dolls. At least she wasn't into playing shooting games with toy guns and knives, thought Abby. She preferred the real ones, of course. Probably not the way to raise a little girl but, after all, extreme circumstances called for extreme measures. Or something like that.

Soon after Juliet went to bed, and they were reasonably certain she was asleep, Noah dinged his glass and got everyone's attention. With a nod from Ted, standing near the back with Abby, he began to tell them about the choppers. He watched Cal closely without being obvious.

As his story progressed, even though he kept it purposefully short and to the point, Cal became more pale and raised a hand to her throat. As she became slightly more agitated, he signaled to Ted.

Ted whispered to Cal, who nodded, and he and Abby helped her to her own cubicle. Abby stayed with her, holding her hand, speaking calmly . . . she told Cal that she understood, they all felt that way sometimes, and that she must get this under control, for all their sakes.

She couldn't tell if it was doing any good at all, but Cal's breathing had calmed and become more even. She gripped Abby's hand tightly, but managed to lie back and try to relax.

Abby could tell that Noah had finished by the sudden murmur of other voices down the hallway. Within a minute, he appeared at the door and took Abby's place. She wanted to stay, but she needed to see Emmy; at any rate, Noah seemed to have things well in hand.

She slipped out of the room and found Emmy staring out the window, looking up at the sky. She put her arms around her and rested her chin on Emmy's shoulder.

"Now what, Abby? Are we ever going to be done with this? What was the point of making it this far?"

"It's okay, Em. It'll be all right. I have a plan." And she told Emmy about the cave.

Her friend almost sagged in relief. "When can we go? Tomorrow? How soon?" Emmy was near tears.

"Not now. But very soon. We have to get more supplies up there. We have to move fast, before . . . before they come back. But we have to take care of Cal, and Pops. We all need to make plans, but let's keep the cave just between us." Abby hesitated, but didn't mention that Noah, too, knew about it.

Noah came out and told them that Cal was sleeping and that she'd be just fine. Ted and Pops were deep in discussion about the new information and trying to formulate some sort of plan. Noah glanced at Abby, but said nothing and joined the men.

Abby and Emmy slipped off to the room they shared with Juliet and whispered long into the night.

By morning, it was snowing again. Ted, Noah, and Pops continued their discussion of the night before. They agreed that some more reconnaissance needed to be undertaken, before any definite plans could be made, but they also knew they needed to move fast.

Finally, it was decided that, as soon as the weather broke, Ted and Noah would return St. Louis. Noah, however, wished to stall a bit until he was sure Cal was okay; he planned to do that without making it an issue, as Cal had requested. He was confident that he could do this, as long as Cal showed improvement.

Abby and Emmy went back to their room after breakfast. They sat Juliet down to explain the situation to her; they tried to give her information that was age-appropriate, but Juliet was smart and asked a lot of questions. They finally gave up and just answered honestly and straightforwardly. Neither of them mentioned the cave.

"Okay," said Juliet, and went back to playing with her toy army. Abby and Emmy went into the living area and began to make lists of needed supplies.

"Do you think she's okay?" asked Emmy.

"She said she was," Abby responded. "I think we should leave her alone for now and just keep answering her questions."

"But she seemed so . . . used to it. Like this is normal!"

"Em, for her it is normal—she's been here almost four years and this is likely about all she remembers. Let it go, and help me figure this out."

The girls kept their heads together for the better part of the morning and no one disturbed them. The snow had stopped by lunchtime, so they took Juliet outside for some much-needed exercise. All three, however, kept stopping to look up at the clearing sky.

Cal joined the conversation that night, after Juliet had been tucked into bed.

"I'm sure you all think I'm a sniveling weakling, but the truth is that I haven't been myself for a long time. I had a nice talk with Noah last night, and he's convinced me to start some medication.

"I expect to be fine, sooner rather than later I hope, and I insist that you all stop keeping things from me." She'd spoken her piece and she sat there, arms crossed, almost daring anyone to argue. Ah, for the moment at least, she was the Cal they all knew and loved . . .

Pops was the first to speak. "I'm taking you out of here, Cal." He held up his hand as she started to interrupt. "Nope, no arguing. I know you love it here and I do too, but there's nothing left for us and you know that as well. You haven't left the site in a long time; me either, much. And, well, it's time.

"We'll head south, see what we can see. The sooner we get away from here, away from any major city, I think things will improve. And that's that." He mirrored her pose, as well as her look, and even Cal smiled at this.

"Okay then," she said.

Everyone let out a collective breath; they had all been expecting an argument. A lot of arguments. Only Noah looked sharply at Cal, but it went unnoticed.

It was Ted's turn. "I was thinking of going west. You know, like those old cattle drives and stuff? It's a thought, anyway; right now I guess I just don't have a clear idea.

"But I'll come up with one, and soon too. I mean, it's just me, and I can take care of myself okay. No real plans to make, I guess."

They all knew Ted was the wandering sort; since they were all kids together, he'd been the one to head off to strange places, cooking his way around the country. He could live outdoors, indoors, any place he could flop. He always ended up back here, though. He'd probably be just fine, as long as he stayed under the radar.

So far, Noah had stayed out of the conversation, but now all eyes turned to him. "At the moment, like Ted, I'm not sure." But he looked only at Abby.

"Abby and I are taking Juliet away somewhere. We haven't really decided either. But we'll probably stay pretty close to the area."

Pops looked sad for a moment. "Sure will miss that little girl." The others looked equally unhappy. Unfortunately, Juliet couldn't be divided and they all knew she'd never go anywhere without Abby.

That broke up the meeting for the evening, and Abby volunteered herself and Emmy to take the news up to Martin. Whether he stayed or left was up to him.

Robin Tidwell

CHAPTER THIRTY-EIGHT

Martin had elected to remain in his new home, as Abby suspected he would. He became downright angry when she told him about Ted and Noah's trip to the city and what they'd seen. He ranted and railed against Co-opCom and said he was tired of hiding and running. If they wanted him, they could come get him. His wife agreed completely, as did his daughter.

They were resolute. They were staying.

Ted and Noah made one more trip to St. Louis, driving as far as they could, going on foot the rest of the way. Their report afterwards was disheartening, at best. The colonel had been busy. All three barracks had been rebuilt, plus a spanking-new command center downtown. There were few signs of civilians. Ted and Noah agreed that this was a purely military area now, one most likely tasked with bringing in strays and serving as an

outpost, given its location in the center of the country.

Abby and Emmy spent the next couple of weeks either on the road or hauling supplies up to the cave. They had to go at night, without lights, so as not to be seen; in fact, all of them had begun sleeping during daylight hours and emerging only under cover of darkness.

Several more weeks passed, and the ground began to thaw. The trees came out, a few wildflowers showed themselves. Ted was still vague about his plans, Noah even more so. He kept watching Abby, but she was too busy to notice; he assumed no one else noticed either, but he was wrong. There was a lot of speculation when neither were close by, and outside of Emmy's presence as well.

And one day, the choppers flew over the camp. As they knew they would.

Preparations had been in place since the beginning of the year; sleeping during the day had its advantages. They were awakened by the noise, but by the time they'd gathered in the main room, the choppers were gone.

Every day, for a solid week, it was the same thing. Noise, blades, whirring, running to the living area. Just as they'd about decided to forgo sleep altogether, the flyovers ceased.

A week later, a lone chopper flew in, very low. Then it left, banking and flying east. The following week, another. This one dipped even lower, flattening the long meadow grass.

That was beyond alarming—the colonel and his henchmen were done checking, they knew, they were playing with them. Pops assigned two to keep watch at all times. Whoever wasn't on duty was supposed to sleep, but no one did. Not anymore. They were exhausted and frightened.

It was time to go.

They huddled together the next afternoon, packing their personal belongings which hadn't yet been loaded into the trucks. This would be the last day, they'd all be going their separate ways. There was no way to communicate anymore, and hadn't been for quite some time but it hadn't mattered until now. Ted had finally decided to head west. Noah claimed to be tagging along, and Ted was okay with this. He figured four eyes were better than two and anyway, he was pretty laid back and took whatever came his way . . . more or less.

Abby had finally spilled about the cave; Pops had already figured it out, of course. He'd grown up right here, back when the camp was just another farm, and he knew every inch of the place. He approved of her choice, while he worried constantly about all three of them.

Emmy was quiet, but resigned. She'd get to stay with Juliet, and with Abby. She was just so very tired of running and hiding.

Juliet, while frightened at least as much as the rest of them, was excited about this new place. She'd been there once, when James and Candy set off that horrific explosion, but she didn't remember it very well.

They were all fairly calm, considering the circumstances, and waited for darkness.

BOOM!

They rushed for the windows, peering outside. That had been close, but not here, not . . . Abby turned pale. She could see the plume of smoke. It was coming from Martin's place. She moved away from the window. Then she noticed Cal.

The woman who had warned them of VADER . . . the woman who had brought them all together, who had survived the threats, death, destruction, and every horrible event, had completely fallen apart. She slid to the floor, pale, trembling, gasping for breath for no apparent reason. Abby ran to her side; the others turned, stupefied.

BOOM!

The walls shook, some of the interior ones fell, and Juliet screamed. Noah was the first to react. He grabbed Juliet and thrust her at Abby, shoving them both toward the back door.

"Run!"

He scooped up Cal as though she weighed nothing more than a small bird and half-ran, half fell into the small kitchen. He saw Abby then, standing by the door with Juliet. "Emmy!" he hollered.

"Get out! Everyone out!"

Emmy and Ted appeared as smoke from the meadow began drifting inside the shattered windows. They were dragging Pops by the arms as the old man clutched his chest. "Noah," he rasped. "Go, go now. I mean it!"

And he died.

That was all Cal could handle. She leapt to her feet, shoved the table aside, and grabbed Noah's gun. One shot to her own temple, and it was over. She slumped to the ground. Dead.

Emmy blinked. She blinked again. She tried to take it all in at once, and failed. Ted, however, recognized the signs and shoved her out the door. Noah was right behind them. Abby was waiting.

BOOM!

"Abby!" screamed Emmy. "Run! Take Juliet and go!" Abby ran.

BOOM!

CHAPTER THIRTY-NINE

Abby climbed up on the large, rocky overhang at the top of the hill behind the cave. She scanned the immediate area, then further afield; this was a routine that she hadn't broken in the last six months since she and Juliet had fled the main camp. Every morning, every evening just before dusk. Satisfied, for the moment, that there were no intruders, she stuck the binoculars in the case and headed down the trail.

Juliet was finishing the breakfast prep; not that there was much to it, anymore. Supplies were dwindling and Abby knew that, in spite of finding some mushrooms and wild strawberries and a few herbs, she'd have to venture out soon.

She'd just about made up her mind to go into town today, leaving Juliet with strict instructions to stay hidden in the cave until she returned, but she agonized over the possibility that she might not make it back. She sighed. Best not to overthink, just do it. Things were getting desperate. Hell, they'd been desperate, but the time had definitely come.

"Thanks," said Abby, accepting a bowl of runny oatmeal with a few strawberries drowning on top. "Jules, it's time. I have to go into town. We're running out of . . . everything. I need to see what's going on and see what's available out there."

Juliet looked at Abby. "I want to go with you."

"Sweetie, you can't go. I have no idea what I'll run into and it's a long way into town. You need to stay here, inside, until I get back."

Suddenly, Juliet jerked her head up and stared at a point past Abby's shoulder. "Someone's coming," she whispered.

Abby was immediately alert, the conversation forgotten as she reached slowly and unobtrusively for her .357. She turned her head ever so slightly as she pulled the knife from its sheath with her left hand. Juliet had already faded back, unseen, into the brush, just as she'd been taught in case of an emergency. Abby quickly rolled to her right, stopping behind a scrubby hazelnut shrub.

She watched and waited. Abby knew that the person walking towards the little camp couldn't yet see them and likely hadn't heard them either. It was amazing how finely tuned Juliet's hearing had become in the last six months, and how well she had acclimated to their life of concealment.

As the intruder reached the remains of their small fire, Abby reached out and grabbed an ankle, giving a hard yank. In a flash, she was straddling his body, her knife at his throat.

"Abby. Do you think you could get off me now? And do you really think I didn't see that coming?"

Abby jumped to her feet. Oh, good Lord. Noah. She didn't know whether to hug him or slap him.

With a sigh, Abby stood up, offering Noah her hand. She smiled. Tentatively. This, after all, was the man who'd sent them away and from whom they hadn't heard in nearly half a year. True, she'd thought he was dead. And he'd sent her out that door to save her life, and Juliet's.

Still.

She whistled, short and sharp, and Juliet emerged from the forest, running to Noah.

The three gathered around the fire, Juliet fetching more wood, and Noah held up his hand. "I know you have a thousand questions, but just give me one second . . . there!"

Abby blinked. Noah set down a can of coffee, something she hadn't seen in weeks and weeks. And he handed her a pack of cigarettes. She looked him suspiciously. She was beginning to think she was hallucinating, but no, Juliet was smiling—that was also something she hadn't seen for a very long time.

"Now," said Noah as they sat back with their coffee, "I'll fill you in on everything." His smile faded.

When Noah had regained consciousness that horrible afternoon, the first thing he realized was that yes, indeed, he was alive. Most certainly alive, as he could feel every broken bone and every single bruise. Which covered most of his body.

The second thing he realized was that the bombs had stopped and the choppers had left. He tried to open his eyes, but it was too bright and the world seemed to be spinning. But it was quiet. Too quiet.

And then, he remembered. Emmy, Ted . . . their bodies were nearby. The old infirmary was gone. Flattened. Somewhere in there, Cal and Pops lay, troubles over and at peace, he hoped.

He became panicky, searching the ground around him, looking for Abby and Juliet. He was afraid . . . He knew his name. He knew what he did. He remembered it all. Then he lost consciousness again. It was too much.

When he awoke again , the sun was just rising. Another day. Water. He crawled to the creek, just 100 yards away, and made it there by the time the sun was overhead. He figured he passed out again at some point along the way. He drank, he splashed water on his face, he drank some more. And he slept.

Noah paused at this point and refilled their cups. Abby lit another cigarette and Juliet squirmed around on a blanket, shifting position.

"You know, Abby, those things'll kill you."

"Right," she snorted. "Yeah, I'm worried about these."

Noah smiled. "Hand me one, will you?

"So," he continued, after a minor coughing fit, "I figured if I got to my truck, I had some bandages and such and some painkillers. My leg was broken, just a fracture really, so I had to crawl. Took me a whole day. And boy, was I hungry too.

"By then, I realized I probably should be watching the skies but it didn't matter. Guess they never came back to check for survivors. Figured their damn bombs did all the work." He sighed. "And they mostly did."

They were all quiet for a while, thinking of those who'd died. Juliet crawled over to Abby and put her head down. Noah continued his story.

He'd camped out by his truck for a week, regaining his strength. Found a sturdy stick to use as a crutch. Saw no signs of choppers or anyone else. He finally decided to try to drive, to go up to see what had happened at Martin's place.

It wasn't anything special. Just the same thing, a different place. The house, the barn, the family—all gone. Obliterated. He stayed there for another three weeks. By then, he was fairly well recovered and not in too much pain. He headed for the city.

He stayed out in the suburbs, moving only at night, scavenging what he could and where he was able. He spied on the troops; learned their numbers, their movements. He considered trying to infiltrate and then . . . what? He didn't know. He might be the last person on earth, he was so isolated. Except for the enemy. Always, there was the enemy.

Two weeks ago, he woke up and made plans to move that night, as he often did to keep under the radar. He packed what little gear he had with him and filled some water bottles. He lay down and tried to sleep before nightfall.

And jumped up, fully awake.

There had been something nagging at him, something still just hovering within his subconscious. He thought of that last day, the bombs, the running, the screaming. Death.

And then, there it was. He remembered Abby climbing the hill, pulling Juliet behind her, looking back one last time.

"So, here I am."

For two years they lived in the cave, the three of them. They watched constantly for patrols but never encountered any, neither in the air nor cross-country. Either Colonel Barton had forgotten about them or he believed them all to be dead and no longer a threat. Regardless, they had some measure of peace for many months.

Juliet continued in her lessons, mostly taught by Noah as Abby still had little patience with sitting still for any length of time. She took Juliet out in the woods often, though, to practice her defensive skills as well to teach her more about tracking and trapping. And shooting, of course. Juliet loved her weaponry.

In fact, for her ninth birthday, Noah gave her a shotgun. It was remarkably similar to Abby's and Juliet was thrilled beyond measure. She gave him a big hug and planted a loud kiss on his cheek. He looked over at Abby. She smiled, but said nothing.

Later that night, she went to him.

The next year seemed to fly past. They watched, still, but were more relaxed. Juliet thrived. Once in a while they drove around the area, still at night, on scavenging trips. They managed to keep themselves clothed and fed. They saw no signs of anyone else.

They never talked about the years they'd spent in exile, even though they were still refugees of a sort. In many ways, it was an idyllic existence.

While their first winter had been rather mild, this second one came in early and harsh. Snow would have been welcome, as it acted as additional insulation for the cave, but the bitter winds only teased them with a remote promise.

The temperatures dipped below freezing on many nights; during the day, the sun barely warmed at all. Finding firewood became a full-time job. Game was scarce, even the animals had sense enough to stay out of the cold and hole up somewhere.

It began innocuously enough. Juliet sneezed. And sneezed again.

As night fell and the temperature dropped, her fever rose. Noah was worried but tried not to show it. He kept Abby busy, warming broth, fixing cold cloths—those were easy to come by, and keeping the fire going. He dug into his stash of medicines, which were running low. If Juliet didn't start to improve soon . . . After four days, the fever broke. Juliet sat up for a few minutes but fell back upon her pallet weakly. Abby was so relieved, she almost cried. She held the girl and stroked her hair.

The worst was over.

A week later, Juliet was moving around the cave easily. She was anxious to be outside, but Abby wasn't taking any chances. There was no reason to go out, it was warm and dry here, and the wind stopped at the entrance. She urged Juliet to wait and tried to distract her as much as she could.

And then Noah sneezed. He was hit hard. Within hours, he was nearly unconscious.

Abby continued to put cool cloths on Noah's forehead as he tossed and turned in semi-delirium. He muttered a few words now and again, mostly indistinguishable, and tried several times to raise his weakened arms to fend off imaginary attackers.

Juliet sat nearby, waiting to assist if needed, clearly upset. She knew enough of what had been going on to know this probably wasn't going to end well. She felt sad for both herself and Abby, as Noah had come to mean a great deal to them. She silently wished she could do more to help.

The night wore on, the stars began to twinkle their last few blips before becoming invisible in the lightening sky. The darkness grew briefly, as Abby and Juliet watched and waited.

Suddenly, Noah bolted upright and looked at both girls through clear eyes for the first time in nearly a week.

"Abby, I love you. I want you to stay here, and be safe, for as long as it takes. My notes are in my pack; you might be able to use them someday. I hope they'll help in some way to stop this; it needs to end, and soon.

"Juliet." The girl flew into his arms, and Noah held her one last time. "My little girl," he said quietly. She began to sob.

Noah took Abby's hand and squeezed, as he lay back on the pallet. One last breath, and he was gone . . .

CHAPTER FORTY

Abby bit down on a stick of pine; it tasted terrible but Holy Mother, the pain was incredible . . . Nothing in her life had prepared her for this, not books, not her imagination, certainly not stories from any parents she had known. She wished Millie were here, or Emmy, or anyone at all. Besides Juliet. Juliet was here, had always been here it seemed, but the ten-year-old could only do so much.

That's it, she thought. Changed my mind. Not doing this. Of course, like countless mothers-to-be in the history of mankind, she had no choice at this point. That's all there was to it, and Abby knew it.

Her body shuddered, seeming to have a life of its own, and Juliet steadied her with a hand. Abby grunted again and felt something wet and heavy slide out onto the pine needles between her feet. A lusty cry sprang up and echoed in the woods.

Abby leaned back against the pile of blankets and gathered up the infant, holding it to her breast; it was a tiny girl, perfectly formed, and Abby let out a sigh of both relief and exhaustion. Juliet handed her a piece of twine, with which she tied the cord, then Juliet herself made the cut. Within minutes, the afterbirth was expelled and Juliet placed it in a bucket to be checked.

Half an hour later, cleaned up and made comfortable with Juliet's considerable assistance, Abby examined her new daughter more closely. Juliet cuddled next to her and they both marveled at her deep blue eyes and fuzz of blonde hair.

"Little Emmy," said Juliet quietly, tracing the baby's soft cheek with her finger. She leaned down and kissed her forehead, carefully.

"EJ," corrected Abby, gently. "There was only ever one Emmy . . ."

Abby dozed, content to let Juliet finish cleaning up the birthing site and gather everything for the return to the cave. EJ slept quietly as well, a small furrow between her pale eyebrows as she appeared to be puzzling over her entry into this strange world.

Soon, Abby awoke and rose to her feet with Juliet's help. The girl looked like she'd fall over with the weight of the pack she carried, but she was tough and strong after all these years. The two made their way carefully through the forest, taking their time, allowing Abby to set the pace.

Juliet settled Abby in the cave and did a quick reconnaissance around the immediate area; she started the fire and began dinner preparations as Abby watched and made the occasional suggestions. Then she fell silent for a few moments, as she gazed at the baby.

"She has Noah's eyes," said Abby. She hadn't spoken his name aloud since he'd left them, and vowed never to do so again.

EPILOGUE

"Jules, Jules! Where are you?" The small blonde girl raced through the thicket, searching for her friend. She stopped abruptly as a hand reached out and yanked her into the undergrowth. She landed with a thump on her little rear end and glared up at her captor.

"C'mon, Jules, why'd you do that, huh?" She rubbed the affected part of her anatomy, still frowning.

Juliet grinned down at EJ, extending her hand to pull the child to her feet. "That's what you get for racing around here like a herd of buffalo, making enough noise to wake the dead."

"Well, if I was making that much noise, at least I'd get to see everyone that you and Mommy are always talking about, right? Besides, there's no one here but us, hasn't been for years and years, my whole life!"

"Not so long, little one. You just turned five, after all. And it doesn't hurt to be cautious."

"Huh," said EJ, scowling and looking so much like a miniature Abby that Juliet found it difficult not to crack a smile. "You think because you're all grown up and stuff that you can be the boss of me! But you can't, so there!" She put her little hands on her hips and glared some more.

This time Juliet did laugh. "So what's so important that you had to come running after me like your tail was on fire?"

"Tail? I don't have a tail, Jules, you're being silly! Anyway, Mommy said to come get you for dinner. I helped her cook and everything!" EJ tugged at Juliet's hand. "Come on!"

The two girls walked hand in hand back to the cave where they'd been living for so long, one tall and graceful, a young woman, long braid falling over her shoulder; the other a tiny, trusting soul who had known only love in spite of living in a world that consisted of just two other people, a dangerous world in which anything could happen at a moment's notice.

ABOUT THE AUTHOR

Born in St. Louis, Missouri, Robin graduated from Parkway Central at the end of her junior year and went on to college . . . five times. Nearly 30 years later, on a whim, she looked over her transcripts and re-enrolled, completing not quite sixty hours of credit in just over one calendar year. Her degree, from Columbia College, is a combined major of psychology, sociology, and criminal justice.

Robin's writing career began at the age of eight, when her grandmother insisted she read Gone With the Wind before taking her to see the movie. Inspired by Margaret Mitchell, she began scribbling little booklets of stories, and was the editor of her elementary school newspaper and a columnist in high school. She submitted a short story to Seventeen magazine and was promptly rejected, but still keeps a copy of the manuscript in her desk.

Robin has worked as a snack bar cook, a salad prepper, a camp counselor, a waitress, a receptionist, a housekeeper, a freelancer, an editor, and an employment consultant and manager. She's also been in car sales, skin care sales, cookware sales, advertising sales, and MLM. She's owned and operated an entrepreneurial conglomerate, a cleaning service, an old-time photography studio, a bookstore, and a publishing house.

Seven years ago, Robin and her husband Dennis moved back to St. Louis after many years in Columbia, Sedalia, Colorado Springs, Durango, and Granbury and Tolar, Texas. They live with their youngest son, a dog, a cat, and a puppy.